DANIEL AND THE QUEEN OF BABYLON

CAROLE M. LUNDE

DANIEL AND THE QUEEN OF BABYLON

iUniverse books may be ordered through booksellers or by contacting:

iUniverse
1663 Liberty Drive
Bloomington, IN 47403
www.iuniverse.com
844-349-9409

Because of the dynamic nature of the Internet, any web addresses or links contained in this book may have changed since publication and may no longer be valid. The views expressed in this work are solely those of the author and do not necessarily reflect the views of the publisher, and the publisher hereby disclaims any responsibility for them.

Any people depicted in stock imagery provided by Getty Images are models, and such images are being used for illustrative purposes only.
Certain stock imagery © Getty Images.

ISBN: 978-1-6632-4311-9 (sc)
ISBN: 978-1-6632-4312-6 (e)

Print information available on the last page.

iUniverse rev. date: 08/01/2022

Contents

INTRODUCTION

The Book of Daniel in the Hebrew Bible gives no information about Daniel's early life and no information about the queen of Babylon. The book is mostly about King Nebuchadnezzar's increasing dementia, and little about Daniel himself. The queen is mentioned only as one who summoned Daniel to interpret the writing on the wall at Belshazzar's feast. She was not given a name.

Upon extensive research into the ancient empires of Babylonia, Assyria, Persia, and Egypt, the story comes forth. She was Queen Nitocris, designer and architect of the rebuilding of the City of Babylon. She was named after Queen Nitocris of Ancient Egypt, who lived 2000 years before her.

Over a thousand years before Queen Nitocris of Babylonia was Queen Samiramis of Babylon, who built a tunnel under the Euphrates River so she could walk from the palace to the temple without passing over the Euphrates River. It was large enough to accommodate horses and chariots. The description of the tunnel was written by Diodorus in 50 BCE and is found in Wikipedia. It is quoted in this story and permission to use it is in the Reference section at the end of this book.

For reading clarity, listed here are modern and ancient names of people and places.

Daniel's three friends, Shadrach, Meshach, and Abednego, were given these names in Babylon. Their Hebrew names that I use in this story are Hananiah, Mishael, and Azariah.

The Seaport of Ur, first home of Abram and Sarai, is no longer a seaport today because the Persian Gulf has receded several miles from Ur. The ancient name of the Persian Sea was Makran. The Strait of Hormuz was called Bazora.

The Chinese City of Guangzhou became known as Canton because of a faulty English translation of the Chinese name Guangzhou. The name is still Guangzhou.

The Amazon Warrior Women were relegated to myth until archaeologists excavated their remains, giving them a place in history. They roamed ancient Scythia, a region that covered what is now Afghanistan and Pakistan.

Chapter 1

DANIEL IN JERUSALEM

———— ❦ ————

The troops of Nebuchadnezzar poured into the temple in Jerusalem. They tore down the woven hangings, carried out the gold vessels, and destroyed everything else sacred to the Jews.

Daniel was almost frozen in shock. A chain was around his leg. He was being dragged along the streets with everyone from the temple and the royal house. The noise was horrendous as the flames of Jerusalem crackled and roared, grew higher, and spread with amazing speed throughout the city. It seemed as if everything was bursting into flame at the same time.

Through burning eyes, he looked around for his friends, Hananiah, Mishael, and Azariah. But it was impossible to see anyone in the dust and smoke that swirled around. He tried to call out to them, but the smoke made him cough and choke until he could barely breathe.

People around him were crying, calling out, and falling over the stones from the buildings and walls. The heat from the fires was suffocating. Those left behind died in the fire and smoke before they could get out of their neighborhoods.

He stumbled outside of the walls and fell down on his face, losing consciousness. He was shaken to half awake because someone was taking the chain from his ankle and dragging him. Still coughing he was helpless to ask or protest.

Once outside the walls of Jerusalem the people of the royal house and the temple who survived were being thrown into wagons to be brought to the palace at Uruk in Babylonia by order of King Nebuchadnezzar.

Everyone in the wagons was in misery. Daniel was not sure he himself would survive. They needed water. Eventually a guard put an urn of water on each wagon. Daniel dipped the corner of his robe into it and crawled to the others. He squeezed water into their mouths from the fabric and wiped their faces.

His three friends, Hananiah, Mishael, and Azariah, were in the wagon behind. The four of them began to attend to those in the wagons behind them as well.

"Use the water sparingly, Azariah. We do not know when they will bring more."

Daniel looked about to determine where they were. The river ran past Jericho and they likely would not go there. It was a long and steep way down from the heights of Jerusalem to the river. But perhaps further north closer to the Sea of Galilee.

"When we get nearer to the Jordan River, we can refill the urns there."

In the next few days the river was in sight. The soldiers stopped to refill their supply of water. Daniel, Azariah, Hananiah, and Mishael picked up the urns from the wagons and headed toward the river. In their weakened state it was hard to fill and carry the urns, but they affirmed with each other that God was their strength.

On their second trip back from the river the guards came by. Azariah, Mishael, and Hananiah were in their wagons ministering to the people.

Daniel hoisted his urn into the wagon bed and was climbing in. The guards grabbed Daniel and dumped him out of the wagon knocking him to the ground.

"Are you trying to organize an escape? You can walk to Babylonia, prophet!"

The travel by foot was hard and grueling. Daniel rubbed his ankle where the shackle was placed again on his chafed skin. He was hungry and tired. In anger and frustration he shouted to the guards who were close by.

"Please, if your king expects you to bring him a large workforce of slaves, these people must have food and rest as they travel or they will all die!"

A guard tramped over to Daniel and took a threatening stance.

"And who are you to tell us what we must do, slave?"

A very young Daniel, with clear eyes, disheveled hair, and ragged clothing, stood up to the guard and looked him in the eye.

"I am Daniel of the Royal House and Temple in Jerusalem. I am a prophet and reader of the stars and signs. Food and rest! Or your king will not have what he burned Jerusalem for, not just the gold but the people. Bring him people alive!"

The guard hit Daniel with his fist and knocked him down. Daniel jumped up immediately as though the blow had not phased him. He stood up to face the guard again and shouted at him.

"Food and rest in honor of your king!"

The guard raised his fist to hit him again, but for some reason thought better of it and stalked away. They were marched on into the night until the guards were weary and they stopped to sleep. But from the next day on the captives were stopped every midday and evening for food and rest.

Weeks later the captain of the guard came to find Daniel, stopped, and looked him up and down.

"So you are a magician? Can you do miracles and magic for me?"

Daniel took a deep breath and resolved to stay calm.

"Sir, I am skilled in all knowledge, learning, and understanding on the earth and above. I read the celestial signs and the universe responds when I ask for wisdom. I am a prophet of our god and a teacher of all men."

"I see...tell me, do you then predict the future? If you do, can you tell me mine?"

"Good captain, you are taking care of these my people as best you can under the circumstances, and your reward will be great."

The captain laughed, half amused and half surprised.

"What reward will that be, Prophet?"

"The reward, sir, is a life of success, peace, and love. Much good will come to you."

The captain's face sobered.

"It is strange that even in your captivity and misery you wish me well."

"It is not so strange, Sir. My god teaches us to be compassionate to others regardless of who they may be. We must abide by these teachings wherever we are, regardless of our condition."

The captain stayed silent. Presently he looked up at the sky and squinted against its brightness.

"Where is your god? Is there a statue where I can see him?"

"My god is within each one everywhere and also within you. There are no statues because you are the living representation of your creator."

"I am the living...what? How can that be?"

"It is the spirit of the Creator that is within us all and gives us life."

"What is your name, Prophet?"

"Daniel, Sir."

"I will remember you, Daniel."

The captain stood thoughtfully for a moment, glanced back at Daniel, and then walked toward a guard.

"Guard, take the shackles off this man."

After many months the bedraggled Jews staggered past the ruins of Babylon and on through the miles and weeks into Uruk. Some in chains, some stumbling, and some heaped on wagons, injured and perhaps dying. Many men and women had already died on the way.

Ninana and her father, King Nebuchadnezzar, watched from a palace balcony. He was smiling and filled with pride. The longer she watched the angrier she became.

"Why are you doing this to these people, Father? What have the captives done to deserve this? How is Jerusalem a threat to us from so far away? Look at them. They are miserable and dying!"

"My daughter, you are a girl and cannot understand governing and war. Only men understand this. It is necessary to bring the people here to enhance our workforce and our slave population. We need more people here to rebuild Babylon, my new capital, and ensure our security. That is how empires are built. Babylon is the greatest of them all! This is how men, not girls, get things done.

"Captives are first paraded through the streets to show our people the power of mighty Babylonia and their king. Then those who have not died will be taken to rebuild the City of Babylon."

Ninana was becoming more incensed by the minute, hardly able to catch her breath. She turned to face him.

"Does that give us the right to take people from their homes and force them to do this work for us? What security are they for us? They are not even soldiers."

He did not answer her. He called for a servant to bring food and wine to his chambers and walked away.

This was how every conversation she attempted to have with him was abruptly stopped. He would be condescending, she would become angry, and he would turn and go.

"He said that war is necessary to keep the peace. That makes no sense to me. Yes, I am a girl. But that does not mean that I am stupid, weak, or will give up! This is not right. I will not give up."

Young Ninana was tall, lanky, with reddish brown hair that was bobbed a few inches below her ear. Her servant begged her not to cut it short, but she liked it that way. It annoyed her when long strands fell into her freckled face as she bent over her drawings. She kept a pair of bronze scissors in a basket in her room and cut it off herself.

"My Lady, it is very...uneven. May I try to trim it for you?"

Ninana did not see the need, but since her servant relented, she allowed her to trim it evenly. Unaccustomed to the clumsy instrument, the servant did the best she could.

"It looks all right. You may go."

"Yes, Your Highness.

Ninana had been drawing buildings of her own design in a secret room in the basement of the palace since she was six years old. No one knew about the room where she spent many delightful hours drawing long straight lines and in-depth images on the smooth walls. They looked quite real to her. She was sure they would become the magnificent buildings in the new City of Babylon.

She carefully closed the door each time she went in and out so as not to disturb the dust and webs. No one must discover her secret.

Chapter 2

YOUNG NINANA GOES TO BABYLON

—— ⟲ ⟳ ——

"Babylon is just rubble from a thousand years of destruction, Ninana. Why do you pester me to go there? What could possibly be of interest to you?"

King Nebuchadnezzar was looking over plans laid out for the rebuilding of the City of Babylon west of present capitol, Uruk. The room was strewn with maps and discarded scraps of plans. He turned and walked away to the other side of a large table for designing and planning. He angrily kicked away the scraps on the floor.

"My dream is to make the City of Babylon my capitol. It is to be the most beautiful city in the world. The master builder, Zaidu, is excellent, but my architects are not. They need to do a better job or I will have them all thrown into the dungeon."

"Your dream is also my dream, Father. I am learning to be an architect. I want to be the designer. I will make beautiful buildings for you."

"Perhaps I will look over your designs when the time comes. Now go along. I have work to do. Zaidu, will be here soon."

King Nebuchadnezzar could not be concerned with what he considered to be his daughter's foolish fantasies. She knew he was just patronizing her and would not remember his promise. But she was determined to be the designer of the most beautiful city in the world.

She gathered some of her drawings and positioned herself where she could see Zaidu when he left the palace. It seemed to take forever. She waited.

As Zaidu was leaving the palace Ninana ran to him.

"Where are you going in such a hurry, Princess?"

"Please, Master Zaidu, take me with you to Babylon. I am an architect. I want to see the foundations of the buildings, what strengthens the structures, and how they are raised. I must see it all. I need to know everything."

"And your father? Have you asked him?"

"My father does not pay any attention to me. He thinks I am a dreamer with foolish fantasies. He is right. I am a dreamer. But I see a great city and it is not a foolish fantasy. Here are some of my designs. Please look at them."

Zaidu stopped and thought for a moment. Then he sat down on a garden bench with her and looked over her work.

"This is better than the architects who are working there. The king has been greatly displeased with their attempts.

"Princess, I will take you to Babylon if your father agrees. But the men are rough spoken and may not be fit for the presence of a princess."

"I will not be offended, Master Zaidu. My work is the most important thing in the world to me and I must see Babylon, whatever it takes."

King Nebuchadnezzar stopped to see Zaidu approaching him again.

"Your Highness, your daughter wishes to go to Babylon with us, but I am not sure that is wise. The sites are rough and so are the men."

"Oh, by all means take her and get her out of my hair. Maybe that will cure her of her childish ambitions and fantasies."

It was true. When Zaidu told the men who were loading the wagons with supplies, they shook their heads. They grumbled among themselves. If she had not been the daughter of a king they would have objected strenuously and demanded that she be sent away.

"A girl cannot possibly understand men's work. She will be in the way. There are snakes and vermin. And what if she gets hurt? The king will have our heads."

Zaidu heard them as he walked by.

"My head, not yours. I am responsible for her and she will be all right. Just carry on. We must be ready to leave at dawn."

"The wagons of supplies will be ready to go before dawn, Master. They are nearly ready now."

Ninana made sure to wear her sturdiest sandals, tunic, and robe. She carefully packed a bag with her drawing supplies. Breathlessly she ran to meet Zaidu at the palace gate. The wagon was already there waiting for her.

"Am I late?"

The men glanced around to see that this princess, this girl, was really coming with them.

"No. You are right on time. Slow down, Princess, and save your energy. It is a long way to Babylon."

Zaidu swung her bag into the wagon where it would not fall out or be crushed. He made room for her beside him in the front seat. The driver, shaking his head, snapped the reins on the rumps of the horses and the wagon lurched forward almost unseating her.

The road was rough and she hung on tightly to the side of the seat. They jolted along around the edge of the city into a large field where the caravan of supply wagons was waiting.

Satisfied that the caravan was organized and ready, Zaidu, his deputies, and Ninana got down from the wagons and walked to waiting horses. They would travel much faster on horseback.

"We will change horses at a stable at the town of Isin, about halfway to Babylon. We will need fresh horses to keep up our fast pace. The guards and drivers will stay with the supply wagons and arrive in a few weeks."

Zaidu looked with a frown at Ninana.

"Have you ever ridden a horse?"

"Well, only a small one."

"A small one?"

Ninana looked down at her hands. She should know better than to lie to Zaidu. He could see right through her.

"Please, Zaidu, I am not afraid of the horses. I am sure I will be quite comfortable."

Zaidu burst out laughing.

"I will pick out a small horse for you."

Zaidu was tall, well-built and even imposing. His black eyes were snapping under the hair that fell over his brow. He moved quickly and efficiently as he checked the caravan one more time.

He picked her up, put her into the saddle on a small horse, a gentle mare. He gave her a harness strap to hold onto with one hand and reins for the other. He fit her feet into the stirrups.

"Do not be concerned. She will follow along so you will not have to guide her. Just hang on and sit easy using the stirrups for balance."

Ninana did her best to look confident as they moved out at a brisk pace. Zaidu rode close to her to be sure she was not sliding out of the saddle. The wagon road was well worn but rough with protruding stones.

They rode through the first day and night stopping only momentarily. The next midday they stopped among some scrub trees for a rest in the shade and food.

Ninana was so stiff and sore she was not sure she could move much less walk. Zaidu eased her off the horse and gently sat her on a bundle that the deputies had put down.

"You will get used to it. When we arrive in Babylon you will be able to find your legs and walk."

"Yes, I will be able to walk and climb onto the ruins. I must see everything. I cannot let anything stop me."

Her voice did not sound as steady and confident as she hoped it would. But she must not show weakness. She was determined.

"Princess, we will not let anything stop you, even if we have to carry you onto the ruins to do your work."

Ninana laughed at the thought of being carried onto the walls of Babylon. She was sure that would not be necessary.

She hungrily ate the food placed on the bundle beside her and smiled. She was going to Babylon. She was actually going to Babylon, her lifelong dream!

Chapter 3

BABYLON IN RUINS

Dawn was breaking on the fourth day of their travel and the light was creeping over the landscape. They ate quickly and continued.

"I did not know it was so far! Will we be there soon?"

"Princess, the Empire of Babylonia is enormous, the largest in the world that we know, and this is just a very small part of it. We will be there soon."

After a few more days the jagged ruins of Babylon came into view.

Ninana's heart began to race with excitement. There it was! Her future was rising before her. She clapped her hands and grinned up at Zaidu. He just shook his head in wonder.

When they arrived at the edge of the ruined city they dismounted. A young man gathered up their horses and led them away. Ninana hobbled a short way and sat down on a building stone. She was not about to admit to the pain, which was momentarily intense.

Slowly she got up, recovered her balance, picked up her bag, and walked forward one step at a time until she was sure of her legs.

Approaching the ruins she looked for the highest point from which she could see everything. Zaidu came along behind her in case she should trip and took her bag.

"Princess Ninana, watch for snakes and vermin closer to the river, and do not step into holes caused by swirling waters. The river floods the city and recedes leaving many soft places."

She shuddered.

"Oh, I do not like snakes and vermin! I will climb up on the highest remaining section of the wall and sketch what I see from there. I will be careful."

"Someone will bring you food and water during the day. We will stay in tents at night. You will have your own. I will be close by mine so do not be afraid."

Ninana could not imagine what there was to be afraid of. She had never known fear. The thrill of being in Babylon overshadowed everything.

Zaidu handed her the bag and lifted her onto the first few enormous stone blocks. She looked around and pointed to what looked like a good place. He helped her up to the place and looked around with her.

"The city seems to go on forever! It will take many buildings and keep me busy for a long time."

"It is many miles square and goes beyond the other side of the river. Please do not go near the river, Princess."

Her bag contained a pile of well cured and trimmed goat skins for her sketches, drawing tools, and charcoal. With her heavy bag slung over her shoulder, she crawled and climbed until she found just the right spot that was flat. It was so exciting that she didn't notice her scraped knees and stubbed toes.

There was a slight breeze that rippled her robe when she spread it on a flat rock. After carefully arranging the drawing tools on it Ninana sat down to quietly survey the city ruins. There was so much to take in. The ancient ruins of Babylon spread out for miles over a much larger area than even Uruk.

Zaidu told her what to look for regarding ancient foundations and narrow streets.

"Here is a map so you will not get lost among the rubble and shells of buildings or walk in areas that are full of holes which could be quite deep. Do not go too far because as the light changes, the shadows make everything look different. It will be hard to find your way back."

"Thank you. I will stay close by for now. It is all so big!"

The city spread beyond her sight. She did not see any way to cross the sluggish river. And then there were the turtles, vermin, and snakes. She wanted to see everything but for now she decided to remain on this side.

As she climbed down to the ground level and walked carefully through the rubble, the sun was bright and sometimes blinded her. She was about to step around a stone when she saw the tail of a snake at her feet as it made its way to the river. She jumped and backed away into a building stone and abruptly sat down.

Her heart was pounding and her hands shaking. Hurriedly she returned back up to her perch. When she felt calm again and her hands stopped shaking, she began to draw buildings on her flattened goat skins. Soon the hours went by unnoticed.

That first day a young man with long sun-bleached hair came up over the stones to where she sat. She looked up at him and smiled.

"I have food for you and a tent to give you shade."

He placed the food on a rock beside her and began to set up a lean-to style tent to shade her.

"My name is Ninana and I thank you."

"No need to thank me, Your Highness. It is my pleasure to serve you."

When the tent was set up and well anchored, he turned to go.

"But wait. What is your name?"

"My name is Daniel. I am from Jerusalem."

Ninana snatched a breath in surprise. Of course, he was one of those herded into Uruk and paraded through the main streets to be jeered and spat upon.

"I am glad to know your name. I am sorry that you are forced to work here."

She was flustered and not sure what else to say. Her heart went out to him.

"No one forces me, Princess. I joyfully and willingly go where my God leads me."

He bowed briefly and climbed back down over the jumble of building stones.

Ninana sat for a while thinking about Daniel and the Jews when they were herded into Uruk. Now she had met one and knew his name. These were real people, not just slaves. She nibbled on the food he left for her and eventually resumed her sketching.

Every day she took sketching materials with her to record ideas as they came to her. She climbed to another perch on the remnant of the wall in the ruined city from which she could survey the layout from a different angle. The streets of the city under the rubble were beginning to emerge. Zaidu told her the city was almost twenty miles square. The walls had been so thick that they staged chariot races on top of them.

Chapter 4

QUEEN SAMIRAMIS

It always thrilled Ninana to watch the workers moving broken stones and clearing streets. The pattern of the city was slowly showing its original order. She could not imagine how long it would take before new buildings could rise from these foundations.

Day after day she could pick out places where the streets had been and made her way carefully among the stones and mud. She envisioned the buildings that must have sat along them. She shivered as she remembered the snakes.

Each evening when the sky was darkening Zaidu came for her. Daniel came with him to take down her lean-to and carry her bag of supplies. As they ate dinner, Zaidu showed a tablet of writing to her.

"I want to show you this. It is about a passage under the Euphrates River built by Queen Samiramis over five hundred years ago. I have found no trace of the tunnel, but I thought you would like to know about her. It reads,

> *"In a low ground in Babylon, she sunk a place for a pond,*
> *four-squares, every square being three hundred furlongs in*
> *length, lined with brick, and cemented with brimstone, and*

the whole five-and-thirty feet in depth: into this having first turned the river, she then made a passage in form of a vault, from one palace to another, whose arches were built of firm and strong brick, and plastered all over on both sides with bitumen, four cubits thick. The walls of this vault were twenty bricks in thickness, and twelve feet high, beside and above the arches; and the breadth was fifteen feet. This piece of work being finished in two hundred and sixty days, the river was turned into its ancient channel again, so that the river flowing over the whole work, Semiramis could go from one palace to the other, without passing over the river. It was large enough for horses and chariots to pass through."

Ninana's mouth dropped open in astonishment.

"So am not the only woman to build in Babylon! A passage under the river seems impossible, but still she did it!"

"As I said, Ninana, I have found no evidence of it. I am sure after five hundred years of many floods and the destruction of Babylon over and over, it was all washed down the river into the Makran Sea. Not one stone of it will remain."

"How sad! I understand, and I certainly will not wade into the river to find it. But it is good to know about Queen Samiramis, another woman architect in Babylon."

Their tents for sleeping were on a raised plateau under a row of scrub trees. She wondered where Daniel and the slaves slept. She saw no other tents.

Her tent was separate from the others by a short distance. Rough robes were stacked in the corner of it for her bed and covers. Zaidu left some bread, wine, and cheese and an oil lamp, for which she was grateful. She wanted to finish her sketches before she slept.

After a short time the wine made her sleepy. Before she knew it, the camp was stirring and the men were going to their work sites. As the sun was barely showing over the horizon Zaidu came to take her to where food was laid out for their breakfast.

"The hour is early, I know. This is how we work every day."

"That is fine Zaidu. I am getting used to it."

He nodded, picked up her bag of supplies, and escorted her to where food was served and then back to her perch on the wall.

"Will you show me where those palaces stood and where the passage might have been?"

"Yes. But do not be disappointed. There is nothing left of the palaces either."

They climbed through the debris for a few miles until she could see the river.

"We will go up onto a fragment of a wall to look over the area. It is not safe to walk there until we build a dam to keep the Euphrates out and let the land dry. Right now it is very swampy and unstable."

Ninana closed her eyes and imagined a palace one side of the river and a temple on the other. The reality of Babylon was growing in her mind and sparking her imagination about what had been, and what she could now create there.

Each day as she sketched, she thought of Daniel's words, *"No one forces me. I joyfully and willingly go where my god leads me."*

One day when Daniel brought her food, set up and checked on the stability of her tent, she asked him to explain joy and how that could be in his situation.

"Is it not true that my father's army destroyed your city? But soldiers brought you and your people here, some injured and some in chains? How can you say you were not forced?"

He sat down on a stone opposite her and pushed his hair out of his face.

"My god is always with and within me wherever life takes me. If I believe that I am forced as you say, then I have forgotten my god and my joy will be gone."

"How does your god lead you?"

"It gives me joy to see my god everywhere and I follow my joy."

He got up from the stone and bowed to her.

"I must go. Zaidu will be displeased if I am away too long. He has much work for me to do. He is a good man and I wish to serve him well."

What he said brought more questions to her mind. There was more she wanted to ask but not sure how to ask it. What words to use.

He follows his joy.

Chapter 5

JAREM MEETS NINANA

Jarem, the elderly architect of the palace and master of the architectural school in Uruk, leaned on his walking stick as he climbed up to Ninana's perch. He was pleased to see the progress in Babylon as he gazed around. She slowly looked up and smiled at him.

"May I see your work?"

"Oh, yes! I hope you do not think my ideas are childish as my father does."

He took his time looking over her sketches.

"On no! These are very good! Yes, very good. Do you have a teacher?"

"Only my heart and my dreams. I have no teacher other than those."

"You may know that I am the master architect of the school in Uruk. I would be pleased if you would come to the architectural school when you return and look at the drawings we have there. You may use a clay or sand drawing board to sketch your buildings. If you wish, you might attend the classes as well."

"I would like that! I have drawn my buildings on the walls of an abandoned storeroom. It is deep underground in the palace. I am the only one who knows it is there. Would you like to come to my secret room? You will see many of my drawings if you promise to keep it a secret."

"Yes. I will go there with you. I promise to tell no one about it."

He began climbing down over the building stones. One of the workers who always came with him helped him over the huge stones.

Jarem knew his days of climbing around construction sites were numbered. The pain in his joints was getting stronger, almost too painful to bear. The physician could do little for him except give him an herbal potion to reduce the pain so he could sleep at night.

Back in Uruk Jarem leaned on his cane as he followed her down three stairways and through a long dark hall into the room under the palace. The wooden door creaked as he pushed it open. She stepped in past him and lit the lamps. The flickering light revealed a cavernous room full of wonderful drawings, a panorama all around him on the walls.

"This is my city, Master Jarem. Is it not beautiful?"

Jarem was almost speechless as he turned around and around, gazing up at the walls of sketches. It did indeed feel like he was in the middle of her city.

"Yes! Yes, it is magnificent! How did you learn to do this?"

"In my mind I see the buildings of Babylon rising and I make them as beautiful as I can. I want to draw more of them, but I am running out of room. Now the oil lamps are darkening the walls. Soon they will all disappear...my city will be gone! What can I do, Master Jarem?"

He turned to her and saw that she was almost tearful.

"Come with me and we will find a place for you in the school to do your work. In my school we have large sand boards, clay tablets, goat skins, and papyrus where my students do their work. There is no need for lamps there. The light from the many large windows illuminates the rooms."

"Yes! Thank you! I will come with you. I want to see your school and do my work there."

Ninana was relieved and wiped away a tear. A plan for saving her drawings was coming to mind. She carefully closed the door and followed Jarem. They went back through the hall and up the stairs to the street where out of breath he hailed his small carriage. The driver stepped down to help them in and drove them to the school.

The school building was a long low structure with large windows as he promised. It was positioned on a rise facing the west side of the city. When they entered, all twelve students immediately stood and bowed to their master teacher.

"This is Princess Ninana Nitocris, daughter of King Nebuchadnezzar. She will be studying with us. She is a gifted architect and an inspiring addition to our school."

The students were wide-eyed. There would be a young girl in their school, a princess! The head student, Shamhar, stepped forward and bowed respectfully.

"Pray, great teacher, how shall we regard royalty among us?"

"She will be regarded with respect. I have seen her work and it is exquisite. Everyone please sit down."

Ninana was shown to a drawing board in a corner near a window and given the supplies and tools she needed to begin. She looked around at the students. They were still staring at her.

"Master Jarem, may I speak to them?"

"Yes, of course, Princess."

She walked out from behind her table and stood before them.

"I wish to be regarded as just a student here without reference to my royalty or that I am a girl. My name is Ninana and you may address me by that name, or Princess if that is more comfortable for you. I will not be offended. I also wish that I not be spoken about outside of the school. It may bring distracting attention that would harm our work here."

There was silence. Jarem smiled at her, amazed at her poise for one so young.

"Thank you, Ninana. Please, everyone continue with your work assignment for today."

Ninana sat down at her drawing table, picked up a piece of charcoal, and set to work sketching. The sand and clay boards were helpful. Unlike the walls of the storeroom, she could easily erase what she did not want to keep. Also, she did not have to climb up on stacks of bundles to reach the top of the walls.

The sun was setting and the students were leaving but she did not notice. She was still concentrating on her drawing. The afternoon had passed so quickly. The head student, Shamhar, cautiously approached her.

"Come, Princess. It will soon be dark. We must all leave and go home."

Ninana jumped at the sound of his voice. Embarrassed, she looked up at him and smiled.

"I am sorry! I was so engrossed in this design. Yes, I will stop now."

Jarem came in and waved for her to come with him. She looked over her table, gathered her work, and put her tools in a box. He realized her concern about where to put her drawings and walked over to her.

"You may leave everything in place, Princess. Just put a cover over your table with everything under it to keep it all clean. The covers are on a shelf behind you."

The students were gone by the time they got into his carriage.

"I hope they will not hate me. I want them to like me or at least be friendly."

"I also hope they will be friendly. Remember, Ninana, you are royalty and that will always create a barrier with the commoners. The students hope to be great architects someday, but you already have it within you. Walk carefully and do not be boastful."

Ninana was sobered.

"I have lived in my father's palace and gone to the work sites in Babylon. Everyone is very kind there. I have not ever thought to be boastful, as you say."

"Yes, I am sure you were not. But your place as royalty in the palace and with the builders is very clear. Royalty is expected in those places. You would not be viewed as competition. Anything you say, even innocently, can be construed as competition to those who are of a lower rank.

"The students here are unaccustomed to royalty and see your presence quite differently. Just be mindful of who you are and who they are."

Ninana came to be aware of the barrier between royalty and commoners as she thought more about it and continued her studies there. She did her best to put them at ease, but there was always a distance, an underlying tension that she could not erase like the drawings on her sand board.

Chapter 6

THE SECRET ROOM

Ninana spent several mornings studiously copying her drawings in the room below the palace. She was determined not to lose them. The walls were already darkening near the ceiling from the oil lamp smoke.

Each afternoon Master Jarem arrived in his carriage to take her to the school. She brought her copies to put with her work there. The students had large individual boxes in which to store their work. She could keep all of hers together in her box.

She went to Babylon for months at a time with Zaidu, the master builder, to follow their progress and work on her drawings there. He patiently answered her many questions. They were well thought out questions and sometimes helpful to his projects. Sometimes he sought her opinion on a problem they faced. Her insights amazed him.

The students were curious about Ninana's work and too respectful to openly ask. She was intense and rarely spoke to anyone. One day Shamhar, the head student, was elected to question Ninana about her drawings and travels to Babylon.

"Dear Princess, my classmates and I wonder about the work you are doing in Babylon. Would you mind sharing about it with us?"

Ninana looked up startled. This was the first time someone spoke to her. They were so quiet and kept to themselves, even with each other.

"I am sorry, Shamhar. I am so focused on my work that I did not think to talk with you. I have always worked alone. Only Master Jarem ever bothered about my work, not my father or anyone at the palace. I am happy to share with you. What would you like to know?"

"Well...why do you go to Babylon? You are gone for many weeks. What do you do there?"

"My father is rebuilding the City of Babylon to be his new capitol. I am designing the buildings. I go to Babylon to learn about their construction. I sketch the city streets and visualize how the buildings could be placed on them. The sketches are like maps that keep me from getting lost. Babylon is so large and the deep piles of rubble prevent me from having a clear picture of where I am when I walk through them. Perhaps I can take all of you there for a few months."

"Thank you, Princess. I am sure we will love to go with you!"

"I need to ask Master Jarem and Zaidu, the master builder. I will do that very soon."

Now there was much excitement in the school. A few other students came forward to speak with her and see her work. Dakuri, Naram, and Rihat were very shy but she stood up and smiled at them.

"Please, what else do you wish to ask?"

"Princess, how do you come to create these designs? Have you seen them somewhere? Did you have a teacher before you came to our school?"

"I had no teacher before Master Jarem. There is something within me that compels me to draw them. I just see them in my mind and my dreams. I sketched them on the walls of a storeroom deep inside the palace. It was a room that was not used and no one else knew it was there. I drew them all over the walls, like a city all around me. The more I drew them, the more ideas came to me."

Dakuri shyly offered his own experience.

"I have some dreams of buildings. I did not think they were important."

"Oh, Dakuri, your dreams are very important. They are the universe sending you ideas for your work. You must begin to draw them. Your teacher is the universe which knows all things. This is what my mother told me and I have learned it is true."

Other students quickly stepped up and plied Ninana with many more questions. Some of them shyly showed her their work and asked for her advice. It seemed that she had become a teacher as well as a student.

She remembered Jarem's cautioning words about not appearing competitive. She remained humble and asked them many questions of them as well. The barrier was lowering but would never completely disappear.

Zaidu drew in a deep breath. He tried to imagine how it would be to have twelve students along with Ninana at the site.

"Yes, Princess, I can arrange to take the students to Babylon. You must have a plan for what they will do while there. They cannot just roam through the ruins unaccompanied. The men are starting to move large stones to rebuild the foundations of the walls and they could be in danger."

"I will give them instructions to follow me and not wander about. They are quite respectful and I am sure will present no problems. This is the biggest opportunity they have ever had to expand their understanding and experience. It is so important to them and perhaps for the future work at Babylon. They ask many good questions.

"I believe you can organize and direct them. I will depend upon you."

"Thank you, Zaidu! Indeed, the students have not traveled outside of Uruk. It will be their first journey."

The students were well prepared, instructed in what to bring, and how long they would be gone. Their families came to see them off.

Their next thrill was to be riding horses for the first time. The guards set them on horses, as Zaidu had done with Ninana a few years before. They gave them straps to hold on and fitted their feet into the stirrups.

They were no longer quiet and shy. They chatted with each other as they never done before. They laughed when they could hardly dismount at Isin to change horses. They held each other up as they walked the stiffness out of their legs.

"Princess, we feel so foolish. Did this happen to you when you first traveled on horses?"

"Oh yes! Master Zaidu had to pull me off the horse and set me down on a bundle of supplies until I could get up and walk on my own. Only my determination to go to Babylon kept me from complaining."

Jarem was delighted for the students and rode in his carriage alongside the slow supply wagons. Even then he was stiff and sore when he arrived, but he could not allow his pain to cause him to miss this wonderful event.

Ninana slipped easily into the role of teacher and guide. It was a most exciting time for her, too.

"My fellow students, I will take you to my favorite perches from which I sketch. You can then choose your own places. Please do not go about the ruins without me. It is very easy to get lost. All the ruins look alike and change when the sun changes in the sky. So even if you are sure you know your way back, the shadows can change how everything looks."

"Princess, what should we do if we get separated?"

"Stop and call out. Do not keep walking. Stand still. The workers and I will find you. We want everyone to be safe."

"Princess, when to we eat?"

Everyone laughed.

"They are preparing a table of food for us right now. Come this way."

Ninana was delighted to show the students her city and take them around the Babylon construction sites. She led them to her favorite perches which had the best views. They chose their places on the wall near Ninana and soon settled in to chat and sketch. Their shared her excitement and at last she felt accepted as one of them, if only as their benefactor and only in Babylon.

Zaidu was pleased at the behavior of the students and Ninana's gentle leadership. The workers took food to the students and they were happy to spend a little time talking to them about the construction. It was turning out to be a good two months for everyone.

Master Jarem stayed in Zaidu's tent during the day and met with the students when they came in from their perches for dinner. The pain in his knees did not allow him to climb over the rocks and debris scattered about from the former destruction.

Ninana and Maser Jarem became co-teachers. They enjoyed the conversations and the insightful ideas of the students. Their excitement was renewed and increased every day.

"I do not know when I have enjoyed teaching so much, even if my knees complain bitterly."

"It has been the most wonderful experience for me to get to know them. I remember what you said about the royalty barrier, but it seems to be less since we have been here."

"I am very proud of you. Not only of your work but your leadership and wisdom. It seems you do excellent work in whatever you choose. Your talents extend far beyond architecture."

"I wish my father could acknowledge that. But of course he has the mind of a king and that will not happen. I may wish it, but I have stopped hoping. You are my father, Master Jarem. You do all those things he will not or cannot do."

"Your wisdom goes beyond what he expects. I think perhaps at times you terrify him."

She laughed at the thought of her powerful father being terrified of her. He always said she was 'just a girl.' It was hard to understand how a mere girl could be terrifying to a king.

The students were sad to leave Babylon. They wanted more of the experience. They extended it by chatting enthusiastically with Ninana all the way back to Uruk.

Dakuri, Naram, and Rihat made plans to share their dreams each morning and get started sketching them. They invited Ninana to join and help them.

"I can help you for a time, but then you must trust your own thoughts. You can always ask me any questions, but your ideas must be completely your own. You will be amazed at how they will come to you more and more."

Chapter 7

NINANA'S WEDDING

King Nebuchadnezzar summoned Ninana to the room where he held public audiences. She was a bit puzzled.

"This has never happened before. What can it mean? Does he want to see my work? Dare I hope he will approve of me at last?"

"I have arranged a marriage for you. Your mother must prepare you for your wedding to Nabonidus who will be king when your half-brother, Evol-Merodach, and I are gone."

She stood still. Frozen in shock.

"M-marriage? Why must I marry? I do not wish to be married! I have my work to do."

"It is time you married. That is what daughters do. They obey their father's commands and I command you to marry."

She swallowed hard. Her father had never commanded her to do anything. A command was ominous. She dared not refuse even though that was on the tip of her tongue. So she took a deep breath and spoke quietly to control her anger.

"But why Nabonidus, Father? He is an Assyrian! Are they not our enemies? Why should I not have a husband from our city, Uruk? Are there none worthy?"

"You will understand some day. For now you must be educated and trained to be a queen, to dress and walk like a queen, to talk like a queen."

Then she began to lose her cool.

"He is not royalty! I am! And yet he will be a king because of me. How is that fair? It will all be given to him and he does nothing to earn it. I work every day for your dream city, Babylon, and you give me no credit at all."

"You are a girl, Ninana, not yet a queen. Go now and talk to your mother. She will tell you what you need to know to be a wife and eventually a queen. Ask your mother the questions about those things."

Ninana's heart sank. She hated to be dismissed as if she were a mere child. She was nearly seventeen, capable and talented as any man. Why could he not see that? Why could he not talk with her instead of at her?

Slowly she walked out of the room. Control of her life was slipping from her grip. Could it be that her life as she knew it was ending? She ran tearfully to her mother's apartments.

Queen Amytis knew what was coming. She was not happy about this marriage either but could do nothing to change it.

Ninana fell on to a chaise and cried for the first time in her life.

"A marriage I do not want! How could he? And to that slothful Nabonidus!"

Amytis gave her a goblet of wine and sat down to wait for the calm after the storm.

"This is so sudden! Marriage! Mother what must I do in a marriage? What happens? I mean...do you enjoy being a...wife?"

The wine helped calm her sobs and hiccups. Ninana sat with Queen Amytis in her apartment drawing room. The queen began describing to her what happens between husbands and wives.

Ninana turned pale.

"Is that just like the animals? It sounds terrible."

"You will get used to it. It doesn't last very long. That is how you will produce a child, an heir to the throne. Have you not seen a man before?"

"No, I have not and do not care to. Once Evol-Merodach pushed me into a corner and grabbed at my robe. I did not know what he was doing. He frightened me. I put my fingers in his eyes, pushed his face back and I ran away."

"Did he come after you?"

"I do not know. I heard footsteps behind me. But I ran to my secret room under the palace where I do my sketches of buildings. No one knows about that room, but I barred the door behind me anyway."

"Bless all the goddesses, why did you not tell me?"

"I stayed there for many hours trying to think of what to do and hoping he would just be gone. I did not think of telling you. What could you do?"

"I have some powers that you are not aware of, my dear. I am more than your father's wife and queen. I am the ruling regent when your father is away and I have the power of life and death over others when needed."

Ninana's eyes grew wide and she gasped for breath.

"I did not know that. No one has ever told me about being a queen."

"Ninana, you are so busy with your architecture, and Babylon, that I hardly had an opportunity to talk to you about anything. You always rushed past me when I tried."

"Can you stop this marriage for me?"

"Sadly, no. I cannot go against your father's command."

Remembering the creepy feelings of that terrible experience with Evol-Merodach, Ninana changed the subject and asked how the ceremony was prepared.

"How long does it go on? Will someone tell me what to do?"

Queen Amytis was about to answer when Adad-happe, mother of Nabonidus, rushed into the room.

"This marriage will not take place! Ninana and her friend Daniel, the Jew magician, are friends and who knows what else! She is not pure or fit for my son."

Ninana was about to object that Daniel was a prophet, not a cheap magician, but Queen Amytis stepped in front of Adad-happe in blazing anger.

"My daughter is pure and more so than your son! He is lazy, stupid, and not even royalty. He is the one not worthy! But the marriage will go ahead because King Nebuchadnezzar has decreed it. You will hush any such talk among your women or I will deal with you as Queen Amytis, Regent of Babylonia."

Adad-happe backed away, stiffly bowed and hurried out of the room.

"Mother! I truly do not know you! I have not seen you so strong and powerful. How did you learn that?"

"When your father is away fighting battles or seeing to our allies, I am in his place as Regent or ruler of Babylonia. While I am holding court with petitioners and visitors, you are at the school of architecture or in Babylon. We have different callings which take us away from each other and our life in the palace."

Ninana sobered a bit trying to fathom what her mother was telling her. She had no idea that her mother was the ruler of the whole empire.

"Thank you for telling me this, Mother. I am certainly not ready for the tasks of a queen, much less being a regent. I am sure I will need to know these things if Nabonidus ever becomes the king. I pray he does not."

"Come, Ninana, first let us talk about your wedding. Those things can come later."

They walked out into the gardens and made some plans about the days to come. The night air though not cool was welcome after the stifling air of the palace. Ninana needed some space to breathe after the events of the day.

To Ninana's frustration her wedding ceremony was long and tiring as they appealed to all the gods and goddesses at each of their temples and altars for good fortune. Then the usual drunken brawl proceeded with men and women eventually dropping their garments and crawling all over each other. She always found those parties disgusting and refused to attend them.

After the wedding ceremony she feigned illness and immediately went to her quarters to avoid the celebration that would start and last for days. Her new husband, Nabonidus, became very drunk and chose to fully participate in the merriment. He seemed not to notice her absence.

She struggled to get her mind back on her work. She went immediately to the school to find Master Jarem. He had been most concerned about the sudden changing of events in her life and met her outside the school door. He welcomed her with open arms.

She leaned on his frail body and tried somewhat unsuccessfully to hold back the tears. She did not wish to fall apart in front of the students. What would they think?

"Come, let us go over your drawings and continue to refine them. Do you remember where we left off?"

"Yes, yes I do. Thank you, Master."

Relieved she went to the box where her drawings were stored and they sat down together to work on them.

"I thought I would die if I could not return to Babylon and my work. I felt like my life was being ripped away from me."

"But you can see that it was not. It is all right here waiting for you."

She smiled gratefully at him and, putting the nightmare of the last week from her mind, set to work.

Chapter 8

BELSHAZZAR IS BORN

In the ensuing days after the wedding servants and women of the royal family gossiped about her. They were careful to speak in whispers. She would be their queen one day and could punish them severely if she knew what they were saying.

"She is so serious for a girl. She keeps to herself. Where does she go for so many weeks? Why does she cut her hair so short? Should it not be long and beautiful like the other girls? Perhaps she does not like being a girl. Maybe that is why her husband avoids her. Or she avoids him. She was not at her own wedding celebration..."

That gossip was put to rest when it became obvious that Ninana was with child. Queen Amytis began to stay closer to Ninana and called the midwife to check on her often.

"I do not understand this. I have seen other women who are with child. I did not know they were sick or that I could feel so bad. I am disgustingly sick every morning. I feel so tired and can hardly continue my work"

"It will pass, Ninana. In a few months you will have a lovely child in your arms."

"All I want in my arms are my drawings and bag of supplies."

"Perhaps you will feel differently when you see your child. That changes a woman."

"Nothing will change for me. I have much work to do and that is what I love."

Queen Amytis was at a loss to respond. She knew Ninana had a calling since early childhood and nothing would change that, probably not even a child.

The months went by agonizingly slow for Ninana. The illness came and went, and then came back. Her back hurt so much some days she could hardly stand. Going to Babylon was out of the question.

One night there was a rush of water from her and terrible pains. Queen Amytis called for the physician and the midwife. The midwife came quickly. She was never far away knowing Ninana's time was coming soon. She checked Ninana's progress and was satisfied that the child was not breech, but in a normal birthing position.

"Mother, did you go through all of this? Why do women keep having babies if this is always the way? It is terrible!"

"Yes, I did. It makes you wonder how humanity goes on. I thought I would not survive, but here you are. You will survive this, too."

Somewhere near morning Ninana's groaning became louder until she emitted a guttural scream. The midwife and Amytis were sitting close by. They jumped up, lifted her out of her bed and helped her onto a birthing stool.

"Push, dear! It is almost here."

Her final scream and push expelled the child into the midwife's waiting hands.

Ninana barely heard his first cry. She slept immediately and for two days until the queen feared she would not awaken. The physician finally showed up, glanced at her from a distance.

"She just needs rest."

Queen Amytis was incensed.

"I summoned you before the child was born and you did not come, so how would you know?"

The physician scowled and shouted.

"I am the royal physician, not a slave to be summoned!"

"And I am Queen Amytis, your queen and regent, if you have forgotten. Guards! Come and escort this negligent physician to the dungeon now."

The physician struggled against the guards.

"Perhaps if and when you are released you will be more prompt when I summon you!"

He turned red in the face and then blanched white.

"The king will hear of this!"

Then he clutched his chest and dropped to the floor. The guards picked him up and carried him away.

Ninana was drowsy and her voice whispery. Queen Amytis rushed to her side.

"What was all the shouting?"

"Thank all the gods you are awake! You have been sleeping for almost two days."

Ninana swung her legs over the side of the bed and started to push herself up onto her feet. She wavered. Her mother took her arm.

"Wait, Ninana. Your body is not ready for you to jump up."

"I guess my legs are a little shaky. I will be alright in a few minutes."

"You have not eaten for almost three days. The servants are bringing some food and a little wine for you. That will help you feel stronger."

Ninana moved to a chaise relieved to be sitting down. Even her arms were shaking. The food tasted so good. She didn't realize how hungry she was. Just as her mother said, she began to feel stronger and steadier.

A servant helped her bathe and change to a fresh tunic and robe. She slipped into her sandals and started out the door.

"Where are you going, Ninana?"

"To the school to continue my work. There is a lot to do and I must catch it up."

"But you have not seen your child!"

A servant brought the baby to Ninana immediately.

"His name will be Belshazzar. The priests and advisors have determined the most appropriate name for him. He is named Belshazzar after various gods and past rulers."

"Then, of course, Belshazzar it is, mother."

She looked curiously at the little face and tiny hands.

"I have not really seen a newborn baby before. I hope he will be prettier soon."

"That is what you looked like when you were born, wrinkled and red. But now you are beautiful."

"I did not think anyone thought I was beautiful, not even me."

Amytis was angry that Ninana took no interest in the child. She took the baby from her and rocked him in her arms, wistfully remembering her young motherhood, so long ago.

"You chose to bring him into the world!"

"No, I did not. I did not even choose his name. You and the priests did that. Who chose mine? What or who is Nitocris? It sounds foreign! And it is ugly. I will never want to be known by that name."

"You are named after goddesses as are all princesses. Ni means 'from the beginning I came from myself,' and Nana was the goddess of Uruk. The name, Nitocris, came from an ancient Egyptian queen and a few thousand years later, a princess. Your father heard of them when he invaded Egypt. Your names take you from being a princess to a queen."

Ninana was aghast.

"But why must I have an Egyptian name? Do you know anything about her?"

"It is said that the queen was very strong, as I hope you will be."

"I am strong! I know who I am and what I am. I am an architect. My calling is Babylon!"

"You are now a mother, Ninana. That should mean something to you."

"He comes from a marriage that was not of my choosing, to a man I loathe. That is what it means to me."

"Your name Ninana means that you come from yourself. You are, indeed, very selfish! It fits you well."

Ninana was shaking with anger. She was still not strong.

"I will leave it to the servants to care for him as royalty always does with their children. He will be just fine without me."

Queen Amytis handed the baby to a servant and walked away shaking her head.

Chapter 9

BABYLON RISES

⸺ ❧ ❧ ⸺

Recognizable parts of Babylon were slowly beginning to rise from the ruins. Main streets were cleared so materials could be brought in. Ninana spent many months on the site, occasionally traveling back with the supply caravans to confer with Jarem, her friend and the master architect of the school.

Her efforts to interest her father in her work were still futile. He barely listened to her description of how the work was progressing and briefly glanced at some of her drawings.

"Zaidu tells me all I need to know. He will come back soon."

"Father, Zaidu sent me to you with this information. He trusts me to bring it to you so he can stay in Babylon and continue to oversee the work. It becomes more demanding on him as the work progresses. Shipments of materials come in all the time and they must be recorded to be sure they are correct. The Euphrates must be contained and channels dug so the city will not be washed away when it floods…"

"I will come soon and see for myself."

Ninana took a deep breath and stepped back.

"Of course, Father. We will love to have you come and see our work and your city rising. When do you plan to do that? I am sure Zaidu would like to arrange a tour for you and go over the records of purchases as well. May I tell him when you will be there?"

"Ninana, you more than test my patience! I will send a message to him myself."

Ninana turned, folded her drawings, and put them into a shoulder bag.

"I am more than just your daughter and a mere girl. I am an architect and a woman of talent who works on your behalf. I am sure you do not know what it is like to be treated like nothing."

"You are a married woman with a child that you ignore. What do you say to that?"

"You married me to a man who ignores me and in a drunken craze he caused me to become a mother when I did not wish it. Now you even rebuke me because of the marriage and child you forced upon me.

"I would like you to recognize me for who I am rather than who you think all women should be. I am not like them. I can never be like them. Please, Father, look at me, hear me!"

"I do not know what you are talking about."

Ninana sighed, bowed slightly, and walked away. As always she was more than a little disappointed at her father's lack of response to her true calling. He never would give her the credit she deserved or consider her of any importance at all.

Immediately she hurried to the architectural school, tears running down her cheeks. Seeing Jarem who always encouraged her work quieted her disappointments and lifted her spirits.

"I tried to make him understand again, Master Jarem. It brought the same result. He sees me as nothing but a baby maker."

"Ninana why do you continue to upset yourself about this? He will never change. He really does not know what you are talking about because he is a warrior king, not a loving father. To him people are to be ruled, commanded, and slain if they do not obey."

"I guess that is why no one ever confronts him, not even my mother. It is a wonder he does not have me imprisoned or killed!"

"It would be best if you relented and returned to your work on Babylon. You do have his permission to do that. Be content."

She and Jarem spent many hours working over plans, designs, the height of buildings that the ground would support. Some areas were sand, some clay, and some rock, and the larger buildings needed to be built on the rock. Ruins were smashed into small pieces for underpinnings and roadbeds.

To her amazement drainage and sewage systems had to be constructed in the foundations. Uruk had no such systems.

"Princess, we must carry away the waste of the residents or it will be dumped into the streets and alleys. There will be water from the river running through the drains to wash it back into the river, and deep holes excavated outside of the city for other refuse to be burned and buried.

With Jarem's help Ninana learned more and more each day about the site.

"Who knew there was so much to building a city!"

Master Jarem smiled.

"There is even more. We will learn it together as we go along."

Before she went back to Babylon, Ninana made a brief visit to her mother and her child. Belshazzar was crawling around the nursery and squealing with delight when the servants played with him. Ninana knelt down and hugged him. He was a little puzzled but allowed her to hug him.

"He does not know who you are, Ninana."

"I know that, Mother. He will one day when the time is right. Thank you for taking care of him for me."

"It should be you, Ninana."

"I do not believe that. He is royalty and will have all the care and education that comes with being a prince. He will be respected as I am not."

"You had another audience with your father. How did that go?"

"It is hopeless. I will keep to my work and not agitate him further."

"I know him, Ninana. I do not bother trying to change him. I simply go about doing those things that are mine to do and be content."

"Do you not want more out of life, Mother? Do you have some dreams of your own?"

"I have dreamed of visiting my homeland in Assyria. But that is not possible now. Your father would never understand that either. My home is where he decrees it should be and I must obey. I was given to him to keep the peace between empires, not to be loved or understood."

"And so, like me, you are considered property and not a person."

"Yes. But you are stepping away from that and becoming your own person. I understand what you need to do. I admire you and I fear for you. Please do not anger your father. Even though he has been forbearing about your calling, he is still a dangerous man and could turn on you in an instant."

"I saw him do that when he abruptly demanded that I marry. His face was hard as stone. I will not say anything further to him. I will stay in Babylon. Master Jarem, Zaidu, and Daniel are my friends and do understand. I will learn to be content with that."

Amytis looked at her daughter with tears in her eyes. Ninana hugged her.

"You are my friend and I love you, my mother. I have never said that to you, but I feel it and it is true."

"I do not think I have ever been loved, Ninana."

They stood embracing each other for a moment.

"I must go. Be well my daughter."

Ninana departed perhaps never to see her mother again.

Chapter 10

A NEW DIRECTION

A merchant from China, Master Fu Ling Yang, was traveling and trading on the on the western part of the ancient Silk Road and came southeast to Uruk. This was his last stop, to trade with King Nebuchadnezzar, before going to the Port of Ur. From there he would sail home to China.

He saw Ninana sketching on a piece of clay in the garden. She looked up to see a strange looking man watching her. Standing up she could see he was not as tall as she, with a yellow hue to his skin and oddly shaped eyes.

"My name is Fu Ling Yang."

With his hands together like a prayer he bowed deeply.

"What a beautiful name. What does it mean?"

"It means rich, spiritual, and always in the light of the sun."

His ability to speak her language was surprising. Many foreigners who visited needed the palace interpreters.

"My name is Ninana. It means 'I came from myself' as the Goddess of Uruk."

Ninana put her hands together like his and bowed momentarily.

"A truly blessed name, Princess. It means you are self-creating and your talent comes from within you. Would you do me the honor of showing me your work?"

"Yes! I am most happy to show you my drawings. Please come with me."

They went to her apartment and she brought out some drawings on papyrus. He spread them out on a table and looked them over carefully for some time.

"Where did you learn to do this?"

"The ideas come from within me, as my name means...I come from within myself."

"These are excellent. You have wonderful inner vision. Should you choose to come to China someday, I would love to show you the wonders of Chinese architecture."

Ninana caught her breath. She did not expect an invitation. He was a stranger and yet she felt a sense of trust regarding him.

"China? I do not know where China is. Is it far? How would I get there?"

"If you are willing I will come for you. You will not make the journey alone. I will bring a wonderful lady of royalty for your company. And I will return you safely home."

"But how would we travel? By horses or carriages? I do know how to ride a horse."

"We would travel by ship from the Port of Ur, sail around the horn of India, and north to China. That is how I will travel home. It is a very long journey, but one I am sure you will find fascinating and instructive.

"That sounds so exciting. I have never been on a ship. I am not even sure what one looks like."

When Fu Ling Yang smiled his slanted eyes nearly closed.

"It is truly wonderful. I will return in a few years during my travels to trade with your father. I will call for you and we will plan it all together."

Ninana thought about this all during the week of his visit to the palace in Uruk. He gave her a gift of Chinese drafting tools. She looked at each one carefully as he explained what they were and how to use them.

"My decorative designs must have hard straight lines and correct angles for strong foundations under the walls. These tools will help me do that! Master Jarem has been teaching me shapes and geometry which are so fascinating. I need to know them for laying out property boundaries. Thank you!

"I must name a building in Babylon in honor of you. It will be the 'Building of 'Yang Light of the Rising Sun.'"

He smiled and bowed.

"I am most pleased. It will be beautiful and I must come to see it one day when it is complete. Ah, I see that my carriage has arrived."

She walked to the palace gate with him, feeling strangely sad to see him leave. They bowed to each other in the oriental style and he climbed into the carriage.

"China! I must know about Chinese architecture so I can build one dedicated to him. I wonder what they look like."

Ninana traveled to Babylon many more times with finished detailed plans for the buildings while the construction continued. Zaidu was pleased with the constant sharpening of her skills. She built small but highly detailed model buildings from her plans to assist Zaidu and the builders.

They studied them imagining them as the huge edifices that would grace Babylon.

Her sketches of the Ishtar Gate and the palaces were her favorites. They were as magnificent as the huge city walls that protected them from invaders and the flooding of the Euphrates River.

She chose the perfect place for Fu Ling Yang's building and wondered again what Chinese architecture would look like.

The years passed quickly and Fu Ling Yang returned to Uruk as he promised. Ninana was thrilled to see him. She had been thinking about China ever since he left.

She questioned Zaidu and everyone else who might know something about China. No one seemed to know any more than she did. It was disappointing. She wanted to be knowledgeable when Fu Ling Yang returned.

King Nebuchadnezzar and Fu Ling Yang met and made a trade agreement for special building materials and plans to create beautiful hanging gardens. It was agreed that Ninana would go to China and accompany these materials back to Babylon.

She was about to burst with anticipation when she saw Fu Ling Yang in the courtyard garden. She wanted to run to him, but she stopped.

They bowed respectfully to each other.

A young woman stood a few steps behind him.

"This is Lishan, Princess. She is of a royal family. She is now in my charge and will be your companion throughout the journey. She can tell you everything you need to know about China."

Lishan bowed deeply and Ninana did the same. Then they hesitated uncertain what to do next. Suddenly their eyes met and they began to laugh. Ninana reached for Lishan's hand and led her to a place in the garden where they could sit and talk.

"Ninana, I wish you to know that I will be your friend always. I have been so eager to meet you. Fu Ling Yang has told me about your visits and your architecture drawings. Please tell me all about you."

"Lishan, you speak my language so well. I wish I could speak yours."

"Perhaps you will someday. I will begin teaching you."

They went to Ninana's apartments where they selected her belongings to pack.

"I know nothing about packing or traveling except to Babylon. I carry only a bag with my drawing tools and goat skins. My clothing is very simple. There are ceremonial garments here that I have never worn."

She was amazed at Lishan's efficiency. She knew what to do and did it so quickly. They were finished before Ninana realized they had started.

"There are many things to learn and see in the far east. We will stop in India and then sail on to China. I am sure you will love how people dress there...in long, flowing garments made of beautiful colorful silks."

"What is silk? I do not think I have ever seen it."

Silk is smooth, flowing and can be brightly colored. We make silk in China. I will show you all about it when we get there."

They were constantly together. They had unending conversations as the preparations for the trip to China progressed. Ninana asked the questions that had been in her mind since Fu Ling Yang first visited them.

"What do the buildings look like? Are they different from ours in Babylonia?"

"They are very different. I think you will like them."

"How can they be different. Surely they have doors and windows and roofs."

"Of course, and many rooms beautifully decorated."

The laughed together over many things. She fell in love with Lishan who was sweet, gentle, and very intelligent. She was also very tiny, short like Fu Ling Yang. Ninana felt like a giant next to her.

"I want to take you to my school of architecture to meet Master Jarem and the students. We can look at my drawings together. You can see what I do there and how Babylon will look."

"That is very exciting! Can we go now?"

A carriage brought them to the school. They stepped quietly through the entrance and Lishan looked around. The students were hard at work. Master Jarem looked up, smiled, and came to meet them.

"Master Jarem, this is my friend Lishan. We will be going to India and China soon to see the architecture there."

"So your friend Fu Ling Yang has returned, Ninana. I am sure this is a wonderful opportunity for you. Architecture is different in other places and you will learn much. I will pray to the gods for your safe return."

The students stood and bowed to Lishan and Ninana as he introduced Lishan of China. Shamhar was enchanted by Lishan. He could not take his eyes off her. She was unlike anyone he had ever seen.

"Your name sounds like music. What does it mean?"

"My name? Lishan, means beautiful, mild, and virtuous. I hope that I am becoming those things."

"I am sure you are already those things and more! I hope we will see you... very often."

Then Shamhar blushed and stepped back.

Lishan smiled kindly at him and bowed.

"It will be my honor to visit you again."

Ninana showed Lishan her work and told her all about her designs how they were now being used in the rebuilding of the City of Babylon.

Lishan sketched a Chinese building for her, putting little upward curves on the corners of the roof.

"Oh, your buildings are very different! I must see more of them so I can design Yang Light of the Rising Sun in the Chinese way!"

They laughed as they talked together. When they were leaving Lishan glanced at Shamhar and smiled.

"You must tell me more about him, Ninana. He has a kind face and a gentle way."

"He was the first student to speak to me and he was very respectful. He seemed quite taken with you. Lishan."

They giggled and laughed more as they rode back to the palace in a carriage. Everything was so new and exciting to them both.

"Master Fu Ling Yang said that you have a boy child. If there is time may I see him?"

Ninana was taken aback for a moment. Belshazzar was not part of her life and she did not think of presenting him to her guests. Perhaps Amytis would have done that when guests arrived. She never asked.

"Yes, of course we can stop in at the nursery as we go in for dinner. Servants care for him as they do for all royal children."

"Are you happy being a mother?"

Ninana hesitated not sure what to say. Perhaps the truth was the only way to be true friends.

"I never wanted to be a mother, but that is the way of women in royal families. We must produce an heir to the throne so our empire will be secure."

"I understand. We also must protect the dynasty with heirs. You are quite different from women I have met. I like it that you have chosen to be free to pursue your work. I do not have a child, so I cannot speak more. Thank you for telling me. I hope I have not embarrassed you by asking."

"I hesitated because that is the first time I have been asked about him and I was not sure how to speak of him."

"You can say anything to me, Ninana. I will not judge but accept you as you are."

"Come with me. I will take you to him. I have not seen him for many days myself."

Chapter 11

VOYAGE ON THE SEA

Ninana had never been east of Uruk. Actually she had only been to Babylon, to the west. She thought the seaport of Ur at the mouth of the Euphrates must not be very far.

Fu Ling Yang sat down beside her.

"It is much closer than Babylon, but still a long very ride."

"I would prefer to go by horse back. That is how I travel to Babylon."

"I assure you the carriage is a better choice. Being in a carriage we can speak with each other. I share your interests. Perhaps I could learn more about you and your work. I would be delighted to join in your conversations."

They taught Ninana to say hello and goodbye in Chinese, please and thank you. Ninana had to practice making the sounds that were foreign to her. Her mouth would not quite make the shapes needed.

"Lishan, it sounds so easy when you say them. I feel very clumsy trying to sound like that."

"Our language is many thousand years old and the words are almost born within us. We come in with mouths that know how to make them. Your language has been strange for me, too, and I have practiced it since I was a child. When I was very young Master Fu Ling Yang said I must learn many languages so I could travel with him and understand merchants from other cultures."

To Ninana's amazement the Port of Ur was nothing like the Euphrates River running though Babylon. It turned into a huge harbor and docks reaching out into the water that were filled with ships of all sizes and descriptions. Men were running everywhere loading and unloading them. Their shouts and the smells of the seashore were overwhelming. At first it made her feel quite ill.

"Do not worry. We will rest at a hotel until tomorrow. My physician will bring you some herbs in a little wine to make feel comfortable again."

At the hotel Fu Ling Yang's physician gave her an herbal potion to quiet her stomach. After dinner Lishan took her to their room. They lay down on a large square shaped bed piled with quilts and pillows. The potion was taking effect and Ninana slept soundly until morning.

Footsteps in their doorway awakened them just after dawn. A servant came into the room with a tray of food and placed it on a table. The fruit, fish, and bowls of creamy kefir looked delicious.

"Eat lightly, Ninana. The ship will be another experience that may unsettle your stomach."

"Oh, please! Not that again. I had enough of that feeling when I was with child."

The carriage took them onto the huge dock where their ship was moored. Again the noise of men shouting and the smell of dead fish was strong, but Ninana was more relaxed and better able to tolerate it. As they boarded the ship, the sailors were busy readying it to set sail.

"Is this our only ship? Will we be quite alone on the open water?"

Ninana had never seen a vast body of water like the sea and felt a bit fearful.

Lishan stayed close beside her as they walked on board.

"Some of these ships at the docks and anchored around the bay are ours. They are loaded with trading goods. We will all be sailing together, but a distance apart. They are slower than ours because of the kind of ship they are. They will catch up with us at various ports. We will stay in each place for a few days."

Lishan did not mention the help they might need in storms and high waves. Nor did she mention fending off pirates. Ninana had enough new experiences to take in and those other things may or may not come.

Again Ninana felt a little unsettled as they walked up the gang plank and stepped on the gently rocking ship. Lishan took her arm firmly and Fu Ling Yang came immediately to her other side. They led her to a small stateroom and she gratefully sat down on a bench.

"Do not worry. You will get your sea legs soon and then be able to walk easily along the decks. When we land in India and China after many weeks at sea, you will need to get your land legs back."

Ninana smiled.

"How many legs to I have? I rode horses to Babylon and had to get my legs back from that too!"

They all laughed.

The oars splashed down and the ship lurched backward. Ninana gripped the side of the bench. Them it turned away from the dock and went forward out into the sea. Soon the rhythmic rocking of the ship and the surge caused by the oars became expected and even comforting. As Ninana became a little steadier she acquired her "sea legs."

Lishan began lessons in Chinese words immediately to help Ninana relax. She was an eager student though still having difficulty producing the sounds as well as the words. "This is how you say hello. It sounds like nee-how and goodbye sounds like shai-jian. Can you say those?"

"Yes, I think so."

Ninana did her best to pronounce them several times.

"Good! Thank you sounds like shieh-shieh. You are welcome sounds like boo-kuh-chi."

"When you introduce yourself you say, 'wo jaio.' Wo jaio Ninana. That means my name is Ninana."

"Oh, I like that. Wo Jaio Ninana!"

"Two more for today. Yes sounds like sheh. No sounds like Bu-sheh."

Ninana faithfully practiced the words all day, checking with Lishan to be sure she was saying it correctly.

Lishan added more words for her to learn each day. They used a few Chinese words in all their conversations so Ninana would become more accustomed to hearing and saying them.

"It seems that I get hello and goodbye mixed up. People will not know if I am arriving or leaving."

"When you walk away they will know. They will laugh and applaud your efforts. They are very kind."

Their lessons and conversations were full of teasing and joyful laughter.

The weather was hot and humid as they sailed out of the breezy narrow Makran Sea. The small fleet of ships bounced on the waves and pitched with the wind. Sometimes Ninana stayed inside. If she wanted to stay outside the sailors tied her loosely to a mast so she could hang on and not be tossed overboard.

Every day she watched the sailors at work and begged them to let her help. They were hesitant but Fu Ling Yang nodded his agreement. They gave her small jobs to do that she could handle easily.

She quickly graduated to more complicated tasks, loving every minute of it. Concentration on the jobs helped her become steady on her feet and no longer needed the security of being tethered to a mast.

"Perhaps I should be a sailor instead of an architect."

"Oh no, Ninana, that would be very limiting. I am sure you will have had your fill of sailing by the time you come back home. This is a very long journey by sea. It will be more than a year before we begin the return."

They sat in a protected area of the deck snacking on fruit. Lishan returned to instructing Ninana on some the history of China and the Zhou Dynasty.

"The Zhou Dynasty has ruled us for almost eight hundred years. They spread civilization throughout the land. Many good things have expanded our culture. We learned writing and made coins for trade. We learned to use tools to eat called chop sticks instead of our fingers. You will easily learn to use them.

"We have great philosophers and schools. Chinese philosophy is taught in the schools of Confucianism, Taoism and Mohism. Our greatest Chinese philosophers and poets are Lao-Tzu, Tao Chien, Confucius, and Mencius.

"Confucius taught love or human-heartedness, as the basic virtue of humanity. It is called 'ren' in our language. Mencius made the original goodness of human nature or 'xing' basic in his teaching."

Ninana was fascinated by the thought of human-heartedness. There was so little love in her experience that she wondered what it would be like if people valued love and cared about each other. Most people she knew would laugh at the idea. Love is for fools and would get you killed.

"I know about empires and kings, but not dynasties. I have not heard of philosophies, just religions and gods."

"You will learn much more about them as you see how they work in China. We will visit the schools of philosophies and we can talk about them together with a teacher.

"The dynasties are a little like your empires, but one family rules for hundreds of years. Mostly when the family dies out other families come to take their place."

"One family, hundreds of years! Our kings are fortunate if they last thirty years, like my father, usually less. My half-brother, Evol-Merodach, lasted only a few years before he was dethroned and assassinated. He was a nightmare."

Ninana flinched at the memories and quickly changed the subject.

"Tell me what your buildings look like?"

"Here, I will try to show you more clearly than when I drew them at your school."

Lishan began to draw pictures of their buildings and palaces on a piece of goat skin. Ninana watched with fascination as Lishan drew upturned roofs and ornate doorways. She drew lanterns and dragons that symbolize good luck. They were strange and like nothing Ninana had ever imagined.

"Tell me about the dragons. What are they and where do they come from? We have not heard of them in Babylonia."

"They come from very ancient times and no one remembers their beginning. They are mythical, or symbols of light, happiness, and good luck."

"And why do the corners of the roofs turn up? They look so graceful and beautiful. Is there another purpose?"

"Oh yes. We have much rain and they drain the water away from the buildings so the foundations will not be damaged by too much water."

"The building in Babylon that I will name after Master Fu Ling Yang must look like these drawings. Will there be architects in China willing to teach me?"

"There are and they will be most honored to share their knowledge and to learn of Babylon's buildings that you design."

"My buildings? They would be interested in Babylon?"

"Yes. They are as curious and excited about other architectures as you are!"

"But I do not have my drawings with me. I will begin to make some to show them."

"You will have several weeks or more to spend at their school. You can explain to them exactly what Babylonian architecture is."

Ninana's head spun with ideas and possibilities.

Chapter 12

INDIA

Their studies were often interrupted by rough seas, storms, and dead calm when the oars had to be used. Ninana kept busy doing the tasks that Fu Ling Lang approved and the crew allowed her to do. She coiled ropes and secured tools when the crew finished with them. They kept close watch that she did not injure herself or be in danger.

After a peaceful crossing of the Arabian Sea, they pulled into a luxurious port near the southernmost tip of India, Muziris. Ninana looked in amazement at the huge port looming up before the bow of the ship. As they sailed in, it seemed to spread out all around them until she could barely see the entrance to the port from the sea behind them.

Marvelous buildings slowly came into view. When they got closer a huge marketplace of colorful tents and waving flags dominated the coastal area of the city. She and Lishan leaned on a rail and watched the sail-in all the way to their dock.

"How long will we be here? Will there be time to look at everything? There is so much!"

"Yes, we will spend a few days while she ships are swabbed and loaded."

"Which building is a hotel? They all look quite grand!"

"We will stay in a wonderful hotel near the market. We cannot see it from here. The port is full of people from many countries. Traders come here from everywhere and the Indian people are most accommodating. We will have an enjoyable time."

They picked their way along the dock and out onto the waterfront, avoiding rushing sailors and stacks of goods piled everywhere.

Along with wonders also came dangers. Lishan and their hired guards stayed close to Ninana as they browsed through the market stalls. Fu Ling Yang knew these guards well and engaged them on every trip. He would trust no one else.

The hotel was the most ornate and luxurious she had ever seen. It had those upturned roofs and many designs on the walls. It was hard not to trip while looking up at them all.

Ninana excitedly gathered many ideas for her buildings in Babylon. Working on sketches in their hotel room far into the night, she created interiors as well as exteriors. Lishan was fast asleep by the time Ninana gave in to exhaustion, collapsed on the bed, and slept as well.

Early the next morning after meeting Fu Ling Yang for a light breakfast, he took them for a tour of the port and city in a special secure carriage. Ninana was fascinated by the saris and head coverings that women wore. They were so beautiful and in such a wonderful array of colors. Ninana wanted to get out and walk around the streets.

"I would like to walk among them and touch some of the silks."

"My dear it is far to too dangerous. Even though we have professional guards, they could be easily overwhelmed by crowds of curiosity seekers if we stop the carriage anywhere. I just wanted you to see the city before we sail. This is the only safe way to see it."

Lishan squeezed her hand and smiled at her. Ninana swallowed her disappointment and smiled back. Then Lishan pulled something out of her bag and handed it to Ninana. It was a beautiful gown with exquisite colors, designs, and workmanship, lovelier than she had yet seen in the market and on the streets.

"When did you get this? I did not see you purchase anything."

"I bought it before my trip to meet you and saved it for you. I brought it all the way from China. I wanted to give it to you at just the right time."

Tears flooded Ninana's eyes.

"You are so kind to think of me, even before you met me!"

She ran her fingers over the smooth silk and the ornate designs sewn into the fabric.

"Beautiful! When we get back to the hotel I will put it on."

They returned to the hotel to rest. Fu Ling Yang went to the docks to speak with the ship's captain. He returned at dinner time and announced that they would be spending more time in India.

Ninana and Lishan were surprised and at the same time, delighted.

"Wonderful! I want to see more of India."

"We will tour a few cities. I think you will be interested in the architecture in India, Ninana. Perhaps you could sketch some of the buildings for me. I want to introduce some of them to the Chinese designers and builders. We have nothing like these pagodas, stupas, and viharas in China."

"I would love to! What an interesting task."

"We will start out tomorrow. I will bring writing materials for you to use."

Lishan was a little puzzled.

"But Master Fu Ling Yang, is there some difficulty with the ships that we are staying in India?"

"No difficulty that cannot be repaired. A few of our cargo ships will leave for China tomorrow and a ship with a fresh crew will return for us. It may even take several weeks."

"Is there a war?"

"Lishan, you are very perceptive. Yes, there is trouble and the ships will return for us when it is safe. I did not wish to worry Ninana."

"Forgive me, Master. I should have spoken to you privately."

"It is all right. Surely she knows there are battles and troubles between tribes and empires."

Ninana overhead and stepped up to them.

"Indeed I do, Master Fu Ling Yang. My father is always battling on one border or another or invading a foreign country. I do not know why that must be. He told me that is how we build empires. He said girls and women would not understand governing and such. Only men understand."

Fu Ling Yang winced at this.

"That is not correct about women, Princess. There are many warriors and governing royalty in other cultures who are women including China. They are most adept and capable at governing, and their warriors most fearful!"

"I am relieved to hear that. I would like to meet some of them. My husband, who is now the king and not a very good one, will not last long. He is hated and if he is killed, it falls to me, the queen, to become the ruling regent until my son is of age."

"I fear it is the same wherever we go. China is very large and tribes believe they are not powerful unless they are fighting and obliterating each other.

Our rulers in the dynasty try to stop them because it ruins the chances of advancing our civilization."

They eagerly set out the next day to see more of India. Following the shoreline they started north, then over low mountain passes, plateaus, and toward the next city.

"We will see tall narrow towers with three to thirteen curved roofs. They are pagodas. They stand beside a stupa, a round building like a dome, which holds sacred objects. Near them is a vihara, or temple, with open porticoes where traveling monks may rest and shelter during the monsoons."

The travel was hot and dusty, but the cities were endlessly fascinating to Ninana. They found local guides who would share the history of the city and admit them to some of the buildings. Stupas and pagodas were not accessible, but the viharas were welcoming.

Ninana watched the wandering monks who came in and out of the viharas. They were smiling and friendly, but silent. She was not sure if that was because they didn't speak her language, or they could not speak for some other reason.

Some young boys approached them and pointed to Lishan and Fu Ling Yang.

"China! China!"

They a pulled the corners of their eyes to mimic the Chinese eye shape. The monks came out of the vihara and chased them away with switches.

The guards pulled one boy out of the carriage who was looking for something to steal.

"This is the danger I mentioned the first day when you wanted to get out of the carriage, Ninana. Today we have guards and monks to protect us, and only a few wild boys here. In the crowded city slums, it is much worse. They roam in gangs of ten or more."

"In Uruk I was always in the palace, the school, or a carriage. Young boys like these did not approach me. In Babylon I had the company of builders and craftsmen who looked after me. I did not need to think of danger except for the rats and snakes near the river."

"There will be danger in China as well because there are many tribes always bringing trouble. Mostly they roam the hills and join renegade bands."

In each city they sat in the hotel dining room evenings and discussed Ninana's findings and ideas over dinner. She spread her sketches on a table for them to look over. Fu Ling Yang was delighted.

"The designers at the school of architecture will be most pleased."

"This construction is so different from Babylon. It must be the terrain on which we build. The building materials make a difference too. We must import wood from Lebanon which is far away. I am making careful notes for Master Zaidu."

"Zaidu? Who is Master Zaidu, Ninana?"

"Oh, I am sorry. He is the master builder of Babylon. We have worked together on every part of the city for many years. It takes every scrap of information we can get to construct a whole city with all its systems and foundations. Information helps us solve the problems that arise every day."

They toured three cities and Ninana wanted to stay and spend time in each one of them. They were gone so many weeks that Ninana was sure the ships would sail without them.

"No need to be concerned. They will be waiting for us. There is still the matter of when the sailors will arrive from Guangzhou. Sailing on the high seas always has many challenges, even more than we have already seen."

This made Ninana wonder what they were not telling her, but she decided not to ask. There was enough to concentrate on with her sketches and notes. She wanted to give Master Zaidu a full report.

Chapter 13

INDIA TO CHINA

—————— ❧ ❧ ——————

When they arrived back in the Port of Muziris, Ninana was secretly relieved that their ship was still there. The sailors arrived the next day and immediately set about preparing everything for the voyage to China.

They set sail on a very hot morning. The moist air was still and stifling. There was no relief in the cabin or on deck. The sails were flat and the oars sluggish. Ninana and Lishan had little energy in the heat and slept on and off during the day.

"It will be cooler as we get past the islands and sail north."

"I hope so! It is hard to do anything but sit still and hope for a breeze."

Some stewards brought cool drinks and frozen desserts. Ninana could not believe what she was experiencing.

"How did these get so cold?"

"They are kept frozen in the cold rooms beneath the hotel in Muziris. Frozen water is brought from high in the mountains in special containers so it will not melt and stored in very cold rooms deep under the ground."

The cooling of the deserts and drinks in her throat were refreshing. They ate and drank them quickly before the hot air could warm them. For a short time she could even breathe more easily.

It seemed to take forever to sail through the islands and start northward. Storms rocked the ship and brought no cool air. It rained and rained until the decks were too slick to walk on. Lishan and Ninana stayed in the cabin even though it was airless and hot.

"Is it always like this?"

"Yes, always."

"Lishan, is there another way to get to China?"

"Yes, over the Silk Road. It is an ancient and busy trade route that comes into China from the west through treacherous mountains and hot deserts. There are robbers and brigands there, too, that rob travelers and often kill them."

"There, too? Do you mean there are robbers here on the seas as well? Are we in danger from them?"

Lishan snatched her breath. She didn't mean to tell Ninana that there were dangers and now she had done it.

"Yes, called pirates. They are a danger here, but we have other ships with us and many sailors to fight them off, so they rarely bother a fleet."

"Pirates! Have you ever seen them? Have they attacked when you were on a ship?"

"I saw them at a distance. They came upon us suddenly in the islands and turned away when they saw our ships."

"Did you pursue them?"

"No. We do not look for battles. To catch them would mean to expose us all to whatever diseases they might have on board. Better to let the ravages of sea life dispose of them."

"I see. There is much for me to learn on the high seas. Have you traveled on the Silk Road?"

"Very little. Master Fu Ling Yang believes it is too dangerous. He travels only on a few parts of it in the far west. Traders travel on camels, horses, donkeys, and on foot. Farther east there are high mountains and arid deserts to cross. Many travelers die along the way from accidents, illness, freezing to death, or from lack of water. They are even robbed and murdered.

"The Silk Road splits to go to cities on both sides of the deserts. One part goes farther to the north and then southeast to meet the part that goes south and comes back to meet the northern route. Then it goes east and south through China. It takes much more time, many more months, than to travel on the sea."

"Lishan, you are so knowledgeable about these things. You must have studied for a very long time."

"I have studied since I was a child. In China we begin education very early. It made me curious about everything."

"Oh, and I have been drawing buildings since I was a child. That is why I am excited to go to China, to see the architecture. But I know of little else. Thank you for being such a good teacher for me."

The stifling hot air came after the storms and lingered for many days with no breeze for the sails. Large fans made of bamboo and bird feathers were brought to the rowers below deck. Servants and rowers took turns fanning everyone.

Some of the rowers fell ill from the heat and had to be moved to the upper deck under a canopy where a physician treated them. Some died and were dumped into the sea.

Ninana was shocked to see this.

"Master Fu Ling Yang, can we not take them home for their families to bury them?"

"No, we cannot. The bodies would decay and sicken us all. We would all die. We send them into the sea with a special blessing. Their families will be notified and compensated. It is expected that some sailors will not come home.

"We will sail into the Strait of Malacca, between the peninsula that is attached to the mainland of China and the islands around it. The next seaport will be Malacca where we will trade for supplies and food. We will stay in a hotel at the port while our sailors scrub down the decks and generally clean the ship."

The accommodations in Malacca were not good like Muziris, but there were no other choices. Fu Ling Yang sent for the guards in Malacca that he trusted, but they did not respond. He sent sailors to look for them. They returned shaking their heads.

"They are dead. Killed by brigands last week. Their brothers told us."

"This is not good. We will all return to the ship now. We cannot stay here without guards."

As they turned to toward the ship two men approached them.

"We are brothers of your slain guards. If you will have us, we will be your guards. We understand you pay well."

Fu Ling Yang's eyes narrowed.

"How did you learn that I pay well? Perhaps you killed these men you say are your brothers and took their wages."

"We would not kill our own brothers!"

"Yes, you would and you did."

The sailors stepped up with knives drawn. The young men backed away. They hurried into an alley and disappeared.

Ninana, Lishan, and Fu Ling Yang returned to the ship accompanied by their sailors. The cleaning was still in progress, but the cabins were cleaned, so they could comfortably stay in them. Lishan approached Fu Ling Yang.

"Master, how did you know they killed their brothers?"

"They mentioned the good wages. And I do not believe they were the brothers. More likely they were the brigands who killed them. They knew that those men worked for us so they killed them and waited for us, hoping to take their place."

The sailors stayed on guard overnight. The next morning the food was loaded on board and the ship was ready to sail. Again Lishan was reassuring.

"We will soon be through the straits, past the islands, and into the South China Sea. There will be cooler air."

A few days later they passed through the straits, past a scattering of islands into the South China Sea, as Master Fu Ling Yang and Lishan said. The welcome breezes came up filling the sails, cooling the air a little.

Ninana and Lishan sat in a favorite sheltered place in the prow of the ship. They so enjoyed sharing their life experiences, practicing Chinese words, and drawing sketches of their homes.

They walked on the decks together letting the breezes blow through their hair. Ninana had become accustomed to the motion of the ship and moved along the decks easily. As they sailed closer to the China coast she was leaning over the rail to catch a glimpse of the land on the western horizon.

"Will we be able to see China soon? Are we close?"

"Yes, we are close but still too far out to see land, Ninana. We will be turning into a very wide river and sailing to a busy port there, the Port of Guangzhou. We will be putting into that port in a week or two, depending upon the weather, tides, and other boat traffic."

China! Ninana's dream of several years now was coming true! She felt the same thrill as she felt when she saw Babylon for the first time so many years ago.

Chapter 14

ARRIVING IN CHINA

They neared the China coast and soon turned into the mouth of the large Zhou Jiang River. The Port of Guangzhou was located on this wide river that carried ships inland to the protected port. Ninana watched carefully as they navigated the river and passed the many islands. Eventually the port and a huge city beyond it came in view.

Before they prepared to disembark Fu Ling Yang sat down with them.

"I want to tell you that the battles nearby have ceased for how. The Zhou Army has beat them back into the hills. I believe the army has successfully secured the city and the whole province, so we should be able to travel safely. I will be checking with the army commanders regularly.

"My people will meet us and take us to our home within the protected city. They will be accompanied by guards. I will be making arrangements for our travels about the city and beyond if no more battles erupt.

"My assistants will locate what your father has purchased in our agreement, Princess. All will be shipped to Ur on a freighter and carried on smaller barges up the Euphrates to Babylon."

"Thank you, Master. I am deeply grateful for all you are doing for me and for Babylon. It has been my heart felt joy for so many years. My focus is now on China. Lishan has told me about the Silk Road and I would love to see a small part of it. Would that be possible? Is it close enough?"

"Yes. It ends in here in Guangzhou near coastal markets where we will be docking. You will be able to experience the excitement of the merchants and see things from many other provinces and countries at this end of the Silk Road. It is a very busy market area…"

"And, yes, it is a very dangerous place."

"Ah so. I am happy you remember that. Stay with our guards at all times. They will take you where you want to go. Lishan will speak to them for you in their language. The few words you have learned will serve to make the required polite greetings."

"Xièxiè, Master Fu Ling Yang."

"Bù keqì, Princess."

They walked gingerly down the gang plank and stepped onto docks that were swarming with dock workers and merchants. Goods were moved on and off ships at a dizzying rate.

"How does everyone know where everything goes and which cargo to move. It all looks like a jumble."

Fu Ling Yang smiled and the corner of his eyes crinkled.

"I assure you that everyone on the docks knows what to do. Everything is marked and the dock workers recognize those markings. Each ship has its own special mark as well. The ships' officers have a list of the cargo and check everything as it comes on and off their ships."

He pointed out one of the officers who was checking the marks. The officer moved with lightning speed from bundle to stack. Then she could recognize that other officers doing the same. The jumble was beginning to make sense to her.

She was transfixed watching everything when Lishan touched her arm.

"Our carriage is here. We will show you some of the market and city on the way to our place of lodging."

Ninana became acutely aware that not only was she taller than Fu Ling Yang and Lishan, but taller than everyone she saw. Feeling like she towered above the crowd, she found herself hunching down a bit.

"Ninana! What are you doing?"

"I feel like a giant here."

"You are not a giant and you will see others who are as tall as you are. Please stand up and be proud of your stature."

Ninana felt a bit embarrassed and straightened her shoulders.

"I have not seen anyone my height since I left Babylon."

Lishan laughed and hugged her.

Everywhere people were smiling and seemed happy as they hurried about their business.

She remembered to bow politely the way Lishan and Fu Ling Yang did and say, "Nǐhǎo, Wǒ jiào Ninana."

They politely bowed to her.

Fu Ling Yang escorted them to a carriage. As they left the dock area and drove through the markets, Ninana watched the buildings they passed with rapt fascination. Ornamentation and designs were on the walls of buildings and everywhere else that she looked.

Streets were decorated with lighted fire breathing dragons and lined with colorful lanterns. The music playing from all around them was in a quarter tone sound. Though strange to her ears, it was pleasant and even joyful.

Guards rode on the back of the carriage and some walked beside it. They stopped at a large bazaar so Ninana and Lishan could step down and approach some of the displays.

Fu Ling Yang watched with interest as they walked through racks of clothing, tables of vases, decorations, and many things Ninana could not imagine a use for.

"Anything you want to purchase here will be sent to a warehouse and included with the items being shipped back to Babylon."

She picked up a beautiful Jade and gold bracelet.

"May I just wear it?"

"Yes, of course."

Fu Ling Yang signaled the seller, marked something on a piece of rice paper and bowed.

The day was waning and the exhausted travelers stepped back into the carriage. They drove through a large ornate gate and stopped in front of a magnificent home on a hill. Lishan touched her arm.

"This home has belonged to his family for generations. I have been honored to grow up here."

"I am so amazed. I want to get my sketching materials and draw them all!"

"You will certainly have time to do that and more."

The family and servants immediately came out to greet them.

"Their kimonos are so beautiful!"

"There will be lovely kimonos supplied for us as well. Come, let us greet them and go in."

"Nǐhǎo, Wǒ jiào Ninana."

They all smiled and bowed.

Ninana dropped into the large, canopied bed and was sure she would sleep immediately. But it was as if she were still on the ship. She felt that the room was moving.

"Lishan, I cannot sleep. I am still feeling the waves of the ocean!"

Lishan rang for a servant and asked for something to help Ninana sleep.

"It takes a few days for the sensation of motion to stop. A servant will bring you a little rice wine. I will light a candle so you can center yourself in the room and ease the feeling of rocking."

Ninana observed that the servants almost scurried in, bowed low, and silently backed out of the room. How different this was from Uruk where the noisy rushing around and clatter of the bowls of food as they were brought in and set down, disrupted conversations.

Feeling incredibly peaceful she was soon asleep. She had dreams of sailing the seas, marketplaces, and shadowy figures moving about. She awakened to see that the shadowy figures were the servants quietly bringing in food and fresh kimonos. Sleep overtook her again for another hour.

Chapter 15

SILKWORMS AND DANCERS

In the morning Lishan came to her bedside with fruit and rice in a bowl.

"Ninana, would you like a little food?"

"Oh, Lishan, I was dreaming that we were still in India!"

"I dreamed that too. Do you feel well? Has the rocking stopped?"

"Yes! The room has stopped moving."

Ninana sat up and realized she was very hungry. Gratefully she took the bowl from Lishan and they sat down together cross legged on a very large pillow.

"Today we can have a day of rest and a walk through the royal gardens. The royal grandmother would like to show you her prize silkworms. She lives at the end of the garden path."

"Worms? Silkworms? What are they?"

"The silk you wear is made from the skin that the worms shed. The skins are spun into threads and woven into fabrics. It takes thousands of worms carefully raised and nurtured. Everyone in China raises silkworms, even the school children."

Ninana remembered the tail of the snake she encountered near the river in Babylon and shivered at the thought of wearing the skins of worms.

"Do not worry, Ninana. The worms do not look like snakes. In fact when they hatch they look like little ants. They are placed on mulberry leaves to eat the mulberry buds and become fat like worms."

Ninana was still skeptical. It is hard to imagine ants producing silk skins and spun into the kimono she was wearing.

They walked through gardens of flowers and ornamental trees, red bridges over streams, and beautiful little buildings with roofs upturned at the corners. Gardeners were carefully tending the plants and pathways.

"Everything is so beautiful! Enchanting!"

"Yes. People's lives are often hard and our gardens are intended to enchant and give pleasure. The grandmother's cottage is just around the corner at the edge of the mulberry tree orchard. We must be very quiet. Silkworms might die from sudden noises."

Ninana was still not sure she wanted to see worms, but now her curiosity was peaked. They fairly tiptoed into the cottage. The grandmother met them and bowed. She whispered as she showed them each stage of nurturing silkworms and how they were cared for. They saw the final cocoons that the worms shed and the women who were carefully soaking them in boiling water to loosen and to extract the silk.

Outside the orchards stretched as far as the eye could see with thousands of mulberry trees that produced the leaves to feed the silkworms.

"It all looks very complicated."

"Yes, and it is one of our major industries. We export silk everywhere and to other lands. Children are taught this skill very young. Schools teach them to raise the worms as well. The silkworm industry is everywhere. There are huge farms dedicated to raising the silkworms."

They walked to the far edge of the orchard and stopped at a small factory where the raw silk was bundled ready to be taken to the houses where it was spun and dyed beautiful colors. The silk was white or yellow before it was dyed.

"Then beautiful clothes, kimonos, slippers, wall and bed coverings are made from the sheets of silk."

Ninana forgot about snakes, worms, ants, and felt a little better about the silk kimono she was wearing, and the silk slippers. She realized that she knew next to nothing about the origin of the rough tunics and robes she wore in Babylon.

They went back to the house for a banquet style meal. Lishan and Ninana were famished.

"We will rest, eat, and be entertained by musicians and dancers for the evening."

Ninana was tired and thought she would like to eat and go to bed, but the dancers came out in amazing costumes and their movements fascinated and energized her. The dance moves they made and the masks they wore were like nothing she had ever seen. The quarter-tone music was strangely intriguing, even haunting at times.

Lishan whispered the story to her, which made it easy to understand what the characters were symbolizing. There were innocent girls, murderous villains, and rescuing heroes.

"I never went to theaters in Uruk because they were brothels and dancers were only enticing the men to come to their rooms. This theater is so different and delightful."

After the performance Lishan took Ninana backstage to meet the actors. They were happy to show her their costumes and explain the theater arts to her through Lishan.

"How do you make those dance steps?"

A dancer took her hand and showed her how to turn her feet and arms and move to the strange music.

"Lishan, it is like trying to make my mouth speak your words as you do. My arms and legs do not want to turn the way the dancers turn theirs."

"They have been dancing all their lives, since they were young children. Their young soft bones naturally adjusted to the movements. It would be difficult for me to make those movements now because I have not danced since I was a child."

"Oh, Lishan, I thought you could do anything!"

"We all have our place in life. It is important that we do that place justice and not try to do everything. You are an architect who builds cities and I am not. You have been doing it since you were a child, just like these dancers."

"I feel very tall and awkward here, but I can climb over the ruins of Babylon with no difficulty. Even if my hands and knees are scratched from the stones, I love it all.

"Lishan I am taller than all of your people, especially the elderly ones. I feel like I should sit down to talk to some of them. Are there none taller among them?"

"We have tall people, Ninana. You will meet some of them. We will visit many different places where people come from tribes far away. They are tall like their tribe's people."

"I thought when I met you and Master Fu Ling Yang, that you were the only two. Now I see it is all of your people."

They laughed and chatted together about all their experiences as they went to their sleeping room. A servant brought small bowls of rice wine for their sleep. Ninana was grateful for this because she was too excited and sleep would not come quickly.

Chapter 16

THE SCHOOL OF PHILOSOPHY

Ninana woke up early, anticipating what this day would bring. Everything had been so new and exciting.

Lishan rolled out of the bed onto her feet.

"Come, let us go to the baths this morning before the food comes. A revitalizing soak in tepid water with herbs and fragrances, and an energizing mint massage will be wonderful."

Ninana was ready to go right into the next adventure, but Lishan was right. It was good to take care of herself and not just charge through her days here. How different this was from camping at the site of the ruins of Babylon, climbing the stones, barely taking time to stop and consider her own needs.

They splashed into the water and floated among the flowers. The fragrances were energizing and the massage wonderful. She had never had a massage in Babylon. They were what the men did that led to something else.

"Today Master Fu Ling Yang and some guards will take us to the school of philosophy. Do you remember on the ship when I spoke of our greatest

Chinese philosophers and poets, Lao-Tzu, Tao Chien, Confucius, and Mencius?

"Confucius taught love or human-heartedness, as the basic virtue of humanity. It is called 'ren' in our language. Mencius made the original goodness of human nature or 'xing' basic in his teaching."

"Yes, I remember. But I still do not know what a philosophy is."

Lishan hesitated over her breakfast and thought for a moment.

"Philosophy is the love of wisdom and intellectual inquiry into the nature of living life. It is beliefs that are stated in an orderly way so people can live by them. We will go to the schools and libraries. The teachers there will explain this more clearly than I can and I will translate when needed."

"Oh. Love of wisdom! My father's philosophy was to rule, conquer, murder, and enslave. This is how he said empires are built. No love of anything except power, pride in his city, and his empire."

"That might be a form of philosophy, but it is about the physical actions. That is not the love of wisdom and the intellectual inquiry into the nature of things. Philosophy is of the mind and thought."

Ninana frowned and finished her food. The difference was not yet clear to her.

Master Fu Ling Yang called for them and escorted them to a waiting carriage. The guards were seated on the back of the carriage and some mounted on horses beside it.

"Why did we not have guards yesterday in the gardens?"

"Because the gardens are protected and the guards are out of sight to preserve the tranquility. We are going into the city and through dangerous places today. We will have guards with us now wherever we go."

The school buildings were low and spread over many acres. They had the same curved roof edges and decorations on the walls that she saw when they docked. Ninana could not read the words on the outside but Lishan said it was School of Philosophy.

"Your writing is like pictures."

"Yes, each mark changes the letter to another one. A student learns twenty-six hundred characters before being able to read the simplest text."

"I was never taught to read our Arcadian writings. I recognize some of the common words and names on the buildings. Mostly my study was geometry for building."

The interior was very quiet and people spoke in low tones. Classrooms were divided only by painted screens. There were shelves of writings along the walls in the area called the library.

A man came to meet them, bowed, and beckoned them into one of the classrooms. A teacher came forth who, much to Ninana's joy, spoke her language.

"How is it that you have someone who speaks my language?"

"He was brought here from another school far away in honor of your visit. They wish you to understand. We will spend many days here and hear the different philosophies. This teacher will present each one."

"How will this help me in architecture? Or will it?"

"If we have a philosophy of the goodness of humanity, how will your buildings reflect that. Will there be art that will express that? Or will there be only pictures of war and slavery?"

"I thought of that only when I wanted to design the building dedicated to Fu Ling Yang. I did not think of that applying to all of my buildings."

The teacher came in, bowed, and began a lesson on Confucianism and then the teachings of Mencius. Ninana asked many questions about how these ideas were formulated into a teaching.

"Master, where do they come from and who uses them? How are they used? Is everyone made to follow them?"

"My Dear Princess, the ideas come from the heart and mind of a person and they cannot be legislated or forced upon others. Each person must see the truth of these teachings within themselves and then express them in what they say and do."

"So, Master Teacher, are those who do battle and attack others not able to see this? My father, the King of Babylonia, he sees only a necessity to rule, command, and enslave. He has built the largest empire in the middle east."

"This creates a conflict between what is within and what is without. Actions do not reflect his inner truth. Do you see any effect from this on his happiness?"

Ninana sat back and thought about this.

"He is never happy. He cares nothing for the desires of others. He is now losing his mind. Some days he does not recognize me as his daughter. He becomes agitated and confused."

Ninana began to think about Daniel and all of their discussions.

"Daniel was surely a man of inner peace and followed the ways of peace and love. He stayed so centered and unruffled. He called it the teachings of his invisible god. Did he mean that this god presence was the truth within him?"

The more the teacher spoke of these things, the more she was sure that she understood them, understood herself, and even Daniel.

She remembered the arguments with her father and how he crushed her spirit every time. Yes, of course! This was the difference She did not know how to protect this inner truth except to bury herself in her work.

"How long will we be here? I want to hear more if possible."

"A teacher of Mencius will be here tomorrow. His teachings are very similar. How are you feeling about this? Are you comfortable?"

"I am comfortable and learning some things about myself, my father, and my friend Daniel. Something within me comes alive when Daniel speaks of his god, and that same something within me was always crushed by my father. I am learning about that. I need to know a little more."

"That is wonderful, Ninana. I was afraid you would not be interested in philosophy. It can be boring for some people."

"I am far from bored. There are so many things to learn about life that I was never taught. You know so many things and I am in awe of you."

"And I of you, Ninana! I could never build a city."

"Can you say that we build a city within ourselves, a thought city of greater awareness of life and love?"

"Yes, Ninana, exactly that!"

Fu Ling Yang entered the room and bowed.

"Are you ready for dinner? You have been here many hours and must be very hungry now."

"Oh yes!" Ninana and Lishan answered together.

They went to the carriage where guards were waiting and started for home. Then tension of the day broke. Lishan and Ninana began to laugh and laugh.

"Pardon us, Master Fu Ling Yang. Lishan has been translating and I have been concentrating very hard to understand ideas that are so new to me. I guess we have not taken time to relax all day."

"Ah yes, the tension must burst forth. Laughter is a wonderful release."

Dinner was a welcome sight. The music and dancers returned to entertain them. Ninana was pleased to understand some of their symbolism now. They always made her forget her fatigue.

The sleeping room was a welcome sight as well. Exhausted they dropped into bed and were immediately asleep.

Chapter 17

SCHOOL OF ART AND ARCHITECTURE

Several days later Lishan and Ninana awakened in the soft morning light. It was raining through the shafts of light. They just lay there watching it until servants brought a tray of fruit, fish, breads, and some fresh kimonos.

"Are you ready for the school for architects?"

"Yes, I am. Are we going there today?"

"I think so, if it is safe.

They washed their faces and slipped into their kimonos. Ninana was delighted that the kimonos were in different colors and designs every day. She kept fingering the silk and imagining how the funny ant-like silkworms produced them.

Master Fu Ling Yang walked into the dining room and announced that it would be a good time to go to the architectural school.

"They are putting up a building and would like to have you come and see it as it has been designed and goes up."

Ninana's interest shifted and she forgot about the schools of philosophy. This was her purpose and her dream. She carefully packed her drawings to take with her to the school. She had some of buildings designed for Babylon that she created recently and some of the drawings of pagodas that Fu Ling Yang asked her to make.

The carriage and guards were waiting with Fu Ling Yang.

"This place is near the outskirts of the city a short way into the hills. The architects and artists require a quiet place in which to create new ideas."

Ninana's eyes lit up in anticipation. Lishan looked concerned.

"Master, is it dangerous with rebels near the city?"

"We do not know where the rebels are, but the city police keep watch on them. We must take some chances. If we let fear rule our lives, we will hide in our houses."

The ride took an hour through the city streets. At last they came into a clearing outside of the city and could see the school on a far hill.

There was a loud cry of warning from the guards as a large band of brigands rushed toward the carriage. There was shouting and clashing of metal. Fu Ling Yang leaped from the carriage, sword drawn. A brigand pushed him aside and reached for Lishan.

Ninana jumped from the carriage almost on top of the attacker. Her height must have startled him. He stumbled backward, his curved dao falling from his hand. She snatched up the sword while shouting and screaming and swung it wildly back and forth. Her hair now long, swirled around her shoulders and face. The attacker scrambled away, sure he had seen a she-devil. The city police rushed in and beat them back, slaying many of them.

Fu Ling Yang stepped over to Ninana, a look of surprise on his face.

"Ninana, are you certain that you are not a first cousin to the giant Amazon Women Warriors?"

Ninana lowered the sword and pushed her hair out of her face.

"Who are the Amazon Women Warriors?"

"They are a fierce tribe of women, tall and great fighters."

"I will ask my mother when I return to Babylonia."

Ninana realized what a mess she must be and laughed.

"This is more how I look when climbing through the ruins of Babylon."

Lishan laughed and reached for Ninana's hair.

"Let me help straighten your hair and kimono."

"It is hopeless, Lishan! I was not meant to be neatly tucked in."

They climbed into the carriage and continued to the School of Architecture. Ninana was glad that nothing would deter them. Her heart was set on getting there.

The school was on a beautiful rise in the foothills. The landscaping was breath taking with gardens and trees, flowers and bridges. The building seemed to loom larger as they approached. The classic turned up eaves were graceful and colorful. It was all like a dream.

As their carriage rolled up to the gate they were greeted by four bowing students who assisted them from the carriage and guided them inside.

"Nǐhǎo. Wǒ jiào Ninana"

Lishan added that Ninana is an architect.

They all bowed. The headmaster, Chaoxiang, came in and greeted Fu Ling Yang. They were old friends. After a short exchange Fu Ling Yang turned to present Ninana to Chaoxiang. She bowed.

"I am pleased that you are so tall. I must look up to greet you!"

Chaoxiang bowed and burst out laughing.

"And I am pleased that you are tall as well, Princess, like the people of my tribe."

Ninana thought she blushed for the first time in her life.

"I am sorry that I look so disheveled. We were attacked and I was in a sword fight, swinging the dao like a wild woman."

"I see. So you are like my distant relatives, the Amazons."

There was that reference to Amazons again.

He invited them into a large theater where master students were working on the plans for a huge building. There were drawings all over the walls, much like Ninana's secret room under the palace in Uruk. It was a wonderland of ideas.

She walked from wall to wall gazing at the sketches entranced by them.

"Lishan, I must build a place like this in the new school in Babylon. I had one in my palace in Uruk when I first started sketching. It was a storeroom under the palace that everyone had forgotten. Now I can see that it must be done so my students can join their work and see how it all fits together."

Fu Ling Yang came to them.

"A meal has been prepared for us. Please come this way."

They entered a garden-like room filled with plants, pots of flowers, and tables where students were being served food. They sat down at the table that Chaoxiang indicated and the food was immediately placed before them.

"A place has been prepared for all three of you to live here with us for a time. I hope you will be comfortable. It is much too dangerous to travel back and forth to Fu Ling Yang's house each day, as you have seen."

Ninana could hardly swallow her food. She was going to actually live here among the architects. Fu Ling Yang nodded his agreement.

"It is wise, dear friend. We are honored to accept your most gracious hospitality, Master Chaoxiang. Guards will return to my house and bring extra clothing for us."

Fu Ling Yang, himself, would travel back to his home and return to the school periodically to see that all was going well.

Chapter 18

MASTER CHAOXIANG

───────── ❦ ─────────

After they were comfortably settled in their rooms, Ninana and Lishan had tea with Chaoxiang. She brought out her drawings and placed them before him.

"Master Fu Ling Yang wishes you to see the drawings of the pagodas, stupas, and viharas in India. I understand you do not have them here, so I agreed to sketch them."

Chaoxiang smiled and the corners of his eyes crinkled like Fu Ling Yang's. He studied them for a few minutes.

"I am most pleased you that have done this. He has described them to me but this is the first time I can see them, thanks to your talent, Princess. What else have you brought?"

"These are my drawings of the rebuilding of the city of Babylon. Babylonia is the largest empire spreading throughout Mesopotamia. Babylon is to be the capital. My favorite sketch is the Ishtar Gate. The gate, palace, and city walls are to be covered in blue and gold tiles. It is a Persian process that is being taught to our builders."

She was about to go on when she looked up and saw him smiling at her.

"Am I speaking too much, Master?"

"I am smiling because of your enthusiasm. You have deep love for architecture and unprecedented skill in your ability to sketch and construct your buildings. I shall add the sketches of the pagodas to our library if you agree."

"Oh yes! They were made for you."

At his gaze and soft voice Ninana felt a tingle go all through her body. She had never felt such a sensation before in her life. Heart pounding and flustered she quickly gathered up the sketches and handed them to him.

The next day she was given a workspace in the area with structural engineers. Again they were all much shorter than Ninana. They were a bit wary at first, not certain what they should do. Lishan was at her side to translate. Chaoxiang came to join them to explain Ninana's presence and how they were to work with her.

Soon they were comparing structures, studying her work on the City of Babylon, and introducing her to the Chinese way of designing and structuring buildings.

"Lishan, I need them to tell me about these hanging gardens my father wishes to have in the City of Babylon. I know nothing about them or even what they should look like."

An engineer took her to a place on the wall in the theater where the hanging gardens were sketched. She could see that they were enormous, with full size trees and bowers of flowering plants. There was running water that was piped from a drain back up into the pots to continuously water them. There were sprays of water coming from fountains on the sides of the top tier.

Ninana began sketches of the garden and imagined how they would fit on a ziggurat with a temple at the top. There would be cantilevered porches and coverings for shade. Water would need to be pumped up from the river into a reservoir so the fountains would have constant flow and the plants would be continuously watered. It was overwhelming.

Chaoxiang asked three of the engineers to work on the project with her. Their sketches were in Chinese structuring and she needed to convert some of it to the structures needed in Babylon. All of this kept Lishan very busy translating.

They would go to bed exhausted every night.

"Ninana, I think I am becoming an architect myself. I could not create designs but I do know something of building structures now."

"You do so well translating. I know it must be a challenge between two languages and an unfamiliar subject. I feel like I am running between two countries. Do you know anything about the Amazon women? I heard it from Fu Ling Yang and now from Chaoxiang. They sound fascinating."

"I know only what you now know. I have never met them or heard stories. Only that they are to be feared when someone attacks them."

Chaoxiang was aware that Ninana was working too many hours and requested that she and Lishan meet him for the afternoon tea ceremony. He did not wish to disappoint Fu Ling Yang by not taking care of them.

"Have I done something to displease you, Master Chaoxiang?"

"Oh no, I am very pleased with you. I have been concerned that you are working such long hours which is not good for your health."

"I have always worked hard and have no concerns that it will hurt me in any way. Perhaps I will shorten my working time and enjoy the gardens here. I have not given myself time to explore them. Also I would like to see the building that is in the construction process."

"That would please me. Has Master Fu Ling Yang determined how long you will stay with us?"

"He has not said. I have so much to learn. I heard about the hanging gardens when my father ordered them from Master Fu Ling Yang. The building of a ziggurat has been in progress since I left, and a temple will be built at the top. That is simple enough. Ziggurats and temples are common constructions there. But the hanging gardens are a complete surprise to me."

"How is it your father did not confide in you? You are his architect."

"Yes, well my father considers me as only a girl and that my work is just a fantasy. Fortunately the master builder, Zaidu, considers me essential and we have worked together on the rebuilding of the city since I was very young. Master Jarem, the master architect of the school in Uruk, saw my talent and invited me to study in the school."

Chaoxiang had a look of concern in his eyes.

"I am so sorry for your father, that he has completely missed the blessing of the precious jewel in his midst. I am glad to hear that others saw your work and supported you as you deserved."

Ninana did not know how to respond. Revealing her childhood pain was embarrassing.

"And your husband? How does he regard you?"

"He is not royalty except through marriage to me. That was my father's choice, not mine. He has no talent and is a failure as a king. The army and the people are revolting under his misguided rule and neglect. My mother, Queen Amytis, is still the regent or ruler should something happen to him."

"So you are not really a princess, but a queen. Is that not true?"

"Yes, I suppose it is. But I do not care to call myself a queen. The only thing I have ever wanted to do in my whole life is to rebuild Babylon. It is my calling and my only joy."

"Your only joy? Do you not have a son?"

"Yes, but he is only interested in himself and parties with wine and women."

"Ninana, have you ever been in love?"

The question shocked her and brought out a defensive response.

"No, have you?"

Chaoxiang sat back and looked at her. She raised her eyes to his and again felt that tingling throughout her body.

"I shall not pry further, Ninana. Know that I wish you love."

Lishan and Ninana went out into the gardens in the evening and sat down by a fountain.

"Ninana, he is in love with you. I see it in his eyes and hear it in his voice."

"How can that be? He does not know me. Should not one know another before they speak of love?"

"No one knows the ways of love. It is a mystery that comes upon us, walking softly like a cat and purring in our ears."

"Have you been in love, Lishan?"

"I was very young and he was a student. He was not royalty and I was told it was not wise to continue with him. Before I had to make a decision, he died of a fever that was raging through the city. I was brokenhearted, but I knew I must move my life forward. Master Fu Ling Yang has been a wonderful help for me all these years since."

"I am so sorry, Lishan. As Master Chaoxiang wishes me love, I also wish you love. You will be coming back to Babylon with me, will you not?"

"Yes, of course."

"Well I think there is a master architect student there who would be pleased to see you again."

"That hope is tucked away deep in my heart, the hope that it will be so."

Chapter 19

LOVE FOUND AND LOVE LOST

Chaoxiang worked intensely with Ninana and a few engineers over the next few weeks to get all she needed to take back to Babylon and establish the gardens.

The more he was with her, the closer to each other they were drawn. Lishan was right, it was like a cat coming on soft paws and purring in their ears when they spoke.

She did not expect a personal intimate conversation with him, but he guided her to a quiet place where he could speak.

"It would be my hope, Ninana, that you could stay with me forever. But I know that cannot be. For me our meeting has been a blessing and a tragedy. A blessing that through the most unlikely circumstances we have met, and a tragedy that we must now part."

Ninana thought her knees would give way. She leaned into is body to steady herself. His arm slipped around her and pulled her close. She wanted to give in to his embrace but knew she should not.

"I have a destiny that calls me, dear Chaoxiang. Babylon is in danger and somehow I must not only rebuild it, but I must also save it. My father kept Babylonia safe. Eventually he lost his mind and could not continue. Those who came after him are incompetent fools including husband and my son. Eventually King Cyrus of Persia will invade us and somehow I must get to him before he destroys my city."

They fell into an embrace again and quickly backed away.

Lishan turned to Ninana and smiled.

"I must disobey Master Fu Ling Yang that I should never allow you to be alone and allow you to be alone with Chaoxiang. Be careful not to make your parting more painful than it will already be."

"But we will not be able to speak with each other while others are close by."

"Will you need to speak? Will not words only be in the way? The light and fire of the dragon of happiness will be enough."

"You never cease to amaze me, Lishan."

Chaoxiang and Ninana decided to observe the tea ceremony in a tea house at a secluded part of the garden. Servants brought all they would need for the ceremony and their privacy.

They walked slowly through the garden paths, over a bridge and stream, and through the trees. The tea house was nestled beneath a wall of flowers. Colorful silk curtains fluttered over the porticoes in all directions.

They entered the tea house and sat down on the soft cushions. Chaoxiang performed the ceremony to perfection. The waiting and anticipation was almost unbearable. Slowly slipping their clothing off piece by piece, they lay down together. This was something Ninana never imagined would happen in her lifetime. The art of lovemaking did not exist in Babylonia, just disgusting assignations on the banquet floor.

They explored each other's bodies with the utmost gentleness and caring. The hours went by unnoticed, they were so absorbed in each other. They savored every moment knowing it would never come again.

Fu Ling Yang came to collect Lishan and Ninana. The work was finished at the school and drawings were carefully packed for the journey back to Babylonia. Ninana said Zàijiàn and Xièxiè to the engineers, thanking them for their help. Lishan and Fu Ling Yang climbed into the carriage. Ninana lingered a bit longer.

Chaoxiang guided Ninana into a small arbor of flowers and gave her an exquisite gold and jade ring. She could feel his energy and his love as he slipped it onto her finger.

She looked into his eyes for the last time and whispered "Xièxiè."

He took her to the carriage, helped her into it, and they drove away. It would be several weeks before they actually sailed. Ninana was glad for the time to process all that had happened including her aching sadness.

"Come, Ninana, let us take a boat ride on the river. The peacefulness of the river and colorful boats going by will be a welcome and healing distraction."

Lishan was right. There were celebrations on the river with some fireworks and lighted dragons floating over the boats. The quarter-tone music came from the shoreline. The boats floated lazily along. Ninana sat back in a comfortable deck chair and closed her eyes from time to time. When she did that she could still see his eyes.

"Lishan, I will miss it all. I have come to love China as well as Chaoxiang."

"I always miss it when I leave, too. There is something magical, mystical, and dangerous about it. The excitement is intoxicating."

When the boat docked, Fu Ling Yang met them with a carriage to take them back to his house. Lishan took the opportunity to discuss a visit to the Silk Road.

"Ninana and I talked about the Silk Road. I promised Ninana that we would see it. We can go to the marketplace and follow it along the banks until we reach the beginning of the Silk Road.. This might be the best time while we wait all these weeks for our departure."

Fu Ling Yang was skeptical, but he would not refuse them.

"I will send extra guards at a distance so they will not spoil your enjoyment. Wear the clothing of the common people and, Ninana, leave the ring and bracelet at home. It would attract admiration from the wrong people."

Ninana fingered the ring, not having taken it off since Chaoxiang put it on her hand. She knew she must leave it and the bracelet and find ways to keep them safe as she traveled home to Uruk and to Babylon.

"Master Fu Ling Yang, I will need a way to disguise them. Something I can wear under my clothes to keep them secure and out of sight. Is there such a thing?"

"Yes, there is. I will have it for you before we sail. Come with me."

They went to a mysterious shop near the market run by an elderly man. When Fu Ling Yang knocked on the ancient door a face slowly became visible in the cloudy window. The man opened the creaky door and beckoned to them. They entered a dark room and passed on through a door he unlocked for them. Ninana was mystified and relieved to be in a room that had light. The old man peered at her face, her hand, the ring, and bracelet. He said nothing.

He guided her hand to a piece of treated rice paper and pressed it palm down. The paper changed color under her hand. He covered her face with a cloth and held a lantern close to it. It was very bright. He took the cloth and paper away and placed them in a box. Then he bowed to Fu Ling Yang and Ninana and showed them out through the doors to the street.

"What was he doing? Will he make the disguise from that?"

"He was measuring your energy and will make a container that can only be opened by you."

"My energy?"

"Yes, the body has unique energies that move throughout your body. No two people are alike."

"Will it last very long?"

"Yes, it will so long as you do not let anyone else hold the container for an extended period of time. Next to your body it will recharge from your energy pattern."

Ninana was almost breathless. There was so much mystery in China. Babylonia had only suspicion and ignorance.

"I wish to know more before I leave. How can I do that?"

"I will take you to a mystery school where there are seers, magicians, and art depicting the mysteries. There are books explaining them for the student of the mysteries."

"Will they allow us to see them?"

"Yes, we may see the art and books, and the seers will explain. We may not practice any of the rituals or enter the inner sanctuary. Those are for the students and dangerous for anyone not trained or unsupervised."

"Why would they be dangerous?"

"There is a world of darkness beneath the earth where the spirits dwell and hold those mysteries sacred, to be imparted only to the initiated. Others would get lost, lose their minds, and never return to this world."

The thought of losing her mind made her shiver. She was remembering that her father seemed to be losing his mind, storming at the priests, and sometimes not remembering her. She thought he just wished she were not there. Now she was seeing something else, but not sure what it was.

Chapter 20

THE SILK ROAD

———————— ❧ ☙ ————————

The mystery school was dark, forbidding, and fascinating. After a short time they were admitted by someone in a long dark robe and hood with strange symbols embroidered all over them. Their faces were hidden. Guests were admonished to speak and walk softly. Silence was essential for the spiritual atmosphere.

There were many rooms of paintings and sculptures. Lishan quietly translated as the seer explained the paintings. They were beautiful and the mysteries were disguised by their beauty. The sculptures were frightening. There were snakes, animals, and strange beings. Ninana had shivers. Their glittering eyes seemed to dance and followed them as they passed.

They were guided to sit down at a table in the library. The seer gave them the books they were permitted to see. Others were behind huge, closed doors. Whispering Lishan began to read the first few pages of them in Ninana's language.

"These books are very old and the stories are thousands of years old. No one knows where they came from or who wrote them."

"I wonder if Babylonia and Assyria have these ancient stories as well. I have never heard of them. The priests and magicians in the palace are very secretive about them if they do. There are even murderous."

"This book says they all come from a deep well in the earth created by a falling star from the sky. It carried the mystery stories and buried them in the hole it made when it hit the earth. The hole is so deep that no one has ever reached the bottom."

They finished their tour of the Art and Mysteries Museum and went home for dinner and an evening of music and a Chinese opera.

"Is the Chinese opera filled with the mysteries, too?"

"Yes, they are acted out to the music. People are fascinated by the stories, but they do not know what the deeper mysteries are. Most do not care. They just want to be entertained."

They went to bed that night and Ninana's dreams were full of strange images. She woke in the morning feeling like she had been in that deep hole where the mysteries were buried.

The next morning it was raining and looked like it would continue for several days. They spent the next few days inside playing Chinese board games.

"This is a new experience for me. Games were not part of my childhood nor was just having fun with others. I guess my fun was drawing my buildings in the room under the palace alone."

"There were no games in Babylon? Having fun is instructive and necessary for cultural growth. Games teach children how to play together and how to compete."

"I suppose the children played games in the streets but I did not go into the streets. I went from the palace to the architectural school or to Babylon. The students at the school worked during their days, too."

The following week the weather cleared and the streets dried out. Lishan and Ninana set out for the market and the Silk Road. Their guards were not far behind.

"I want to see everything. I love the different cultures, the sound of the languages, and all the beautiful displays. Uruk seemed to have fewer markets, and certainly not so colorful."

Music was different from kiosk to kiosk as the cultures changed. Some of it was rather clangorous with drumbeats and not very pleasant. The market was spread out for five miles. They walked for a while and then sat down in a kiosk for food. They were exhausted after walking through it all and looked for a place to rent a carriage.

At the end of the market where the Silk Road began, someone offered to rent them a carriage. They gratefully paid the fee and climbed in. Lishan instructed the driver to take them a few miles up the Silk Road and then turn back to Guangzhou. They assumed the guards were following along at a distance.

The gentle rocking of the carriage lulled Ninana and Lishan into dosing off. Lishan woke with a start. She asked the driver if they have turned back. He said yes, they were heading back to Guangzhou. She looked around for their guards. No guards were in sight.

As time went on, Lishan realized they were getting further and further from Guangzhou. She shouted at the driver. He did not respond. Ninana was now awake.

"How far have we come? Where are we?"

"We are not going toward Guangzhou but away from it toward Xian."

"How far is Xian?"

"Over a thousand miles."

The driver urged the horses to go faster and faster.

"Surely our guards will find us!"

Ninana was now alarmed and held tight to the side of the seat.

Late in the night the carriage stopped. The driver got down and unhitched the foaming horses. He led them away. Lishan and Ninana were alone in the dark.

"This looks like an encampment filled with brigands and rebels. We need to get away before morning light or they will kill us and worse."

"What do we do?"

"We will find food, blankets, perhaps a donkey, and slip away into the foothills."

Lishan found a donkey with its packs still on its back. She put a scarf over its eyes so it was blinded and would not call out to other animals. Quietly she and Ninana found the edge of the encampment and walked quickly away into the darkness of the wooded foothills.

"Where shall we go? How do we find our way? Should we not go back toward the Silk Road and follow it?"

Lishan whispered back.

"They might come after us on the road. We must keep walking as long as possible and hope we are not missed. A soft plant grows on the north side of the tree trunks. We can feel for it in the dark and know which way is south."

A moon began to show between the clouds. For a few moments at a time they could see around them. Lishan was glad the clouds were still there keeping them in darkness and revealing the landscape only momentarily.

"I have never been so tired, Lishan. But I am sure we must keep going."

"I am tired too, but our lives may depend upon our continuing to move."

They walked throughout the night, morning, and on into the day. There were flat grassy areas where they stopped to rest.

The thunder of horses' hoofs came suddenly and warriors. Lishan and Ninana were about to run and hide, but it was too late. There seemed to be a hundred that surrounded them. A warrior dismounted and strode toward them.

"Who are they, Lishan? Is that a woman?"

Chapter 21

THE AMAZONS

—————— ⧸⧹ ⧸⧹ ——————

"They are the Amazon warrior women."

Lishan spoke with them at length in their language.

"What are they saying?"

"They are taking us with them."

Ninana and Lishan were quickly hoisted onto horses and they all rode away. The donkey followed along, bellowing a complaint at the fast pace.

Ninana saw the similarities that caused Chaoxiang and Fu Ling Yang to say she was like an Amazon. They were tall and slim but she did not have their slanted eyes.

Lishan rode beside Ninana. She spoke in a low voice.

"They battled and destroyed the rebels in the camp. I do not know if they came for us because someone told them where we went or if they were just traveling through and came upon us."

They rode for several days, stopping at night to rest until the moon light faded. No one spoke to them They rode in silence keeping to protected areas. Early one evening they stopped in a hidden area and made camp.

Food was passed among them and some given to Ninana and Lishan. Ninana did not know what it was, but she was too hungry to care.

"Lishan, please tell them about me and that I wanted to meet them. Ask them if they will take us back to Guangzhou. Dare you ask them questions?"

"When we are settled around the campfire I will ask permission to speak."

"Permission to speak?"

"Yes, it is wise to treat them with deepest respect."

The lead warrior turned to them.

"I am Polydora, Queen of the Amazons, descendant of the great warrior queen, Penthesilea. We came to find you because one of the rebels said there was an Amazon woman with you."

She pointed to Ninana.

"One of ours is missing and we thought it was you, but we see you are not. We were in danger where we found you, so our choice was to bring you with us. The other choice would be to kill you so you could not reveal our whereabouts. We do not kill those who do not war against us."

Ninana gasped. "Kill us?"

They ignored Ninana's gasp and nodded to Lishan. She spent some time telling them the whole story from Babylonia, the sea voyage, and to how they came to be there in the rebel camp. They listened with interest and pointed to Ninana.

"Someone said that you are an Amazon?"

"No. But two people said that I fight like you. We were attacked. I grabbed a dao and began swinging wildly at the attackers. Others said because I am taller than everyone around me, I must be a cousin of Amazons. I do not know if any of that is true, but it caused me to want to meet you."

"Stand up."

Ninana stood up. They looked her up and down. The others stood beside her and measured her. They looked at her eyes and her teeth and shook their heads. They gave her a jian to swing. A warrior stepped forward to show her how to use it.

She sparred with her for a few minutes so Ninana could get her aim and swing aligned. She went for it with gusto, hair flying around her shoulders and face. The warrior soon knocked the jian from her hands and they all laughed.

"You are not much like us except in height, but we welcome you as a sister. When it is safe we will take you back to where we found you. There is a village close by that place. You can find shelter there and your way to Guangzhou. We cannot go closer."

"Will you tell me more about who you are and where you come from?"

"We come from the desert and Scythia. We ride from the far west along the Silk Road east to China. We are joined by other Scythian tribes from time to time, but prefer to ride alone. We have fought and defeated Egyptian kings, Persians, and others who attack us."

Ninana thought of King Cyrus. Was he the one they were referring to? Most assuredly. She decided not to mention him. He was too close to her and next to Babylonia. She did not wish to make enemies of these warrior women.

Two Amazon women rode into their camp and indicated that the dangers were past, but there were soldiers from Guangzhou coming this way, yet many days off. Lishan assured them they were safe from the soldiers.

"The are looking for us, not seeking battle. So long as they find us unharmed, they will be satisfied."

"Have we harmed you?"

"No, you have been most kind. You have saved us from danger. We thank you."

They traveled many days with the Amazons back to the place where they had met. Somehow the donkey found them and began to follow.

"We will leave you here. We give you this dao for your protection. It is smaller than the jian and easier to conceal."

Ninana smiled at her, took the dao, and tied it around her waist. She bowed in the Chinese way.

"You will always be our sisters. Farewell."

They turned and galloped away.

Ninana was sorry to see them go. They were rough spoken, courageous, and excellent in battle. She wanted to ride with them and know more, but there was not time. Nor was she a warrior.

They walked south for a day. Night came again and they could see a small fire down in a valley ahead. The appearance of moonlight revealed a small village of perhaps fifty homes, all poor and run down. They stopped and watched for a while. There was no one moving about.

They ate a few bites of food, wrapped themselves in the blankets they had packed on the donkey, and lay down to wait for morning.

"Who knows what the next day will bring!"

"Yes, who knows. I will pray to Nezha, our ancient Chinese god of protection, to keep us safe."

Ninana thought about Daniel and his god, their god. She knew that the blessing of protection came from within. Silently she said prayers, too.

Chapter 22

THE DYING VILLAGE

―――――――― ❦ ❧ ――――――――

The sun rose over the eastern hills. The brightening sky woke Lishan and Ninana.

"Lishan, where are we? Do you know what village that is?"

"No, there are hundreds of little villages scattered over the foothills and along the rivers. Let us approach and sit by their well. The well is the gathering place. Strangers stop by the well and wait to see if there is a welcome."

They packed their few belongings on the faithful donkey's back and started for the village well. They sat down quietly at the edge of the well and waited. Then the donkey suddenly announced their presence with a plaintive bellow.

Slowly the villagers came out of their huts. They peered with squinted eyes toward the well and called to their neighbors. Presently a small group of them approached the well.

Lishan introduced herself and Ninana in their language and explained how they got to the village. The villagers turned to talk among themselves. They were nodding and glancing at the two.

"What will they do, Lishan?"

"They are discussing their food shortage. Their sons have gone to live with renegades. They do not know what to do with two more people in their village."

"Tell them we have some food to share with them. Tell them I am an architect and builder, and I will help them repair their homes."

Lishan looked a little puzzled.

"Look at that pile of building materials near the trees, Lishan. Someone was going to repair their homes, probably their sons who went off to be with rebels. I can do that for them and teach them how to do it."

Lishan was a little skeptical but what else could they offer until they could find their way home to Guangzhou. The people listened intently to Lishan and looked curiously at Ninana.

"They do not understand. Let me show them."

Ninana went to the pile of materials and brought out some pieces. An old man motioned to her to follow him. She went with him to his hut which was sadly in need of repair. It was nearly falling down.

Ninana spread the materials on the floor pointing to how they should be put in place. Other villagers came to watch. Lishan translated all Ninana was saying and what they were saying back. A few more men stepped up and helped them put the rafters into place. She showed them how to cut notches in the uprights and lay the beams in the notches. Then Ninana shook it to show how much stronger it was.

"Ninana, there are so many homes here that need repairs. How will you get to them all?"

"I am a teacher, Lishan. When I teach a few of them, others will learn and help, and soon they will take care of all the places themselves. They just need to know how to do it."

The villagers crowded around and soon even the women were going to the pile and distributing the materials. The place was a flurry of activity for the next few weeks.

Lishan asked if anyone knew how to get back to Guangzhou. They all shook their heads.

"Ninana, soon we will need to find our own way. Guangzhou is to the east where the sun rises. The Silk Road slants from north to south to reach Guangzhou. Walking east we would soon come to the Silk Road and be halfway to Guangzhou."

They sat with the people at the evening meals and talked about who they were and why they needed to go back to the city. The people tearfully pleaded with them to stay. They knew nothing of ships, oceans, Babylonia, or why Ninana could not speak their language. It all fell on deaf ears.

"I am not sure they will let us leave!"

"Yes, they will. We just need to ease them into it."

The next day two of their sons came into the village. There was rejoicing at their return. Lishan explained to the sons what Ninana was doing and asked them to help.

"We are most grateful to help. There are so many homes that need repair and we were overwhelmed. We did not know how to do it."

"Go with Ninana and she will show you. Already your parents and grandparents are learning how. You must learn from them. Are more sons coming back?"

"I do not know. The rebels moved out quickly and no one knows where they are going or what may have happened to them. We became afraid and left. Others may leave, too."

"Were you with the encampment on the Silk Road a day's walk from here?"

"Yes. Some Amazons came and drove everyone out. They are terrifying."

They sat around the fire after dinner and Lishan talked with them all again.

"We must return to Guangzhou as soon as we can before soldiers come looking for us. Will you show us how to get back to the road?"

They put their heads down or turned away.

"You do not want soldiers to come here. They might not understand why we are here. They could think we are your captives and do much harm. They might tear down the homes we just repaired. That would make us sad."

Soon two of the elderly women nodded, stepped forward, and agreed to help Lishan and Ninana get back.

"Grandmothers, are you sure you can find the way?"

They nodded vigorously and pointed north and east.

"Lishan, you said we should go south and east."

"The Silk Road goes northwest to southeast. We will get to the road more quickly if we go with them a little north."

The grandmothers tapped Lishan on the arm.

"We came here as children. We remember."

"Will you take us tomorrow morning?"

Again they nodded and smiled nearly toothless grins.

Two more sons came into the village that evening, exhausted and half starved. The others told them all that was happening. The village was coming alive with the whole community excited to restore their homes.

"We can leave quietly now. Their sons are returning and the village is beginning to thrive again. We will not be missed."

They retrieved the donkey from the wooded area and began packing food and blankets to tie on its back.

"It is amazing that this donkey has stayed with us even following the Amazons. It must have been sent by the gods, Lishan."

"We have had more gods watching over us that we can imagine."

In Guangzhou Fu Ling Yang waited for the soldiers to return bringing Lishan and Ninana. But they were gone for several weeks already and had not returned. He went to the end of the market and found where the carriage was rented. The owner said his carriage had not come back and assumed it was stolen, his driver joined the rebels taking the women with him, or they are all dead.

Fu Ling Yang and his guards plus other soldiers began frantically searching along the Silk Road. After a few days returning soldiers met them on the road and said that no one had seen the women. They had gone over halfway to Xian with no sighting or word of them.

The carriage was found in a wooded area where the encampment had been. No signs of Lishan, Ninana, or their purchases at the market were found in them. They went back to the road and followed the trail of the rebels who had moved on, thinking they took the women with them. Far to the west they found the rebels slaughtered, their broken bodies scattered everywhere.

No one was left alive except one young man. He crept cautiously out of the brush not certain if it was safe, but he was starving and needed help. They beckoned to him to come to them.

The soldiers were sure Lishan and Ninana were dead. Fu Ling Yang refused to give up.

"If you did not find their bodies, there is a chance they are alive. We will keep looking."

"Where do we look next, Master Fu Ling Yang? We have been looking everywhere for weeks."

Chapter 23

JOURNEY HOME BEGINS

———— ᥬ ᥭ ————

The young man who came out of hiding and approached them. A guard took is arm and guided him toward Fu Ling Yang.

"We are looking for two women. Have you seen them?"

"No. Perhaps the women found their way to my village. I am returning to my home there in the hills. If you will take me with you and give me some food so I will not die on the way, I will show you where it is. It is only two day's walk from the Silk Road."

Fu Ling Yang and his men agreed to give him food and take him to his village. They had no other ideas or options.

When they arrived at the young man's village everyone met them. There was rejoicing and stories of these wonderful women who helped them rebuild their homes.

"I know that is Ninana. She is a builder."

"Yes!"

"Where are they now?"

The villagers pointed in the direction the grandmothers had taken them. The soldiers and their best trackers started out immediately.

Fu Ling Yang was relieved that they were really still alive. The news quelled the fears that ran through his mind for weeks that they might be dead. He started out immediately in the direction the villagers pointed.

The grandmothers stopped and turned around.

"Why are you stopping? Are we lost?"

"No! They are coming. Be quiet and listen."

Sure enough Lishan and Ninana could hear the horses and faint shouts of the soldiers calling their names. The grandmothers kissed their cheeks, bowed, and headed back to the village.

The guards and Fu Ling Yang came bursting through the trees. They swung off their horses and ran to Lishan and Ninana. Fu Ling Yang was the first to reach them.

"Are you all right?"

"We are good, Master Fu Ling Yang. We are so happy to see you. We have had many adventures to share with you."

"How did you get here? The villagers said the grandmothers were guiding you home. Where are the grandmothers now?"

"The grandmothers of the village brought us here to find the Silk Road. They heard you coming, knew we were safe, and returned to the village."

"I briefly saw a few of the homes you helped repair in the village. The villagers are still working on them, praising the two of you, and happy to have their homes and their sons back."

"Yes, Master, it is fortunate the sons are alive. They left the rebels to return home before the Amazon warriors attacked and killed them all. We have been under the protection of the Amazons. They have declared us to be their sisters. Ninana told them about being thought a cousin of the Amazons."

"Did they think you are an Amazon Warrior?"

She laughed.

"No. I lost a sword fight with one of them and it was obvious I am not skilled. We just sparred and my jian flipped out of my hands. I was not in any danger. But I am honored to be considered a sister of the Amazons."

The soldiers found the carriage near the rebel encampment, cleaned it up, harnessed a horse to it. They brought it to a point on the Silk Road where they would meet Fu Ling Yang.

Lishan and Ninana unloaded their donkey, hugged him, and turned him loose. Gratefully they climbed into the carriage. Ninana felt the sudden drain of energy from her body.

"It is such a relief to be riding in a carriage. Now that we are on our way home, exhaustion has taken me over."

Lishan sighed.

"My eyes are closing already."

Entering the courtyard of Fu Ling Yang's home, the entire household came out to meet them and almost carried them into the house. The next few days they were pampered and rested. They regaled Fu Ling Yang with all of the stories of their adventures.

Bidding farewell to Guangzhou was a sad moment for Ninana. She had learned to love China. And then there was Chaoxiang...a love that would be in her heart but gone from her life forever.

It would be a few days until the ship was ready to sail. They spent the time floating in the pool with the flowers, packing, and buying a few items in the market they had lost when the carriage was taken by the rogue driver.

"I am so glad I do not have to leave you behind, too, Lishan. I would feel alone and friendless. I can hardly believe I am leaving."

"I will not leave you, Ninana. Fu Ling Yang has given me away. He knows I have another destiny in Babylonia with you and perhaps Shamhar if our stars are aligned."

Everything seemed to change when they were preparing to board the ship, the Guangchuan. The items ordered by Nebuchadnezzar were already on a ship that headed out to sea days earlier.

Someone shouted her name and she went to the rail. It was Chaoxiang. He was running up the gangplank.

"I could not stay away. Perhaps it is foolish of me, but I wanted to hold you one more time."

She rushed to him and they stood on the deck in each other's arms.

"I almost was not here, Chaoxiang. We were lost on the Silk Road for weeks."

"I know. Fu Ling Yang forbid me to go with him. He said I would be in the way and he was right. I would have run wild everywhere shouting your name and they would have wasted time keeping track of me."

"I cannot imagine that you would do that!"

"I am sure I would have."

The crew was ready to pull up the gangplank and waved to him.

"I am trying not to cry."

He kissed her. Squeezed her tight, reluctant to let her go. He knew he could not ask her to stay. Then he turned and headed for the gangplank. It was over … again. Tears she had held back for weeks gushed forth. Lishan put her arms around her and cried with her.

The oars hit the water. The ship lurched back and away from the dock. They caught the river current and moved out of the port, eastward down the Zhujiang River, and out into the South China Sea. A strong wind rippled through the sails as they were hoisted to the top of the mast. The oars were pulled up and the ship picked up speed.

Lishan and Ninana stepped back from the bow of the ship and walked to the cabin. Ninana was surprised that her legs remembered the rocking of the deck and quickly adjusted. The stiff breeze had dried the tears on her cheeks, but tears threatened to gush forward again as the coastline grew smaller and smaller.

Chapter 24

INTERRUPTIONS

Fu Ling Yang was in the cabin looking over records, lists of sailors, dates and times of arrivals and departures.

Lishan and Ninana spent the time talking, sleeping, and doing whatever tasks they could find to do. Once again Ninana eagerly assisted the crew doing the things they taught her to do on the voyage to China. It took her mind from her sadness for short periods of time.

After a week they caught up with the freighter carrying the materials for the hanging gardens in Babylon. It seemed to be drifting.

Alarmed, the captain ordered the sails to be brought down and the oars dropped into the water. They slowed the speed of the ship and pulled as close to the freighter as they dared. The crew threw ropes with grappling hooks onto the rails of the freighter and climbed along the ropes to its deck.

There were no sailors on the top deck. They were found lying below groaning and sick. The captain of the freighter staggered onto the deck when the sailors came on board.

"Everyone is sick from bad food. They cannot move from their bunks."

The sailors began shouting messages back to the Guangchuan. Fu Ling Yang immediately ordered baskets of fresh food and fruit sent along the ropes for them.

The captain of the Guangchuan came back to report to Fu Ling Yang that all the cargo was still safely stowed.

"It will take a few days for them to recover and sail the ship again. Their food went bad and the baskets of fresh food are reviving them. Since the seas are quiet for now, we will stay connected to the freighter to stabilize it. Our oarsmen went over to clean the decks and feed the men. All should be shipshape soon."

"Thank you, captain. How fortunate that we came upon them in time, and no pirates found them first. We could have lost everything."

Ninana was on deck observing while doing some of the tasks.

"Not to worry, Master. I can and will do more to help. Climbing over the ruins of Babylon has made me strong."

Ninana took on more tasks, working day and night, until the sailors could return. Fu Ling Yang was concerned for her safety but did not object. Even he turned to physical tasks where he could. Lishan hurried to help prepare food and brought it to everyone.

On the third day the crew members of the freighter were getting their strength back and ready to assume their duties. Their ship was clean. The fresh food healed and strengthened them. They threw the grappling hooks off the rails. The sailors of the Guangchuan reeled them in and secured them. The sails went up and they were both underway again.

The weeks stretched on as they passed the large islands into the straits of Malacca and into the port to get fresh food. Again the air was hot and stifling with hardly a breeze. They stayed aboard the ship while the food was purchased and loaded.

Without guards that he knew and trusted, Fu Ling Yang did not want to leave the ship and encounter the trouble they had before.

Ninana hoped they could stop in the fabulous Port of Muziris, India, again.

"Oh yes, we must stop there to prepare for the voyage across the Arabian Sea and into the Makran Sea. If you remember, it is quite a long distance."

"I am eager to return to Babylon again. I must be patient."

Lishan laughed her musical laugh.

"And I, too! Do you think Shamhar will remember me?"

"Yes, I am sure he will."

She and Lishan laughed and looked out over the water from the rail as the ship got underway toward the tip of India, and the Port of Muziris.

Muziris was as glorious as she remembered it. When they docked Ninana eagerly disembarked and walked along the dock. Lishan and Fu Ling Yang hurried to catch up with her.

"Please, wait Ninana. Even though we did not encounter trouble here, that does not mean it is not waiting just around the corner."

"Well, my patience did not last long, did it? It is wonderful to get off the ship and walk on land for a while."

They arrived at their hotel and sat down for dinner. As the evening wore on, Ninana began to feel quite ill. She and Lishan went up to their room early.

"What is the matter, Ninana?"

"I have terrible pains in my stomach."

"Lie down and I will…

Suddenly there was a gush of blood on the floor and a groan from Ninana.

Lishan summoned the servants to bring a midwife.

"A midwife?"

"Yes, Ninana. You are or were pregnant."

"Oh no! I am losing Chaoxiang's child?"

She burst into sobs.

"Ninana, it is sad and fortunate at the same time. You could not bring Chaoxiang's child to be born and raised in Babylon! Seeing it was a Chinese child, the servants might even poison it."

The midwife came a few minutes later. She examined Ninana. A piece of tissue came out into a cloth. The midwife showed it to Lishan.

"No worry, Ninana. You are no longer pregnant. That was only the beginning of a child. We will give it an appropriate burial."

The midwife bathed Ninana and put her to bed.

"Chaoxiang's child! I cannot believe it. I want to be sad and thankful at the same time. It was his child but I could not take it with me, so it is gone just as Chaoxiang is gone."

Ninana had dreams of Chaoxiang all night. She would awaken, see his face, weep, and go back to sleep. She woke in the morning with Lishan's arms around her.

"Along with all we experienced on the Silk Road, Ninana, and the hard work you did when we rescued the freighter, probably caused you to lose it. You must remain in bed today. If you feel well enough we will go to the markets for a little while tomorrow."

Fu Ling Yang came to their room during the day to check on Ninana.

"Lishan told me of your misfortune and I am sorry. We will not sail until you are well."

"I am sorry, Master Fu Ling Yang. I do not want to delay our voyage."

"You are in my care, Ninana. I promised your father to return you safe and in good health. But, my dear, we are not always in charge as we discovered on the Silk Road. Life will have its way. Rest now and do not worry. I am going back to the ship and I shall return later."

Chapter 25

GOING HOME

In the several days they remained in Muziris, the freighter caught up with them and pulled into port. Fu Ling Yang was relieved that the freighter was making good time and all was well with the crew.

"Yes, Master, all of our sailors recovered. We lost no one thanks to your help."

"That is good news. We will be waiting for you after we dock at the Port of Ur. Flat bottom barges will be waiting to load the materials and float them up the Euphrates River to Babylon. In a few weeks another shipment will arrive from the west for you to take back to Guangzhou. You will all have time to rest before a voyage back to China."

"Thank you, Master. The crew will be happy to have a rest."

Ninana was exhausted and a little longer in recovering that she hoped.

"I am so sorry to delay our departure, Lishan. I just cannot seem to get my energy back."

"Ninana, you have had a hard time. I know how you love Chaoxiang and he loved you. Your body was doing three jobs. You rode with the Amazons, rebuilt a village and helped maintain the ship, all the while creating a baby. You just need time. There is no need to rush."

Fu Ling Yang took all his meals with them every day. He was very concerned about Ninana, but Lishan reassured both of them.

"Master, even though I do not have children of my own I have assisted many women. I have been with you since I was a child but now I, too, am a woman and know many things."

Fu Ling Yang burst out laughing. The corners of his eyes crinkled and his eyes nearly closed.

"Perhaps I have forgotten, Lishan. Yes, you are a woman. Please accept my apology."

Ninana and Lishan began to make short forays into the market area. Ninana felt a little stronger each time. They made some purchases and handed them to their guards for safe keeping.

"Shopping heals many things!"

Lishan laughed at Ninana as she nearly danced from kiosk to kiosk.

"Yes, I have noticed that too! I love to shop."

The two ships docked at the Port of Ur within a few days of each other. They watched the building materials being unloaded and stacked on waiting barges. Fu Ling Yang had sent word ahead to Zaidu before they left Guangzhou. He was at the docks to take stock of the materials and supervise the loading of the barges.

Ninana was happy to see Zaidu and ran into his arms.

"Is all well with you, Ninana? Fu Ling Yang said there was some trouble at sea."

"Yes, the sailors on the freighter were quite ill from bad food and their ship was drifting. We got to it just in time before pirates spotted it. Some of our sailors boarded that freighter so I learned a lot about maintaining a ship while they were gone. It was hard work."

"So now you are a seasoned sailor!"

"One of my many unexpected talents!"

She told him about the architectural school, but not about Chaoxiang. That was still too painful. She recounted being kidnapped and how that led to the rebuilding of a village in the foothills of China while waiting for rescuers.

"Why am I not surprised. What a blessing for that village. They received the best architect! Much as been done at Babylon. The ziggurat is nearly complete and ready for the gardens. I hope you brought plans to construct them."

"Of course I did. I had two or three engineers in the school in China instructing me and helping me draw how all the parts fit together. Master Fu Ling Yang will be staying in Babylon for a time to help us as well. The design is typically Chinese, but I am sure it will be more Babylonian when we are done."

Many days later they all arrived in Babylon. Ninana and Lishan stood in the carriage to see all they could as they went through the Ishtar Gate, now complete.

"It is breathtakingly beautiful! It is your masterpiece, Ninana!"

Ninana became engrossed in seeing her palace and markets. Soon Lishan could see that Ninana would have many royal responsibilities in Babylon. There would be little time for them to be together.

Fu Ling Yang would be traveling to meet some of his merchants.

"Would you like to come with me, Lishan. I know you wish to be with her, but she needs to attend to the building of the gardens and other areas that must be finished. We shall return at a later time when she is free."

Lishan agreed to go with him. She and Ninana were sad to part, but they both understood.

"We will be together again soon, when we return."

Ninana had returned to the capital of the largest empire in Mesopotamia. The City of Babylon now extended to both sides of the Euphrates River. It covered five hundred acres.

Zaidu walked with her and explained the progress. They climbed to the top of the ziggurat and viewed the city below. Ninana was nearly breathless.

"Many of the houses are three stories high. The flat roofs are buttressed with timbers packed with mud. Not all could afford the luxury of wood and built circular mud-brick huts supported by a center post. The walls are packed with reeds and mud from the river."

Nebuchadnezzar's palace was built with five courtyards, his private quarters, and his harems. The enormous new palace was nearing completion.

"The royal family and their entire entourage have moved into their quarters. They are resplendent with draperies, coverings, mosaics, sculptures and paintings. Some of the buildings are still rising from the foundations, but some essential government buildings, the palace, the walls and the gate are nearly complete.

"The king loves to show off the magnificent shrine to his city god Marduk, contained in the small temple behind us. At his orders the walls and roof of the building are covered with gold and embellished with alabaster, lapis lazuli, and precious stones. The altar, the throne, footstool, and statues of the god are made of over eighteen tons of gold."

"That is a lot of weight! You can tell me how it is supported later. How is the king faring in his mind and body?"

"He is not strong but does not wish anyone to notice."

The engineers and carpenters went to work immediately assembling the hanging garden supports, frameworks, and containers for the plants and trees. They constructed the irrigation system that brought in water from the Euphrates River. As the weeks went by the plants began growing magnificently. They were blossoming and would be perfect to enhance the shrine at the top.

Ninana's work was nearly finished as the overseer. Babylon was becoming the magnificent city she had dreamed of while sketching on the walls of her secret room.

When the army brought the captives from Jerusalem into the city they were put to work immediately to move the construction forward. They were herded into a makeshift encampment where they would live in misery.

It was disappointing to Ninana that the captives were not only forced to work on her buildings but were still living in squalor in small mud huts or goat skin tents, and barely subsisting. All of the glory of Babylon was not of any benefit to them.

"I will change this abomination!"

She began to search for a place on the outskirts of Babylon to build a Jewish section, a place to build decent housing with paved streets, and clean water.

She went to where they presently lived to speak to them about their lives in Jerusalem. She wanted them to tell her about their homes. Hopefully from their descriptions she could design a place that would resemble their original homes.

Nabonidus showed up in Babylon and greeted Daniel and Ninana coolly. They offered to show Nabonidus a possible location for the Jewish settlement. He scoffed and declined.

"It is a waste of money to spend it on slaves. Let them live where they are. That is good enough for the rabble."

Daniel was not bothered by the insult but Ninana was enraged. She could barely keep her anger in check.

"Dear husband, those people have been dragged out of their homeland and brought here. They had a good life once and it was destroyed. They are beaten down and hungry for a decent life again. I want to offer them that and I will."

"Why can you not see the futility of your efforts? It would all be a waste of time. Slaves are worthless except to work and die when they cannot work."

"If you cannot see the success of my efforts all over this city, then you are blind."

Disgusted Nabonidus walked away.

Ninana's effort was met with fear and skepticism by the Jews. They were hesitant to speak with her or give their names. Undaunted Ninana sat down among them with her sketch board in hand.

"Please, tell me what your homes looked like. I want to build them for you."

She simply begin to draw a home and show it to them. They shook their heads.

They remained silent. Along with their fears at being summoned and perhaps punished there were language barriers and difficulties with speaking to a royal Babylonian princess.

"If I may, Princess, I will help you. My name is Daniel. Even though I have a high office in your palace I am still one of them. These are my people."

"Daniel. Yes, I remember you. You spoke to me of your god and his teachings. You are close to my father as an interpreter of… higher things. Please. I welcome your help. I think they fear to speak to me."

"They knew me from the temple and palace in Jerusalem. Now in Babylon they come to pray with me regularly."

They became animated as he spoke. He introduced Ninana as a caring person who truly wanted to help them. Hesitantly they began to smile. They could believe Daniel.

At his instruction they began drawing pictures of their homes in the sandy soil around them. Ninana copied them onto her board. They shyly looked at her copies and helped her refine them. She would point and they would nod or shake their heads.

"This is a wonderful collaboration, Daniel. They are a great help. Please thank them and tell them I promise to return soon."

Chapter 26

THE JEWISH COMMUNITY RISES

— CR ᔭC —

She was eager to show Daniel the place she had chosen for the community. It was a good location and there were no plans to build anything else there.

"You have chosen the area near the perimeter of the city where they will have water, clean air, and small gardens for their food. You have been very thoughtful, Princess. Let us mark out the area so it is officially claimed."

"Perhaps you would tell me more about your god and what you believe to be true. What I know about prayer is the priests who shout at the statues in the temples. They look ridiculous shouting at stone. The assault should cause them to shatter. How do you pray?"

"This is how we pray.

"Blessed be the Name of God from age to age, for wisdom and power are His.

He gives wisdom to the wise and knowledge to those who have understanding.

He reveals deep and hidden things.

He knows what is in the darkness and the light dwells within Him.

I give thanks that You have given me wisdom and power and have revealed to me all I have asked."

"Is this how you know the mysteries of life? Because your god gives you his knowledge?"

"Yes. God's wisdom is available to all who believe."

"How can I believe when all I have known are many gods and none of them seem wise or care about us? They bring bad things on a whim and the suffering of people means nothing."

"You believe with your heart in all that is good and true. Your heart will tell you."

Ninana had only begun to understand something of this through his compassion for the people. His actions were in accordance with his teachings and his god. Love, heart, and compassion were slowly coming together in her mind.

A sense of peace filled her whole being just as when she heard the teacher speaking of the teachings of Confucius in China. Human-heartedness he called it.

Daniel picked up some large stones and piled them up as a marker. He scratched a word on a flat stone with an arrow and placed it on the top. They walked the perimeter to another point where they created the next marker and the next until the area was completely marked out and they were exhausted.

Evening was approaching and Zaidu became concerned about Ninana. She had mentioned her plans for a Jewish community area, which gave him an idea of where she might be.

"I saw your markers and I knew just where I would find you. A very good job!"

Daniel smiled, dusting the dirt from his hands.

"I hope you were not worried, Master Zaidu. May we show you the area we have chosen?"

"I will meet you here tomorrow. It will soon be dark and the servants are preparing the evening meal."

Zaidu and Ninana started back to the camp. Daniel walked a short way with them and then bid them good night. He went to his dwelling where his special foods awaited him.

Nebuchadnezzar showed no interest in Ninana's project, nor did he object. He did not even recognize her at times. He would look at her quizzically and asked her name.

"Father, I am your daughter, Ninana."

"Yes, yes, of course. What is it you want again, Ninana?"

"I want to build a neighborhood for the captives so they will have decent places to live and serve you better."

"So you have said. And who are these captives of whom you speak? I have so many things on my mind, you know."

"The ones you brought from Jerusalem, Father."

"Oh, so I did."

"My Lord King, your daughter is an architect and wishes to add a neighborhood to the great city of Babylon. Would you agree to that?"

Daniel was always close by. He knew that King Nebuchadnezzar was beginning to lose his memory.

"Of course. Yes. Whatever she wants. I am tired now. I need to rest."

Ninana was happy and sad at the same time. Her project could continue to go forward but her father did not know her.

Daniel escorted Ninana from the reception room and promised to speak with her again soon about the project.

Then he called the servants to assist the king to his chambers. The king's body was becoming somewhat feeble and he often stumbled. He would get lost in the great new palace if we went about alone.

King Nebuchadnezzar always trusted Daniel's wisdom and kept him close by. He appointed him to the high position of Chief over the Magicians, Enchanters, Astrologers, and Diviners who he knew were not trustworthy.

Ninana abruptly turned to Daniel, clearly perturbed.

"How is it that my father knows and trusts you, keeps you close to him, and does not even remember me? He turns to strangers and not to me, his own daughter!"

"Princess, I am sure this must be upsetting to you. But you are not forgotten in the great realm of the universe. Each of us is known and precious in the sight of God. He created each of us individually and responds to everyone who asks. Others may forget us, but not God. We are forever in his heart."

"Is that enough for you, Daniel? That your god remembers you, even when my father eventually forgets you, too?"

"Yes. God is forever. Humanity is not. You are remembered forever."

Chapter 27

DANIEL AND ARAKHU

Someone else was waiting for Daniel. It was the captain, Arakhu, who had spoken with him on the road from Jerusalem to Uruk many years ago.

"I hope I am not disturbing you, Daniel. I have been searching for you since our conversation. It seems so long ago now. I became ill and left the army. I wish to become your student. I must know more of what you were telling me that day."

Daniel needed a moment to gather his thoughts and the memory of that day. He barely recognized the captain. He seemed lame, sad, and perhaps ill.

"I am amazed that you found me in the midst of all this."

"I asked among your people. At first they were suspicious, but when I recounted what you had told me, one who had been near you recognized me. He did not know where you were but sent word among your people. Many months later when they decided to trust me, word came back to me that you were building a settlement here for the Jews from Jerusalem."

"This is true. It is here where we stand that the construction will begin."

"Do you live here?"

"No, I live in the palace of King Nebuchadnezzar and am chief of his magicians. You may reside there if you choose and I will sit with you when I can.

"Be aware that none of the magicians hold my beliefs or worship my god. You must keep to yourself. You are there only as my humble student. If you speak of my god or make them suspicious, they will quietly poison and kill you."

"As you can see, I have already been poisoned and my life may be short. I might not be healed by your teaching, but I will go to my grave at peace with your god."

"The poison is in your thoughts, my captain. Your healing is there also."

"What must I do?"

"I mentioned to you that love and good would be your reward for having compassion for the people. That is still true. Now have love and compassion for yourself, much as you had for the people. Think on that and we will speak again."

"I should bring you a gift for your kindness, Daniel. Is there something you need?"

"I have need of nothing, Captain. Give yourself the gift of understanding and that will be enough for me."

Arakhu bowed his head and turned away as tears rolled down his cheeks.

"I will await you at the palace in the place of the magicians."

Daniel and Arakhu met often and Daniel taught him about his god and teachings. Then they began going together to the Jewish settlement to assist in the construction. Daniel noticed that Arakhu began to strengthen and heal day by day. His countenance was brighter as he began to pour out his love and compassion upon the people.

Hananiah, Azariah, and Mishael noticed the difference in Arakhu as they worked together. Hananiah approached him.

"Arakhu, I understand that you live at the palace among the magicians. They might well do you harm. You are not safe there. My friends and I would like you to come and live with us. Our living quarters are sparse, but you are welcome to join us."

Arakhu was surprised and even relieved.

"I will be glad to leave that place. There are so many strange rituals and incantations that go on day and night. I have begun to fear for my sanity as well as my life among them."

Daniel joined them and was delighted that Arakhu would be coming to live in the Jewish community with his friends.

"Daniel, you were right. I am eager to see where my life will lead me now. It is filled with the good of which you spoke. Your god's promises are true."

"Not just my god, Arakhu. Your god. Take the God of All as your own. God belongs to each of us and we to him."

"It is hard, my friend. I was taught that gods were remote and even threatening. A god that cares for me and all people is strange. But I will remember."

"God has cared about you from the beginning whether you knew that or not. Now that you know, you can let God into your heart."

That evening, Arakhu thought the food in his quarters in the palace did not taste right. Immediately he set it aside and rinsed out his mouth. He realized that his escape must be immediate or his death would come that night. He quickly packed his meager belongings, ran down through the kitchens of the palace, and out of the servants' entrance.

Hananiah and Mishael met him outside the palace wall.

"Daniel told us there was gossip among the servants about you and we feared you would be dead before we got to you. The servants were about to let us in and lead us to you when, thankfully, you appeared safe and unharmed. Come with us."

"I was very near to death. The food did not taste right and I spit it out of my mouth, packed my belongings, headed for the kitchen and the servants' entrance."

They left the palace grounds through the back gate, and headed for the home of Hananiah, Azariah, and Mishael. Yes, it was sparse, but it felt like the whole universe had opened up for Arakhu. There were conversations about their god, now Arakhu's god, singing and prayers.

Daniel arrived later in the day. He brushed off his robe and hands and embraced Arakhu.

"Thanks be to God that you are here and safe."

"I am so thankful to you. I have never experienced a home so filled with peace and good will. Your god is surely my god."

They shared food and wine. The evening was filled with blessings and conversation about goodness. Arakhu was a happy man for the first time in his life.

Chapter 28

NINANA'S PROJECT

"Princess, I am chosen by my god as one of his faithful prophets. It is because of my unshakable honesty and faith in my god that I was appointed to this position beside the king.

"Though you may not believe in my god, you are still divinely guided on your path as an architect. Who else do you know can do that? It is yours. I am not an architect, you are. There is no difference between us. We are called but not to the same path. These callings have nothing to do with your father. His mind is failing. I must constantly remind him of who I am, too. Please do not let it spoil your happiness."

"I am sorry, Daniel. I do not mean to speak to you harshly. It is so frustrating that he dismisses me no matter what I do to please him."

"Our path or faith should you choose it, is not to please others but to please God. Others will disappoint you, but God never will."

Daily Daniel sat in the court behind the throne and whispered the words when the king could not think of what he needed to say. He could not remember things he always knew and feared to appear weak or foolish in front of his subjects when he held court.

In his position as the chief among the magicians and astrologers Daniel had the power to dismiss the court when the king became weary, which happened more often as time went by. He would assure the petitioners first places on the following day.

In Jerusalem Daniel was one of God's most faithful prophets. Even though he was taken from his home country and brought to grow up in a kingdom strange to him he never lost his faith, his honesty and clarity.

Ninana did not trust the Babylonian magicians and so called wise men. They were dishonest and always maneuvering for power. Daniel did not seem to be maneuvering for power or taking advantage of his position.

Over time she learned that Daniel was indeed different. He had insight, intelligence, and wisdom. His promotion reflected his keen mind, knowledge, and understanding. He had the ability to interpret dreams, explain riddles, and solve difficult problems.

Fortunately for her father Daniel was someone he could rely upon more each day. She called him a stranger, but even though he was a foreigner, he was certainly not a stranger.

She sensed his deep connection to his god and she wanted to know more. Her only devotion had been to her work and the rebuilding of Babylon.

"Can I understand his devotion? Can I have that as well? Where do I start? Perhaps by knowing him more, I might come to know his god."

Babylon had seven gods, An, Enki, Enlil, Ninhursag, Nanna, Utu, and Inanna. Ninana had a hard time keeping track of which god meant what. Some were evil, some were good, but why? Where did these beliefs in these so called gods come from? Other than building temples dedicated to gods, people didn't pay much attention to them. It all made no sense to her. The gods and goddesses of Babylonia did not interest her. They were remote and seemingly of no consequence in her life.

Her only respite was friendship with the man from Jerusalem. In a society such as Babylon's, it might have been imperative that she blend in with her people, join them in their hedonistic antics, and shun someone as righteous as Daniel. But she did not do any of those things. She befriended Daniel and grew to know and respect him.

Daniel was gentle and kind to everyone. Ninana was fascinated with their conversations about his god and the goodness of the teachings. He would speak to her of his god as they worked, and the value of love and compassion for people.

They spent many months planning the Jewish section and took the Jewish people there often to approve or make suggestions as the building continued. Ninana loved the hands on work side by side with Daniel as they measured out streets and foundations.

The master builder, Zaidu, was glad to supply the materials she needed for her project. He sent left over stone that was not suitable for buildings but could be used for retaining walls, walkways, and foundations. When he had time he came by to see how it was progressing and advised her when they ran into difficulty with the terrain along the Euphrates.

The friendship between Daniel and Zaidu grew as they worked together on the Jewish community in Babylon. They spent hours talking about their lives and beliefs. Daniel's friends Hananiah, Mishael, Azariah, and many others joined in the construction of houses of worship, homes, a marketplace, walls, and walkways.

The greatly anticipated day arrived when the dwellings and the synagogue in the project were ready for occupants. Zaidu and Daniel brought wagons and wheelbarrows to help people move their meager belongings. Street by street the places were filled.

That evening there was singing, dancing in the streets. Daniel and his friends drew Ninana and Zaidu into the merriment. Soon they were all dancing in the circles with the residents, learning the steps and singing their joyful songs. This was the second time Ninana experienced such happiness with a community of people who were foreigners, and yet they accepted her.

Daniel sat down beside her for a rest and the food that was offered.

"They accept you, Princess, because you first accepted them. You cared enough to relieve some of their misery with the great resources that were yours to give. They may not approach you because you are royalty, but they love you."

She smiled as her thoughts went back to China and the village she helped repair. They could not speak to her or she to them, and they knew nothing of her royalty. They saw that she had compassion for their plight and they seemed to love her, too.

"Yes, Daniel's god is right. Love and compassion are most important. My father and other kings destroy communities, but I will build them."

Her heart was full of joy.

Chapter 29

BABYLON RISING

———————— ❦ ———————

Between the Jewish settlement and the continued rebuilding of Babylon, Ninana was very busy. She and Daniel rushed by each other in the hot sun and dusty streets putting finishing touches on everything.

"Princess, come with me to the Jewish community. Have some food and rest."

"There is so much to do! It seems I am needed everywhere all at once! Tomorrow large groups of artisans and brick makers are coming from Persia. They need to set up brick ovens and will teach the workers to make the glazed bricks of to cover the buildings, walls, and the Ishtar Gate."

"Yes, and that will give you time to rest while they are setting up and training your people."

The Ishtar Gate was Ninana's masterpiece through which everyone coming to Babylon would have to pass. As the blue and gold tiles were applied they reflected in the sun so the city could be seen from long distances. The city walls also received the same tiles that shone in beautiful colors.

The barges coming up the Euphrates with the materials for the gardens were secured and unloaded. Lines of workers carried the materials from the barge halfway up the ziggurat.

Ninana was laying out the building plans on the stone steps to share with Zaidu when he arrived. Suddenly they reminded her of Chaoxiang. Tears filled her eyes, ran down her cheeks, and dripped onto the plans. She heard Zaidu coming, quickly wiped them away, and blotted the plans where the tears landed.

They sat down with the plans and Ninana went through them as the Chinese engineers had taught her. They climbed the ziggurat to discuss the location and how it would be supported as a cascading garden over the steps, and how the water would be piped in from the Euphrates. The plants and trees would need constant water in this dry climate.

A team of Zaidu's engineers met with them for several days until they understood what needed to be done. They were amazed at some of the innovations of the Chinese to keep plants alive during the long voyage. Their systems to maintain everything were exacting and unique. The packing structures were a complete mystery to the sailors. Within the structure was a desalination system that enabled them to be dampened with sea water.

The workers and engineers soon had anchors inserted in the stone steps, supports constructed for the huge garden boxes, and braces for the irrigation systems. Plants and trees were moved into the boxes by palace gardeners who lovingly set them in place with the right amount of dampened soil. They seemed to know what each kind of plant needed. Flowers were already beginning to bud and open under their care.

Construction of homes, shops, temples, and markets spread out quickly in all directions. Ninana could not imagine how such a large city could be completed, but it was happening.

More and more workers became skilled artisans. Materials continued to flow up the Euphrates from the seaport for the builders. The little girl who drew cities on the walls of a secret room in the basement of the palace in Uruk saw those dreams blossom and grow in huge dimensions.

The blue and gold bricks were applied to the exteriors of the nearly complete Ishtar gate, palace walls, and the city walls. Golden lion sculptures were cemented into the walls.

Atop the Ishtar Gate was a tomb that Ninana had created for herself. She wanted everyone who entered the city after her death to enter under her tomb which was supposed to be an ill omen for anyone with bad intentions toward Babylon. Word about it got around and it so disturbed merchants coming to the city that a side gate was created for them to enter.

Chapter 30

NEBUCHADNEZZAR'S PASSING

During the forty-third year of his reign Nebuchadnezzar died. His mind had completely failed. Daniel stayed by his side and assisted him until it was not of any use.

He no longer recognized Daniel or Ninana, not even Queen Amytis. He just stared into space and mumbled unintelligible words, sometimes flailing his arms as if still commanding the empire. Restraints were necessary to keep him from pitching himself off his bed. Months later Queen Amytis, Ninana, and Daniel stayed by him as he quietly passed away in the night.

He was succeeded by Evol-Merodach, Ninana's older half-brother. Upon the news of Nebuchadnezzar's passing, he boldly marched into Babylon with an army like the conquering hero.

"Ha! Now that I am the king I can do whatever I want! Everyone must bow to me and scurried about carrying out my commands! All the women I want are mine to take."

Ninana found him disgusting. She stayed at the school of architecture as much as possible to avoid seeing him. She hated the memory of his leering grin and hot breath as he attempted to rape her before her wedding. He still seemed to consider Ninana fair game for his sexual attentions.

"Come now, Ninana, we should be friends. Have dinner with me in my apartments tonight."

"You are a pig, Evol-Merodach. I want nothing to do with you now or ever."

"Oh? Does that weakling husband of yours satisfy you in your bed? I am sure he does not. Perhaps you should allow me to awaken you to the pleasures of sleeping with a real man."

"Do not speak to me of these things. They are none of your business."

"You will come to me one day, Ninana. Sooner or later, you will see."

"Never!"

She avoided being in his presence unless it was ceremoniously necessary. She insisted that Nabonidus accompany her during those times. He hated that duty.

"Do you satisfy your wife, Nabonidus? Or are you impotent? Or maybe you are a male temple prostitute! I will be happy to take her and do the job for you!"

Nabonidus had no clever words to refute those taunting's. His only recourse was to be angry at Ninana.

Nabonidus was in line to the throne after Evol-Merodach, but for now he was left in limbo without a purpose of his own. He had no talent to do anything of consequence.

Evol-Merodach was unable to counteract the danger to Babylonia arising from the Medians. He was a poor general mostly given to bragging and parading. He disposed of those in the army who opposed him, especially the officers.

That created such an uprising in the army that elderly King Neriglissar returned from retirement in a far province to quell the dissent. He was feeble and in ill health. Upon his arrival he immediately dethroned Evol-Merodach and ordered his assassination.

Shortly after that Neriglissar himself died. The exertion of the confrontation with Evol-Merodach proved to be too much for his frail body.

Ninana rushed to his bedside to thank him, almost too late.

"You have freed me from a terrible menace, Sire."

"Yes, and all of Babylonia…"

He smiled, patted her hand and passed away with a sigh, a happy man.

Being a king did not interest Nabonidus. He enjoyed the parties, women, and the soft life. He preferred to escape the duties of a king by accompanying Ninana when she went to Babylon. His excuse was to protect and help her, or find something useful to do.

She made it clear that she did not desire his company. She did not need his protection or help. The builders had seen to her safety for many years and her talents were far beyond his understanding.

"Nabonidus, you must take on the role of the King of Babylonia! There is much for you to do and the armies at our borders are a threat to our safety!"

"But I do not wish to be a king, Ninana! I never wanted to be a king."

"You allowed yourself to be married into royalty which put you in line to be the king. I am sure your mother had something to do with that."

"My mother tried to stop the marriage! She knew you were not worthy but your father, the all-powerful King Nebuchadnezzar, insisted."

Ninana, blazing with anger, screamed, picked up a vase and threw it at him. It missed him and smashed on the floor all around him.

"Enough! You are the one who is proving your unworthiness to rule the greatest empire ever known. Go and attend to your duties...*King* Nabonidus."

He stood as if frozen. He had never seen her so enraged. She seemed to tower over him and her anger was terrifying.

"The might of the Mesopotamian military is concentrated in Assyria. Without Assyria to keep foreign powers in check, Babylonia is exposed. We are in danger! See to your duties to keep Babylonia safe."

His mouth dropped open but no sound came out. Before she could pick up another vase he abruptly he turned and stalked away.

Now that Nabonidus was the king, Ninana was happy to have him be occupied by demands that he be elsewhere, not following around after her in Babylon.

Being of Assyrian heritage, Nabonidus began spending the majority of his time traveling to the Assyrian city of Harran with a small troop of his faithful guards. He pretended to oversee the rebuilding of temples and other projects there.

The population of Babylonia became restive and increasingly disaffected under King Nabonidus' neglect. The priesthood of Marduk hated Nabonidus because of his suppression of the god Marduk's cult and his elevation of the cult of the Moon-god Sin. Worse, he planned to centralize this religion in the new temple of Marduk at Babylon. Now the alienated local priests were in a rage at losing their temple.

"Dear husband, you cannot use my temples in Babylon for the worship of the Sun God, Sin. The temples are rightly dedicated to Babylonia's gods and goddesses."

"I hear that you worship an invisible god, Ninana. So you will not need a temple for that one. There will obviously be an empty temple since his temple must be invisible as well!"

He laughed at Ninana when she tried to explain Daniel's god to him.

"What do you need with another god? Our gods and goddesses will be insulted! An invisible god you said? Maybe he will build an invisible temple. Ha!"

That was Ninana's last hope that Nabonidus would understand anything about love. He only knew about other women and wine. He sold them as slaves when he tired of them. He would sell her if he could, she had no doubt.

Chapter 31

A QUEEN REGENT

Ninana kept to her beloved architecture and building projects. Those were the only things that seemed rooted in reality and worthwhile.

Belshazzar was growing up and rejected any signs of what he considered mothering. Feeling spurned Queen Amytis planned to travel to Haran with Nabonidus. Babylon had never been home to her.

Now that she was free of Nebuchadnezzar's control, she wanted go to her home to visit her temples and enjoy the familiar Assyrian culture.

She wondered if the Assyrian prince who once loved her was still there. Would he remember? The hope caused her heart to beat faster. Years with Nebuchadnezzar disappeared from her memory at the thought.

"Ninana was right. I do have a dream for myself and my own life. I can see the prince waiting for me at the palace gate as he did so long ago. Oh let it be true. I must know."

Appointed by his father, King Nabonidus, the Crown Prince Belshazzar became Regent of the city of Babylon. King Nabonidus chose to live in northwestern Arabia, not too far from Babylonia and let his son rule the City of Babylon.

Nabonidus established a camp among his Arab subjects in the desert of Arabia, near the southern frontier of his kingdom, leaving his son Belshazzar also in command of the Babylonian army.

With Nabonidus gone Ninana became the Queen Regent of all Babylonia. It had been Ninana's intention spend more time with her son and teach him about being the regent of the city, but he was more interested in his friends and the mischief they created together.

Belshazzar became immersed in the social life of Babylon, wine and women. He sequestered himself within the city walls that were so high and wide that he was sure Babylon must be impregnable. He loved cheering the charioteers who raced over the top of the wide walls which could accommodate chariots and spectators.

The military despised Nabonidus because he left the defense of his kingdom to Belshazzar, who only cared for wine and wild parties.

She tried to remind his of his duties to rule wisely and lead the military.

"The city has been destroyed many times. The Persians are now encroaching upon the territory of Babylonia, capturing much of the outlying territory, and we should not let the city be destroyed again."

"Mother, you designed this city and its walls. So we must surely be safe since you are the great architect. No one can breach those walls or gates. You made sure of that, did you not?"

He laughed and like her father, walked away. Belshazzar was not interested as long as he thought the city was a fortress and the stores were filled with wine and food. He took over his father's harem and drew out the daughters that were born there into his parties. His supply of wine and women was inexhaustible.

The parties became more raucous and servants were hard pressed to clean up after one before another one began. Without a leader the military began little by little to disappear into the outer provinces of Babylonia and even to join the Persians.

Soon there were only the palace guards and decimated ranks of the army left. The citizens of the city went about their own usual rounds of parties and trips to the brothels.

Ninana despaired of ever bringing back the order her father had established.

Sadly, Master Jarem became so feeble that he stayed in his bed. He was delighted when she shared her plans with him for the new school. She stayed with him on his bed, her arms around him, until he quietly passed away in the early morning.

Ninana became the head of the new Architectural School of Babylon, as was expected. Plans were already underway to move the school from Uruk to a special building in Babylon that she and her students designed.

The students were busy moving into living quarters and workspaces that were light filled with easy access to the building sites. Their present task was to assist her in designing Babylon's marketplace and banking complex.

They had learned well and built a huge agora that contained the markets and banks. It was a marvel of beauty and convenience. Built close to the side gate, merchants could bring their goods in and out, and banks created a lucrative system of finance.

The school became famous as the popularity of the City of Babylon increased. The number of students doubled again and again. It was an honor to be educated in the school headed by the queen herself. Their skills grew and were in great demand far beyond the Babylonia.

Chapter 32

YANG LIGHT OF THE RISING SUN

The building of her heart was the one dedicated to Master Fu Ling Lang, her Chinese benefactor and friend. He and Lishan were due to return soon.

"My heart yearns to see them again. My life with them was fulfilling. Will it ever be that way again? Can I manage my calling and our friendship in the same heart? It must be possible. Living without them is unthinkable."

He not only sponsored her to visit China but shipped many statues, artifacts, silks, and wall hangings for the building. He even had a small temple dismantled and shipped to Babylon to be reassembled as an entrance just inside the building.

She visited the building often and wandered through it remembering her experiences in China and, of course, Chaoxiang. She kept his jade ring in a special place in the temple area and wore it only when she was in the building. His love seemed to radiate from it. She would close her eyes and see his face smiling at her.

Tears rolled down her cheeks. She missed Chaoxiang as she fingered the gold and jade ring he had given her, slipped on the bracelet, and touched the silks of China.

The foreigners criticized Babylon and laughed the idea of a woman creating all of this. She placed her huge ornate coffin at the top of the Ishtar Gate so they would have to bow to her as they came into Babylon. It was considered a bad omen to pass beneath a dead body. By their own superstitions they believed they would be cursed.

She had an inscription placed on the outside of the tomb where all could read it.

"A great treasure lies within this tomb. If any King of Babylon is short of funds, let him open my tomb and take what he needs, but only in dire circumstances. The treasure will do him no good if it is taken for greed."

Daniel read the inscription and laughed.

"You are teaching them that God takes care of those who stand fast in truth and those who are greedy will get nothing. You have learned well."

"Yes, I have. But they will not understand the blessing I just gave them. The wisdom of it is rich, but the tomb is empty."

They walked through the gate together as the sun lowered toward the horizon. The gate and buildings shown blue and gold like a city floating in the sky.

At last Lishan and Fu Ling Yang returned. Zaidu guided them to the building that bore Yang's name where Ninana was waiting. She came out into the Chinese style gardens to greet them. Lishan rushed into her arms. The three sat down together on garden benches to take in the scene, the buildings, and each other. Ninana was content and happy.

Fu Ling Yang, Ninana, Zaidu, and Daniel were going through the building that bore his name, "Yang Light of the Rising Sun." His small Chinese temple at the entrance of the building gave it a sense of the divine. The rooms were filled with many vases, art pieces, carpets, silks, and extra wall hangings painted with Chinese poetry and birds. She wanted it all to be perfectly Chinese.

Hananiah, Mishael, and Azariah came to assist with the temple. They worked for many hours putting the interior of the temple together. Fu Ling Yang guided them in placing each item while he spoke the appropriate blessings.

"Tell us what this means, Master."

"Everything must flow according to a system of laws called feng shui, considered to govern spatial arrangement and orientation in relation to the flow of Qi or energy. Feng means wind and shui means water. Opposing the wind and water brings conflict."

Lishan, too, was thrilled with everything in the building.

"It is all so beautiful! It takes me back to China the minute I walk in. I love spending time here. Thank you, Ninana, for creating this temple in the middle of your wonderful Babylon."

"It has been the center of my joy."

She did not mention Chaoxiang, but Lishan knew the anguish of her heart and put her arm around her.

Often Shamhar accompanied Lishan in her visits to Yang Light of the Rising Sun. She also missed China.

When Shamhar graduated he became the head of the School of Architecture as Ninana's assistant. His fame grew. He was in demand as an architect in other areas of Babylonia and Assyria. He would bring news of Amytis to Ninana.

"She is well, happy, and has found her prince. She said they are happy to spend the last years of their lives together. She sends you love."

He and Lishan spent many hours walking and talking about China and his work as an architect. He was still besotted with her and she found him to be loving and kind. It was not surprising that they fell in love.

"Lishan, who do I ask for your hand in marriage? If you will agree, of course."

She laughed and took his arm as they walked through the Ishtar Gate, awed at its immensity and beauty.

"You may ask Master Fu Ling Lang. I have no family now. He is my appointed royal guardian."

"Do you think he will agree and give his permission? I might die if he does not!"

"I do not think you will need to die...we will ask him together. It is customary. We should also ask my dear friend, Ninana. She and Fu Ling Yang would stand in for my deceased parents. I am sure Daniel and his friends will stand with you."

They went to the building named for Fu Ling Yang and found all the workers and cleaners were just finishing. Lishan turned around and around, squealing with delight. It was the first time she had seen it all arranged, polished, and looking splendid.

"It is so like my China!"

She and Shamhar walked through all the rooms thrilling to everything they saw. She explained the meaning of some of the artifacts and read the poems on the wall hangings to him.

One evening Fu Ling Yang and Ninana were sitting on a bench in the building talking about the time when he would regretfully have to return to China.

"It will be a very sad time for me. It might be years before I can return, but I will look forward to that time."

"Then two men I love will be in China and part of my heart will always be there."

They became quiet, walked together, each immersed in their own thoughts.

Lishan and Shamhar came in, approached Fu Ling Yang and bowed.

Ninana sensed this would be a very important conversation for the three of them. She excused herself and went to another part of the building.

Shamhar almost stumbled on a carpet and stammered. Lishan held tight to his arm.

"Master Fu Ling Yang, we wish to marry. Please, we ask your permission and blessing on our marriage."

They bowed and waited. Shamhar tried to stop shaking. Lishan held his arm tighter. Fu Ling Yang smiled at his nervousness.

"Come and sit in the temple with me."

Ninana was about to leave them but he motioned her to come, too.

They sat, drank ceremonial tea, and repeated the appropriate blessings.

After a long discussion among the three of them, Fu Ling Lang was satisfied that all requirements for a Chinese marriage were fulfilled and happily gave his permission.

Shamhar nearly fainted. Lishan shook his arm to steady him.

Ninana hugged Lishan.

"I was sure he would remember you."

Lishan giggled.

"I was a little afraid that he might not. I am so happy!"

Chapter 33

A CHINESE WEDDING

—— ❧ ❧ ——

"There is much to be done for the ceremony. You must have a long red dress, Lishan. And the gifts for the parents and the altar must be prepared."

Lishan smiled at her and took her hand, a few tears in her eyes.

"You have learned much about the Chinese ways from our voyages and travels. I am so happy that you know and honor these things! We will do them together."

Ninana sent a servant to find Daniel. Of course the servant announced that the summons was from the queen. He was curious about what this summons could be and hurried to join them.

Shamhar drew him aside as he entered the temple area and the three sat down. Lishan explained everything with Shamhar expressing his happiness.

Daniel smiled and shook Shahar's hand.

"I am honored to stand with you, Shamhar."

Lishan smiled, bowed, and continued.

"During the Chinese wedding ceremonies, the bride and groom stand at the family altar, where they pay homage to heaven and earth, the family ancestors, and the kitchen god, Tsao-Chün. Tea, with two lotus seeds or two red dates in each cup, are offered to the parents.

The wedding ceremony is performed in the evening, which is a time of good fortune."

The ceremony was set for the next evening. Everyone shifted into high gear to create all that was needed for the event.

"I brought a red dress with me from China in the hope that this day would come. Let me show it to you."

It was a gala marriage observed in Chinese fashion and customs. Ninana and Fu Ling Yang acted in her parents' role. Mishael and Daniel stood with Shamhar.

After much joyful celebrating, Shamhar took Lishan to his new apartment in the architectural building. It was quite separate from the students' quarters and beautifully furnished. They could at last be alone. They stood in the doorway to savor the moment before they went in. She took his shaking hand and led him in.

After a few days, Lishan and Shamhar bid them all farewell with many hugs and thanks. They traveled to the north by horse back with a large guard to experience a small portion of the Silk Road.

Lishan was excited to meet the traveling merchants coming from the east and west, see their wares, and speak with those whose language she could understand.

Their guard made the arrangements for their lodging and short travels on the Silk Road. There were camel caravans, spice and silk merchants, travelers from the far west with even stranger languages. The guards advised them not to go far where the possibility of danger would increase.

Shamhar was astonished at the variety of travelers from many countries and the goods they brought to be marketed in the east. His ears were assaulted by a cacophony of languages and music he had never heard before.

Lishan knew some of the languages and could translate. She sent messages to Fu Ling Lang's royal family by a merchant who was going to China.

"How can you be sure they will deliver them?"

"Master Fu Ling Lang is royalty and it is an honor to carry messages for royalty. It will bring the messengers many rewards in trade and riches. Even if the first one who carries the message dies, another will gladly pick it up and deliver it."

It was wonderful and exhausting. Now Shamhar was eager to return to Babylon to continue his work. Lishan wanted to return while Fu Ling Yang was still there.

"I prefer to travel by sailing ships, Shamhar. Some day we must travel to China so you will see the architecture there."

She bought paper from the west and sketched the buildings for him. She even bought some paintings from a Chinese merchant.

The guards knocked on their hotel room door before dawn.

"We must leave immediately. There are threatening situations arising."

Lishan was curious but they did not say what those situations were.

Shamhar knew that their word was to be trusted. They quickly packed up as the sun was about to rise in the east. The horses were saddled and ready. They left in haste for Babylon. Lishan rode close to Shamhar. They said nothing to each other until they were far away from the Silk Road and safe.

The sight of the glorious buildings of Babylon shining in the sun filled them with relief and anticipation of what their coming days would bring. Shamhar knew there was much unrest in Babylonia under King Nabonidus and the borders were being threatened. They went directly to Yang Light of the Rising Sun.

Meeting them immediately, Fu Ling Yang needed to convince Shamhar and Lishan to return with him to China.

"We must all go quickly. It is a long ride to the Port of Ur where we can leave Babylonia and the dangers that are coming."

Lishan was immediately distraught at the thought of leaving Ninana.

"We must take Ninana with us!"

Fu Ling Yang explained to her that sadly they must leave Ninana.

"She is now Queen Nitocris and Regent of Babylonia, and she cannot leave. This is her destiny. It is not yours or mine. You and Shamhar may be killed in an attack that is sure to come from King Cyrus of Persia."

"I remember the Amazon Women Warriors speaking of the threat from Persia. I know they were talking about King Cyrus and his attacks on their people."

"Yes, Lishan. You and Shamhar must decide quickly. Your decision will determine whether you live or die. Come with me to the Port of Ur now where the ship is waiting. I have spoken to Ninana. She agrees with me."

Ninana and Daniel met with them and encouraged them to go with Fu Ling Yang.

"I will miss you Lishan, but I wish you to be safe and Babylonia is no longer safe. Daniel and I will pray to his god, now our god, for your journey.

"Please, go and if you should see Chaoxiang when Shamhar goes to the School of Architecture in Guangzhou, tell him that he always has my love."

"We will..."

They embraced and said tearful goodbyes.

Chapter 34

THE POWER OF NITOCRIS

Ninana and Zaidu sat in a high place on the wall that was created to be a lookout.

"Zaidu, my name is Nitocris. Do you know that name?"

He pulled at his beard and squinted his eyes in thought.

"I heard it long ago in my travels. It is an Egyptian name as I suspect mine is as well. The legend is that the name Nitocris belonged to an Egyptian queen who was strong, outspoken, and did not bow before men. She lived many centuries ago."

"My name Ninana is my childhood name. It was created by my mother after a goddess. It has a special meaning, I know. But I need to feel more centered in a purpose, rooted in something more..."

"Ninana is your childhood name. It is very soft and spiritual. In this world you need to be powerful. Nitocris is a powerful name. It was a queen's name and now it is yours. You are no longer a princess. Your husband has abandoned Babylonia. He lives in Arabia. You are the Queen Regent. Your life will no longer be as carefree as it once was. You will need to be aware at all times of the dangers around you and fight to establish your rightful place. Your survival will depend upon it."

Ninana searched her mind for who she thought of as powerful.

"My father was when he had his mind and Sennacherib was a powerful destroyer. Could I be powerful without being destructive of other nations? Daniel had a special power that I could not define and his survival had depended upon it."

She needed time to put her thoughts in order.

"Thank you Zaidu. I must go and think upon this. I know what you said is true. I must find my own way and stand my power. I must find who I am now as Queen Nitocris."

She and Zaidu climbed down the stairway from the lookout. He went to the marketplace and she went to the Chinese building to sit in the temple.

"I must dress as a queen like my mother did. I must select capable and trustworthy guards to be around me wherever I go. I must learn to command rather than to meekly ask. Command and govern. That is what I said was my father's philosophy. Babylon's rebuilding is complete and beautiful. Already there are those who desecrate it with brothels, street fights, and garbage strewn around. The Jewish community is settled in and in a safe place between the Euphrates and the city wall. No attacks on the city will likely come their way. King Cyrus is threatening and yet I understand him to be compassionate. I must go to him myself."

She reached out to King Cyrus by emissary to ask his advice and help. Perhaps her father was right that women did not understand governing. But she was never taught and now Nabonidus and Belshazzar were making a mess of things and weakening Babylonia. She needed the most powerful king she knew to guide her. She waited patiently for the next few weeks hoping he would answer her.

Queen Nitocris, Zaidu, and Daniel became confidants. They advised each other and planned for the eventual governing and defense of Babylon. She told them of her emissary to King Cyrus. Zaidu caught a quick breath.

"When he responds, you will be ready as the queen. We have gathered information from every part of Babylonia. You have all you need to speak with him."

Daniel was very quiet for a while. Then he spoke.

"I have been praying about this for a long time. I could see it coming and I needed wisdom. I can feel the guidance of the spirit of God speaking to me. Are you willing to pray with me and hear what I have heard?"

Nitocris and Zaidu were agreeable. It felt like the settling in of a higher way, peace and understanding.

They knelt down in the Chinese temple and Daniel began the prayer. It went so deep that a few hours passed before they realized it. When Daniel said, "It is done," they stood up together. Zaidu had not heard Daniel pray before.

"Yes, Daniel. I know it is done. I do not know exactly what that means, but it feels right. Thank you."

After a few weeks a message from King Cyrus arrived inviting her to visit him. She had heard about him from his brick makers who helped her with the blue enameled bricks. She hoped he was the kindly person they spoke about. The kings she knew were mean and thought she was not worth talking or listening to because she was a woman. She continued to strengthen her mind and heart.

"My father was talking to only a girl, but I am a queen. I must release his disregard of me. I will strengthen my resolve to be a queen and only a queen, no matter what kings or disdain I may face. I am the powerful Queen Nitocris now and forever."

She traveled by horseback with her special small guard. Cyrus' entourage met her at the border of Persia to escort her to Susa and his palace. The Persian palace was immense and resplendent with colors, paintings, tiled floors and gold guilt doorways. There were rich hangings, flowers, gardens and fountains everywhere.

She drew in her breath and remembered that her palace was as imposing and glorious as this one. She could not allow any doubts or diminishing thoughts to enter her mind.

King Cyrus met her in an ornate receiving room. She introduced herself as Queen Nitocris of Babylonia. It sounded strange in her ears and almost frightening, but she drew another deep breath and focused upon her mission. He graciously led her to a pleasant area with comfortable chairs and gentle fragrances of flowers where they could talk.

"What do you need from me, Queen Nitocris? I am most happy to help you in any way I can."

"Gracious King, I have never been a ruler. I am an architect as perhaps you know since I have called upon your artisans to assist in the outer finishing of the Ishtar Gate, buildings and walls of Babylon."

"Yes, I am aware of that. I understand from those who returned that your city is most beautiful and your designs are exquisite."

She acknowledged his compliment.

"My father's last days were not as a king's should be due to his loss of memory. The rule of Evol-Merodach, Nabonidus, and now Belshazzar is a disaster for Babylonia. Evol-Merodach was assassinated by order of King Neriglissar. Nabonidus and Belshazzar are weak and cowardly and have no taste for ruling an empire.

"The city is impregnable from direct assaults. The way into the City of Babylon will be open to you. I implore you to preserve my city. I did not oppose you as you took over provinces at the edges of the Babylonian empire. I have no appetite for war."

She knew he had become king of all Persia and was engaged in a campaign to put down a revolt among the Assyrians. She wanted to trust his kindly demeanor. She was not sure her father would think that wise, but what other choice was there?

"When will you come?"

"Soon. I can save your city but perhaps not your throne, Queen Nitocris. Once we capture Babylon, your position will be changed."

"I do not want the Babylonians to fight against you, but I cannot stop them. Only Belshazzar can do that. I know he will not leave his drunken parties to stop them or even encourage them to fight. Nabonidus is living in Arabia as a disgraced king and has not returned even to see the building of the city finished."

"You are wiser than you believe you are, Queen Nitocris, and I admire your courage. You value your city and your people more than your throne. Most queens would be killing even their own people to keep their thrones."

"He admires me? This is so unexpected. How I would love it if my father could hear that. But I must keep my focus."

She had to stop and take another deep breath.

"I have a friend from Jerusalem, the prophet Daniel, whose god teaches him to love and serve others. I have learned much from his teaching. I believe it is a true teaching and I find much wisdom and comfort in it."

She plied Cyrus with many questions about governing and relationships with other countries. He patiently answered them all.

Finally King Cyrus sat quietly and looked at her. Not only was she beautiful, but every inch a queen. The power in her humility was awesome.

"I will do everything I can for you, Queen Nitocris. We will speak again soon and you must introduce me to this prophet, Daniel."

"I will be happy to do that. I wish him to be safe for he is the only good left in Babylon. I thank you for your kindness."

Queen Nitocris stood, bowed, and was escorted back to her guards and her horse. She felt as if she were flying, her heart pounding. The long ride to Babylon on her horse was calming. The time gave her the opportunity to settle her mind and to sort out the things King Cyrus told her.

She quietly thanked Zaidu for introducing her to Nitocris, the queen. She had come into her own power.

Daniel and Zaidu were on hand to greet her. They went to the Chinese temple together and she told them all that had transpired between her and King Cyrus.

"Zaidu, what do you wish to do when Cyrus comes? Will you leave Babylon?"

"No, I will go to reside in the School of Architecture and be with the students. It is a peaceful place and will be safe if there is an attack."

"Daniel? Will you go back to Jerusalem?"

"No. There is nothing there for me. Jerusalem is destroyed and the people scattered. My place is here with you, Queen Nitocris, and wherever you go. My god is in Susa and everywhere I travel."

Chapter 35

THE QUEEN

———— ❦ ———

Queen Nitocris stood on a balcony on the roof of her palace and looked out over her city, the city she designed, Babylon. The Hanging Gardens were resplendent. The terraces were five stories high. The waterfalls, exotic trees, vines, pathways and acres of flowers were enchanting. Many of the plants she brought from China were now matured and visible from everywhere in the city.

They awed visitors and travelers. Guides were provided for travelers to tell them about the gardens, what was in them, the construction, and where they originated.

One of her favorites, along with the Chinese building, Yang Light of the Rising Sun, was the Gate of Ishtar with its blue enameled bricks and golden lions. It was the most beautiful gate ever built and visitors stood in awe when they approached it. She placed her burial sarcophagus in at the very top so everyone who passed through would remember her as the architect of Babylon and bow to her long after she was gone.

Seeing her city all around the palace and for many miles in every direction, the questions always plagued her mind.

"How could Sennacherib destroy this beautiful ancient city with its canals, water dams, and sluice gates? He wantonly destroyed their engineering genius and let the Euphrates to flood into the city, to slowly dissolve its mud and clay brick buildings. How could anyone destroy someone's city, their homes, and their businesses? Their very lives. Yet my father, King Nebuchadnezzar, had done just that. He sent his armies to Judah to destroy Jerusalem and the temple, loot it, and take its residents into exile."

Much as Ninana loved peace, harmony, and creativity there was little to be found in her life except the creativity she expressed in designing and rebuilding Babylon. There were nightly drunken parties in the palaces and brawls in the streets. Brothels were everywhere. The pristine city she imagined and designed was besmirched by the wanton lifestyle of its residents.

The military was incensed that she called upon them to clean up the streets, but she did not care. They took wagon loads of debris out to the Euphrates, but they could not keep up with the garbage and excrement that residents daily tossed from windows into the alleys. Sometimes it landed on them as they worked.

They began to cover the filth with mud and clay instead of carrying it out to the river. It would harden in the sun. After so many layers of clay the alleys became so deep that the residents had to build steps from the streets down to their doorways.

Cyrus' troops were advancing across the Tigris and swamps of Babylonia. Nitocris heard of it and went to Belshazzar who was with two women in his chambers. He was not happy to be disturbed.

"My son, King Cyrus is coming and will be at our gate soon. What will you do? It would be wise to open the gate and surrender. Your troops are scattered and without your leadership they cannot defend us. They have all but given up. Some are defecting to Cyrus' troops to fight with him."

"You worry too much, my mother. Keep the gates closed. You built this city to keep us safe against attack. No one can get in...the stores of food and wine are nearly full and we can hold out longer than Cyrus. Please do not bother me with your fears or I will order the guard to take you to the dungeon."

"You will rue the day you said that to me. The prophecies are not in your favor."

"I thought you did not believe in prophecies. What does Daniel's god say?"

"You shall know soon enough."

The women began laughing and teasing him. Nitocris quietly left. Daniel was waiting by the back gate with their horses. They rode out to meet an envoy from Cyrus. She gave him a message.

"Belshazzar is unprepared. His troops are scattered and have no leader. King Nabonidus remains in Arabia and will not defend Babylon."

A message came back.

"Wait by the back gate. My guards will meet you and Daniel there. They will take you to a safe place."

That evening the usual drunken party was in full swing. There were brawls in the streets. When Nitocris and Daniel returned they went through the servants' hallways and to the magicians' quarters. The quarters were empty. A servant rushed up to them.

"Your Highness, please come. Your son is in great trouble and summons you to the party."

"Oh, has he run out of wine? Surely there is more in the stores below the palace. I assure you he does not want to see me."

"I beg you, Your Highness, it is something else! Some strange writing has appeared on the wall of the banquet hall. None of the magicians or priests can read it. Everyone is afraid and running from the room."

Nitocris followed the servant to the party room. People were screaming and running past them. Wine was spilled everywhere and the sacred gold goblets from the temple in Jerusalem were smashed on the floor. Half-naked women were grabbing up their robes and hiding in the corners behind statues.

Nitocris looked at the wall. It was something sinister. A warning.

"Mene, Mene, Tekel, and Upharsin."

The magicians cowered before an enraged Belshazzar.

"Your majesty, it is strange to us! We do not know the language. We have never seen it before."

"You priests and magicians are supposed to know about strange things you fools! Get out!"

A furious Belshazzar grabbed the objects around him and threw them, smashing them on the walls and floor, driving the terrified priests from his presence.

Nitocris pushed the servant woman toward the door.

"Find Daniel! Find him now."

The servant bowed, ran out of the door and down the hallway.

Nitocris drew herself up to her queenly stature. She knew he could order her to be imprisoned for entering uninvited. Calmly walking in through the mess she addressed her son in the usual courtly manner.

"O Crown Prince, son of King Nabonidus, live forever. Let not your thoughts trouble you. There is a man in the kingdom whom King Nebuchadnezzar appointed chief of the magicians. I have summoned the prophet Daniel to assist you. He will explain their meaning."

Belshazzar turned on her, red faced and panting. He stumbled toward her crazy with wine and rage.

"What are you doing come in here? I did not summon you!"

"The servants came to me saying that I must come. I thought you summoned me through them. I have called for the prophet, Daniel."

He glowered at her and raised his fist. She stood tall and did not back away.

Just then Daniel came into the room and bowed low to Nitocris and Belshazzar.

Belshazzar was wide eyed and stopped at the sight of Daniel.

"Well, Prophet, what does it mean? Can you read it? Your so called wise men cannot!"

"My apologies, Your Highness. The writing is not from their gods, but from mine."

Belshazzar grabbed Daniel by the front of his robe. His hot breath smelling of wine and vomit blew into Daniel's face.

"And just what god is that?"

"It is the god Queen Nitocris has been telling you about, but you would not listen to her. Now hear the words directly from my God."

Belshazzar wavered almost falling down. Daniel wrenched the front of his robe from Belshazzar's grip and turned toward the wall.

Belshazzar threw himself back onto his couch and reached for more wine.

"Speak now or I will have you beheaded!"

Daniel's manner was calm and authoritative. He spoke in a loud steady voice.

"Mene. Mene. God has numbered the days of your kingdom and brought it to an end.

"Tekel. You have been weighed in the balances and found wanting.

"Upharsin. Your kingdom has been divided and given to the Persians. You, Crown Prince Belshazzar, have refused the word of God and lifted your fist against the god of heaven."

The writing suddenly disappeared. Belshazzar shouted in horror, dropped to his knees clutching a golden goblet. It smashed in his hands.

Chapter 36

THE SIEGE OF KING CYRUS

———— ❧ ———

A panicky guard ran into the palace banquet room and shouted at everyone.

"The soldiers of King Cyrus are at our gates! They have found the way in and are rushing toward us!"

Belshazzar sat bolt upright and scrambled to his feet, nearly toppling over from the wine.

"Let no one in! Even if they claim to be Belshazzar himself!"

"Yes, Your Highness!"

Suddenly crazed, suffocating, and overcome by sickness, Belshazzar ran from the room, down hallways, and stairs, and out of the palace by a rear exit. He looked wildly around, barely able to stand up or determine where he was. He staggered along the walls, calling for his guards. No one heard him.

Panting and dizzy he found the door to the palace. The doorkeepers stopped him from entering.

"I am Crown Prince Belshazzar! Stand aside!"

He tried to push past them.

"The prince has ordered us to slay anyone who tries to enter, even if they claim to be Belshazzar himself!"

They pulled out knives as Belshazzar screamed that he was really Belshazzar and vomiting he fell to his knees. Immediately they slew him.

Nitocris stood in the emptied banquet hall. Everyone had fled. The roar of the Persian Army could be heard in the distance and gradually rose to a great crescendo. Cyrus' army was now outside the palace walls and the shouts echoed throughout the banquet room.

"Daniel, we must get to the back gate now. Cyrus' guard will be waiting to take us to safety."

Nitocris fought off the worrying thoughts that intruded as they ran from the room, through the halls, down the staircases, and toward the palace back gate.

"Belshazzar believes the walls of Babylon will hold off any attacker. They would except Cyrus' army will find the open gate I left for them. My son believes because of this we can outlast Cyrus since the wine cellars and the food stores are full. He is sure Cyrus will give up and turn away. Cyrus will not turn away. What will become of us with Cyrus at our gates? Will he keep his word? Will his guard follow their orders to keep us safe?"

Lords, ladies, and servants were running everywhere in terror. Some were trying to get into the palace through its gates for safety. The guards were hurrying to bar the entrances.

Daniel and Nitocris slipped through a rarely used doorway into the alleys behind the palace walls. It was nearly three miles to the gate that Cyrus designated.

Daniel grabbed Nitocris' hand and pulled her after him. He knew the back streets well and just where to go. The streets were full of garbage and refuse. People were lying in the streets and hanging out of windows. Crowds were amassing in the main thoroughfares.

The stench of the alleys was overwhelming. Nitocris had difficulty breathing and thought she would be sick. They hung onto each other as they tripped and slid through the mess. Daniel spotted an archway and they stopped for a moment in a doorway to cover their mouths and noses with their robes.

Daniel looked through the archway in the direction of the back gate. No one was there. They left the doorway and continued to run. A few miles of streets were still ahead of them. Nitocris thought they would never get there, but she called up the resolve of the Queen of Babylonia to strengthen her mind and legs.

The people had rushed toward the palace. The crowds were thinning near the walls. Thankfully their exit was in sight. As they burst through the back gate they desperately looked around. Cyrus' guards came out of the dark and immediately to pulled them into a carriage. The driver cracked the whip over the horses backs and the carriage lurched forward. Soldiers were racing past them entering the gate with swords drawn.

Soon the sounds of soldiers shouting and people screaming faded behind them as they drove away. They continued to travel at a slower pace for hours. Nitocris was soon asleep on Daniel's shoulder. When the carriage stopped she was jolted awake.

"Where are we? How long have I been asleep? Was it all a terrible dream?"

"We are nearly to the Persian border where we will spend the night. Are you hungry?"

"After the smell of that garbage filling the alleys of my beautiful city? Not yet. I still feel a little ill. And Belshazzar? Is he captured or dead?"

Nitocris knew she should weep for him as his mother, but she could not. He hated her, derided her, and would not heed her warning that Cyrus would not turn away.

There was no one to stop Cyrus' invasion, as Queen Nitocris had promised. His troops entered Babylon with little resistance. Some people wisely stayed in their homes and did not go into the streets.

The Babylonian soldiers were nowhere to be found. The palace guard had fled and the body of Belshazzar was still slumped by the entrance to the palace where he died.

Someone reported that King Nabonidus had returned from Arabia with a small guard. It was obvious he was not there to fight and did not know what was happening. No one knew why he was there. They presumed he was bored with life in a small community in Arabia and was dead in one of the brothels.

Chapter 37

NITOCRIS AND DANIEL
IN PERSIA

They arrived at the palace in Susa tired and disheveled. The driver and Daniel helped the queen down from the carriage. The palace before them was enormous with torches lighting the walkways. It was night causing the place to look different than when she visited King Cyrus not too long ago. She fervently hoped her beautiful palace had not been defaced or burned. She feared for her whole city.

The guards placed them in a protected suite of rooms designated by King Cyrus. He would decide what to do with them when he returned. Their rooms were sumptuous and beautifully decorated. Bowls of fruit and vases of flowers were set around. Nitocris took one room and Daniel the other. They could spend some time in a common area between them to eat, talk, and pray.

"I do not know what will become of us, Daniel. But King Cyrus has kept his promises so far."

"Do not doubt that good is coming, Queen Nitocris. God is here with us always and we are faithful."

The next day news came by envoy that Babylon was secured in the hands of Cyrus' troops. Belshazzar and Nabonidus were killed.

"Nabonidus? Dead? But he lives in northern Arabia. How could he be slain? Where?"

"Your Highness, he returned to Babylon with a small contingent of guards and rode right into Cyrus' troops. They did not know who he was. We do not know why he came there. Surely it was not to fight mighty Cyrus with a few guards."

"Nabonidus was never interested in leading the army, war, governing, or even being a king. He was truly not wise. I am sure he came out of curiosity, low wine stores, or boredom with his women."

"Belshazzar was killed outside of the palace entrance. The guards did not recognize him and slew him."

Cyrus did not return to Susa from Babylon but took his army to the far east and into western China. Nitocris wished she could be back in China, too. She hoped Cyrus would love it as she did and not destroy the cities, especially Guangzhou. She prayed that Fu Ling Yang, Chaoxiang, Lishan, and Shamhar were safe there.

A special teacher was assigned to Daniel and Nitocris to teach them about Chaldean ways, gods, and rituals of worship. Daniel was compliant, but steadfast in his worship of God and still prayed openly three times a day from a palace window that faced Jerusalem.

Nitocris joined him in his prayer time when she could. She spent much time thinking about her precious Babylon and hoped she might return someday soon.

She wanted to tell King Cyrus about the building dedicated to her friend Fu Ling Yang, Yang Light of the Rising Sun. She so longed to see it again hoping that the treasures adorning it were safe. She prayed that Cyrus kept his word that her city would be saved.

"We left so much behind during these dark and dangerous times. I cannot bear to think of it all being destroyed again. It was my purpose in life and my great love."

Envoys came back and forth from Babylon to Susa and reported to Nitocris that they had secured the Chinese building and no one could go in or out. The people of Babylon were quiet and going about their business under the watchful occupation of Cyrus' troops.

Daniel began to write his memoirs spending hours, days, and weeks in the Susa libraries. He also prayed that the Jewish quarter of Babylon was safe and undisturbed. It was his fervent prayer.

"They are your people, God. Keep them in the palm of your hand as you have kept me."

Cambyses II, son of King Cyrus, was regent while Cyrus was away in China. He commanded some of Cyrus' troops to secure the rest of the Babylonian empire. Cambyses was focused on his duties and not involved in the petty politics around him. He hated the priests who were constantly maneuvering for power and position.

He did not speak often with Nitocris, but they agreed on how they disliked the priests and magicians.

"I would like you to know that Daniel is not like them. He never seeks power or favor. That is why my father, King Nebuchadnezzar, trusted him."

"How did he trust him? With what?"

"He was a wise advisor. Later when my father was losing his memory and becoming feeble in body as well, Daniel assisted him in court when he could not remember ordinary things. Daniel never let him look foolish or weak in front of anyone. He protected him to the end."

"Oh. So you are saying I need not fear Daniel or distrust him?"

Nitocris was feeling tested. She drew herself up in her mind to her queenly stature and responded in the affirmative.

"Regent Cambyses, we were defeated in Babylon because in order to save the city that was my life's work I opened the gates. I told King Cyrus that the people would not fight but welcome him, and that most of the Babylonian army was already in his employ.

"I gave up the throne I did not want to save what was more important, my city and my people. I am not your enemy. King Cyrus has been most gracious in preserving the city and people. I would like to trust that you will be so as well. We owe him and you our loyalty."

Cambyses' mouth dropped open.

"You did not want the throne? You gave up your throne? For a city?"

"Yes. I have been an architect since I was a child. It has been my whole life, my purpose and my love. I designed and rebuilt Babylon after King Sennacherib completely destroyed it. My father was cruel, my husband and son were debauched fools who used their power pursue drunkenness and women, which was wrecking Babylonia. I could not let them have my city. So I gave it to King Cyrus who promised to take care of it."

"You are unbelievable! I could not have done that! I would have fought to keep it. I want the power and I want the throne! It will be mine and no one will take it from me. I inherit it and I deserve it!"

"It is right for you to want the throne and inherit all that goes with it. It is just not right for me. The power I loved was in my ability to create something magnificent, Babylon."

"So you do not aspire to the throne of Persia?"

"Never. It is all yours, Prince Regent Cambyses. Someone must lead these empires. You must do that, not me."

Cambyses was silent. Still puzzled as he bid her good night and departed.

Years went by before King Cyrus returned to Susa. Nitocris spent time sending messages to her mother in Haran, and to Fu Ling Yang, Chaoxiang, Lishan, and Shamhar in China. She wanted them to know that she and Daniel were safe in the care of the king.

She read them to Cambyses before she gave them to an envoy so he would be sure she was not conspiring with someone against him.

"We are growing older, Daniel. I do not know what life will hold for me from now on. I am accustomed to being busy and creative. Wandering around a palace and arranging a few flowers is not much to look forward to."

"There is more for you in this life. Stay faithful and it will all unfold at the right time."

Cambyses looked for messages every day from King Cyrus. Especially the one that would say the king had been killed in battle so he could at last be the king.

The magicians were jealous of Daniel who was trusted by kings. They reported to Cambyses that against the law, Daniel still prayed to his god three times a day in a window that faced Jerusalem.

Cambyses did not care. He always ignored the magicians. He hated them but would never admit that he feared their plotting and scheming. He had his guards chase them off whenever they appeared anywhere near him.

Chapter 38

LIONS AND FIRE

The magicians spent many days deciding what to do about Daniel. One suggested they throw him to the lions.

"Yes, we will do that! Good idea. We will make it look like he wandered around and accidentally fell into the lions' den. They will eat him before anyone knows he is gone."

So they planned to have Daniel thrown into the Lions' den while Cyrus was still away.

"That foreign queen will know. She will miss him eventually."

"By then it will be too late. We could throw her to the lions as well."

"No! King Cyrus would have us hanged. Let us leave her alone."

They grabbed Daniel during his prayers, bound and gagged him, and dragged him away to the dungeons. Daniel was not so strong as in his youth and could not resist them.

Nitocris began to look for Daniel when he did not return to his room from his prayers as he always did. She alerted the guards.

"King Cyrus will not forgive you if something happens to him. Please find him."

"Yes, Your Highness, we will go immediately."

"I am going with you!"

They wanted to object, but she marched out ahead of them and they had no choice but to follow. She found his sandals and marks in the dirt where they had dragged him. The guards began to run.

"They are headed for the dungeon!"

Nitocris followed them into the fetid filthy dungeon halls and slippery steps. There was a low growl from up ahead.

"Lions!"

They ran to the den gate. The lions were laying down, even sleeping. Daniel was standing among them apparently unharmed.

"Jailer? Where are you? What happened?"

"I am here, Your Highness. I heard what those rascals were planning and made sure the lions were well fed with a double portion before they got here with the prophet. Well-fed lions do not bother anyone. They prefer to sleep and sleep they did."

"I shall see that you are rewarded for saving my friend."

"Thank you, Your Highness. But I require no reward. Daniel has been good to me. He has taught me much about love and goodness. I do not want the rest of those liars and blasphemers to know I did this. They would kill me next.

"The priests will lie and pretend to be amazed but the guards let me know they are watching over me."

The guards went immediately to the quarters of the Chaldean priests and magicians to take them to the dungeons.

Daniel and Nitocris returned to their quarters. Nitocris was exhausted and angry.

"Thank our God that you are safe. That is so fortunate about the lion keeper!"

"That was not fortune but God who always holds me in the palm of His Hand. I never know how He will take care of me. My place is to trust and not fear."

"I do not know if my faith would ever hold up in a lion's den."

"I have spent a lifetime with God. You are new to the faith. Do not worry about it. God loves you as you are and does not hold only favorites in His hand."

Daniel's friends, Hananiah, Azariah, and Mishael, had left Babylon a few years after the siege and came to Susa to be with Daniel. Now they all prayed together in the window that faced Jerusalem.

The priests demanded that Cambyses sign a decree that all should pray facing the east since that was their law and religion. They did not mention the incident with the lions. Cambyses signed the decree to get rid of their presence in his court.

They seethed as they tried to catch Daniel praying facing the southwest. The priests feared that Daniel had cast a spell on the lions and would do it again to save himself. They hatched another plan. This time they would throw Daniel and his friends into a fiery furnace to burn to death. There would only be ashes left.

When they caught Daniel and his friends praying facing Jerusalem to the southwest, the guards could now arrest them because they were breaking the law. The priests ordered the furnace to be prepared.

"Guards! Bind the Daniel and his friends and bring them to us. We will counsel them in the ways of the Chaldeans."

The prison guards were terrified of the priests and did what they demanded.

The priests dragged the prisoners deeper under the palace where the furnaces were keeping the upper rooms warm and burning away the waste from the kitchens. The fire was rather low, so the priests demanded more fuel for it. Those who tended the fires scurried to bring more to burn, threw it into the furnace, and rushed back for more. The flames slowly grew higher and higher.

Daniel stood before the furnaces quietly. He was not afraid.

"Be at peace, dear friends. No harm shall befall us. God is ever present and holds us in His hand."

King Cyrus arrived in Susa that same day and the lion keeper rushed to meet him.

"Your Highness, the priests have taken Daniel and his friends from their quarters to be thrown into the furnaces. Please save them. They have caused no trouble."

King Cyrus sent his guards to the furnaces just in time. Those who tended the fires had deliberately thrown too much refuse into the furnaces and smothered the flames. The guards helped Daniel and his friends from the furnace unharmed.

The king ordered the priests thrown into the fire instead and their families slain. It would not have been Daniel's choice to kill them and also their innocent families, but this was the Chaldean way. He uttered no objection. Cyrus was the king and his decrees were law.

Daniel continued to serve King Cyrus faithfully until one evening as he faced Jerusalem in prayer, he died. Nitocris went to find him when he did not return to is room. She found him slumped over, his hands still folded in prayer. She deeply mourned the passing of her great friend and wished she could go with him.

As she held him in her arms by his window toward Jerusalem she wondered if this was all there would be to her life. His friends came in and quietly mourned with her before they took his body away.

She knelt down at the window Daniel always prayed in and for the first time began her own prayers without Daniel's help.

"My God and Daniel's God, I pray that you will show me the path I must take as you always showed Daniel. I will be joyful as he was always filled with joy at your presence in our lives. I will remember the love and wisdom you have showered upon us and be grateful. Shelah."

Without Daniel she felt very alone. Soon his friends attended the prayers with her when she went to the window three times a day. They were reassuring in their conversations with her that God was with them and responding to their prayers.

She built small flower beds on the balconies of the palace and planted flowers that would grow and hang down over the railings. They reminded her of the hanging gardens in Babylon.

She found the artisans in Susa that made the blue enameled bricks like the ones on the Ishtar gate and walls of Babylon. They helped her line a few of the balconies and flower boxes with blue and gold bricks. True to her prayers she remained joyful wherever she was and whatever she was doing.

Chapter 39

RETURNING TO BABYLON

Cambyses was restless, so King Cyrus sent him to Babylon to bring back reports about conditions there.

"Take Queen Nitocris and Daniel's friends with you. I am sure they desire to see Babylon again."

"I will go, Father. Give me a list of what you want me to inspect. I want to go to Egypt as well. I will be sure they are not planning with Assyria to attack Persia."

"Be watchful in Egypt, Cambyses. Egypt fears an attack from me. The Egyptian pharaohs are proud rulers and do not give up their secrets to strangers. They will be as watchful of you as you are of them. They enjoy poisoning those who threaten them. Choose one of the population to test your food and pay them well to keep silent."

Cambyses was arrogant and power hungry. Out from under his father's watchful eye he would discern what powers he could gather in those places. He was not pleased that Queen Nitocris was to go with him. He was sure she would be spying on him for the king. He still wondered why anyone would give up a throne. Was she lying? He would find out.

"I am pleased that King Cyrus will send me to Babylon with you. I so want to see my beloved city again. I know you think I will be spying on you, but I have never done that and I never will. I want to show you my work that rebuilt Babylon. I am sure you have not believed me so you can see for yourself."

He disregarded her remarks. He would require her to travel to Egypt as well to prevent her from returning to Susa and reporting to the king.

"I will be going on to Egypt, so you will need to accompany me there as well. I cannot bring you back to Susa before I go there."

"Egypt! I would love to go to Egypt. When will we depart for Babylon?"

Cambyses was puzzled at her quick agreement and the excitement in her eyes.

"Does Egypt mean something to you? Might you want to stay in Babylon and I will collect you on my way back to Susa?"

"I am pleased to travel on to Egypt. I wish only to see Babylon, not live there."

She would not tell him that it was her chance to search for the ancient Egyptian Queen Nitocris. He already thought she was crazy to give up her throne, and now she wanted to search for a dead queen.

Daniel's three friends heard the news and were delighted to accompany her to Babylon.

"We heard that the Jewish community was not destroyed. Some of the Jews might be making their way back to Jerusalem. We would like to accompany them. There is probably nothing left of Jerusalem, so they will need help to establish a community there again."

"It might be possible for me to take them with us as far as Jerusalem if they are willing. We need say nothing about this to Cambyses. He will be riding so far ahead of us that he will not notice who is following."

Cambyses sent a message that he was leaving for Babylon tomorrow morning and that she should meet them in the courtyard. Nitocris immediately sent a message to the friends.

Everyone was excited. They all lined up before dawn ready to start for Babylon. Cambyses had already ridden on ahead as Nitocris knew he would. That relieved her tension at having to be in his presence.

She was helped into a royal carriage. The friends were led to a carriage that was occupied by several servants making it quite crowded. Nitocris sent a message with a guard that the friends should share her carriage since she was alone.

Nitocris remembered the same trip she and Daniel made escaping Babylon. Sometimes tears came to her eyes. She sat quietly contemplating how they had all built the Jewish community together. So many thoughts and fears ran through their heads that not much was said as they traveled over the rough terrain.

"I miss Daniel and wish he could be with us. He would love to see the Jewish Community again and even go to Jerusalem. I do not know what happened to Zaidu and perhaps I can find someone who knows."

At last Hananiah, Azariah, and Mishael began to chat and drew her into their conversation.

"Your Highness, what most troubles you?"

"So many things, Hananiah. Is my city still beautiful as it was when we finished building it? Is the Ishtar gate undamaged? It was my favorite.

Will I find Zaidu or is he dead? Is the Chinese building 'Yang Light of the Rising Sun' still there? It held many treasures from China. You helped us put it all together, even the temple in the entrance."

Hananiah saw her tears and touched her hand.

"It is painful, I know. But we are still alive and we will face it together. Our God will strengthen us, guide us every step of the way, and heal our hearts."

Nitocris smiled at them.

"Yes, thank you for reminding me. Often I forget to give my fears over to God and find my joy again. Daniel taught me that when I first met him. I was a child and he a slave. To follow God was to follow his joy wherever he was. If he forgot joy then he forgot God. I guess I have forgotten God."

"Yes, but God never forgets us. That is the blessing. We can always return and God is there."

Even though the way was bumpy, they still dozed in the heat of the day. The entourage stopped midday to rest the animals and let the highest temperature pass before they continued. Even though they were eager to get to Babylon, it was good to have the rough ride stop and let them rest as well.

Chapter 40

THE ISHTAR GATE

Nitocris could see it from a distance. It was her Ishtar Gate shining in the sun as if it were floating. It was the entrance to all of her childhood dreams. It was a symbol of her success. They came closer by the hour and everyone's excitement heightened.

Nitocris could hardly breathe.

"Yes, the walls are still there. Dear God let the buildings be there too...the palace, the temples, and the hanging gardens. Let the Jewish community be untouched."

As they approached the gate, Hananiah, Azariah, and Mishael jumped from the carriage and ran through the gate. Nitocris had the carriage stop within the gate so she could walk through it and into her city.

The friends stopped and turned toward her.

"Your Highness, we are sorry to leave you so abruptly."

Carole M. Lunde

"It is all right. Go and find your people. We will meet here at the gate again when it is time to go to Jerusalem. Bring the people who want to go with us."

Personal guards walked with her into the city. It had the look of an occupied city, a little worn and neglected in places. The army was living in the palace with all their equipment and horses. The stench of uncleaned streets, garbage, waste, and dead animals was overwhelming.

The carriage driver followed with the carriage and Nitocris was grateful. She told the driver what she wanted to see, the Chinese building, the School of Architecture, the hanging gardens, and the Jewish project.

"I will be happy to drive you to these places, Your Highness. They may be farther away than you remember and the streets are filthy."

"Yes, drive me there. I am tired as well as excited to see them. I hope they are undamaged."

Later Hananiah came back to the gate to meet her.

"Your Highness, many people are ready to come with us. They have told me that the pipes carrying water to the hanging gardens broke long ago and the gardens are all dead. The school of architecture is empty except for homeless people who are squatting there. The students went back to Uruk to the old school building."

"Thank you. Tell me no more."

He got into the carriage with her and they drove to the Jewish community. She was almost afraid to look. To her amazement the streets were clean and the market orderly. Everything looked almost like it did the day they completed it and the people moved in.

The people rushed out of their homes and came to meet her. They helped her out of the carriage and took her to their gardens and the temple.

"You built this for our people and we are grateful. We take care of what God has given us through you. Many of the old people who danced with us on that day are gone now. Some of our young men and women want to go to Jerusalem to find their roots. We have told them there is nothing left of Jerusalem but rubble. They still want to go."

"I am sad that my father tore your lives from you in Jerusalem. This settlement was the least I could do for you. I know it is not Jerusalem but I wanted you to have decent homes and a nice community."

"Please do not be sad, Your Highness. It was not you who took our city from us, but you gave us another one. No one else has ever done that for people who are helpless and enslaved. No one in the world is as loving and kind as you are. No one."

Tears threatened to come as she reached out and hugged them.

"We will be leaving tomorrow. All who are coming with us should be at the Ishtar Gate before dawn and we will start for Jerusalem. I wish I could rebuild that for you, too, but my time for building cities is past."

Many hugged her again before she stepped into the carriage. It was unusual to touch royalty, much less hug them. Nitocris loved it. She always longed for the moment when the divisions would disappear and they were all equally God's people together.

Hananiah got into the carriage with her, not wanting to leave her alone. They stopped by the Chinese building but she did not go in. If it had been looted and the beautiful interior torn apart she could not bear to see it.

"We will go back to the gate, climb up into its towers, and spend the night there. I can see nowhere else for us to go. That will be the safest."

"Your Highness, you and I will be here when the first people arrive, but do you know where Cambyses and his guards will be?"

"You can be sure they have already gone. They were camped somewhere outside the city. They came in through the back gate so he would not have to enter under my tomb at the top of the Ishtar Gate. I am sure he conferred with the military there and left."

The interior of the gate was cool and they slept wrapped in carriage robes on military cots until the first people began to arrive. Hananiah rushed down through the tower steps to meet them. Azariah and Mishael were leading them and helping them get organized.

Nitocris' carriage arrived just as she came from the tower entrance. She climbed in and began to move out of the gate, leading nearly one hundred men and women. Hananiah came to her carriage and got in.

"We have made sure that everyone is strong enough and well equipped to make the journey. We have donkeys, tents, and wagons of food supplies. Anyone who needs help can ride part of the way. You need not worry about them. They are survivors and all will be well."

"Thank you, Hananiah. I know now that I could not make this journey without you. Did you find any trace of Zaidu? Or Arakhu?"

"No, Your Highness. Some thought they went away together into Assyria. No one thought they were dead."

"We are not getting any younger and neither are they. I pray they are well and happy. May they find a peaceful place to spend their days."

For weeks they followed the trail left by Cambyses and his guards, but they never saw them. Nitocris was happy to be on her own with her adopted people. There would be no derision from him, no royal proprieties. She had a wonderful sense of freedom and joy.

She felt the exuberance of Ninana coming back into her bones and the excitement energized her.

Chapter 41

RUINS OF JERUSALEM

—— ❧ ❧ ——

As Hananiah said, the people were survivors. They took care of each other on the long journey. Some became injured but none fell ill. The supplies were well calculated and there was more than enough for everyone.

"Cambyses will not know we are taking Jews to Jerusalem. He will not even care."

"Some people are asking if this is the way their ancestors came in chains from Jerusalem so long ago."

"Only the ancestors could answer that and Arakhu, if he is alive. He was one of the army captains. There are not very many ways to choose from, so I think this would be the likely one."

"I wonder how they made it alive as captives."

"Daniel told me that he demanded food and rest for them or they would all die and their king would not get the slaves he burned Jerusalem for. Surprisingly they heeded his warning and gave them food and rest every day."

It was a long, hot and dusty journey. Nitocris did not mind. She had much to think about. She had much to pray about. The sense of Daniel's god became stronger within her. She reminded herself every morning to remember joy. It was a wonderful teaching that he shared with her the first time they met.

"How young we were. Lives and adventures ahead of us that we could not have imagined. How Daniel might love to be with us today. But no, he said he had no wish to return."

They passed Damascus and the beginnings of the Jordan River. Another few days and the stones and foundations of Jerusalem were visible but barely above the surface of the land. It was hard to believe a city once existed there. It was built on a hill, but even the hills around it looked sad, beaten down, and devastated. Nitocris and the people stopped a distance away.

"Hananiah, it is almost too much to take in. How are your people doing? Do you think their hopes will be dashed? It looks so discouraging."

"They are survivors, Your Highness. They will take a proper amount of time to mourn Jerusalem, and then they will organize and decide what to do."

"Are there not enemies all around? Different cultures and foreign peoples driven from their homes, too? Might they resent the Jews returning?"

"Yes, that is very true. There have been many enemies who resent the Jews, and the Jews have some responsibility in this. They have been closed and even hostile to all other people, religions, and customs."

"But Daniel spoke of caring and having compassion for others."

"Daniel was a prophet, and very close to the true teachings. The rulers of Jerusalem were Jews and a few might have been observant of the teaching, but most were just political and vying for power."

They came closer to the ruined walls. The gates were torn down and most of the walls torn down. There was no easy way to enter the city. Stones were piled on stones. Others were scattered so deeply that there was not the smallest pathway through the streets to be seen.

"Who goes there? Who are you?"

"I am Mishael. I am with Azariah and Hananiah. We are friends of Daniel the prophet of the royal family and temple of Jerusalem. We are returning from exile in Babylon."

An old man hobbled out from behind a stone at the edge. He peered at them shading his eyes with his hand.

"Daniel? Is he still alive? Is he with you?"

"I am sorry to tell you that Daniel passed away in Persia not too long ago. He was not a prisoner or slave. He was well cared for by order of the king. May we come and sit down with you?"

"I am Nehemiah and yes, please come and sit. We have little food to offer you."

"We have brought much food and will gladly share it with you."

"Who is this woman and the guards?"

"She is our friend who has saved us and brought us home. She is Queen Nitocris of Babylon."

"It was the king of Babylon who destroyed Jerusalem! How can you call her a friend?"

Nitocris stepped forward and spoke to them in the little Hebrew she learned over the years.

"Yes, it was my father who did this. I was a young child. I was very angry with him and could not understand why anyone would do such a thing. King Sennacherib destroyed the beautiful City of Babylon a thousand years ago. We rebuilt it many years ago."

A few more people ventured out from the rocks at the edge.

"Queen Nitocris is an architect. She built a beautiful community for us Jews on the edge of Babylon. We all worked beside her and the master builder, Zaidu. No other royalty who enslaved a people ever cared for the welfare of those enslaved. But our Queen Nitocris did that very thing. She helped build a market, temple, homes, and gardens for us as close to our Jewish culture and traditions as possible."

"Then welcome, Queen Nitocris. We are grateful that you cared for our people and have brought them here."

They spent a few days together. Soon it was time for Nitocris to continue toward Egypt before Cambyses got too far ahead. He would not look back to see if she were coming but she had her own purpose for going to Egypt.

She hated to leave the people in Jerusalem so abruptly, but there was nothing for her there. She could not be of any further help to them. She bid a tearful farewell to Hananiah, Azariah, Mishael, and the few people around her. She would probably never see them again. This was another terrible loss to her and it tugged at her heart as her carriage drove away.

Her driver and guards found the road to the coast of the Mediterranean Sea. As they approached the coast there was a caravan road that ran north and south. Nitocris was on her way to Egypt at last. But the exuberance she felt until now left her and she felt empty.

The sight of the Mediterranean Sea on the horizon reminded her of her sea voyages to India and China. She quickly turned her mind away from the memories as tears filled her eyes. She would never return to China and those golden days of traveling with Lishan and Fu Ling Yang.

The carriage stopped. Nitocris was startled when two of her guards got in with her.

"Your Highness, we are entering very dangerous territory crossing the desert into Egypt. It is not very far, but it is a stronghold for brigands, renegades, and thieves. We have hired local guards to come with us. They know the territory well. We may find the bodies of Cambyses and his troops if he did not heed the warnings."

Nitocris laughed. She was grateful for the company and the distraction from her gloomy thoughts.

"I cannot imagine that he would heed anyone's warnings or advice. He is headstrong and arrogant. Hopefully he made it through, a sign that we will not be troubled at the border."

If she had told Cambyses her reason for going to Egypt his derision would be too much to bear. Indeed, she was chasing a dead queen who had no bearing on her life except for her name. It might all come to nothing.

An hour into the crossing there was a shout and the carriage halted. A guard handed Nitocris a sword.

"Your Highness, do you know how to use one of these?

"Yes! I am a sister of the Amazon women warriors and they taught me well!"

The guards rode out after the brigands who were accosting some travelers. A few already lay dead in the sand.

"Driver, take me closer!"

"Yes, Your Highness, if you think that is wise."

"Wise or not, get closer."

She left the carriage, grabbed an extra horse, and rode into the fray. The guards were driving the surviving brigands off. She stopped beside a body. It was not Cambyses, nor the next one she came to. And then she saw him lying face down, his sword still in his hand.

"Cambyses! Cambyses!"

He raised his head, groaned, and turned over.

"Thank all the gods you are live!"

She dismounted and waved at the carriage driver. Two guards came to assist getting him into the carriage.

"Where are you hurt?"

"My leg, they got my leg."

She tore open his legging, poured some water and wine on the wound to cleanse it and bound it.

"It is not deep. It will heal. We will carry you in the carriage the rest of the way into Egypt."

"Perhaps if you had followed me closer, this would not have happened. Why were you so far behind?"

She would not tell him about Jerusalem.

Chapter 42

QUEEN NITOCRIS OF EGYPT

"We heeded the advice at the border and waited until we could get extra guards. It seems you did not heed them and rushed on ahead, my prince. Nevertheless we are here just in time to rescue you."

He growled something unintelligible and sank down in the seat. He drank the wine she offered and fell asleep snoring loudly.

The crossing into Egypt was delayed by the tide coming in from the Mediterranean. They needed to wait until morning. Nitocris got out of the carriage with some blankets and lay down on the sand where the guards were bedded down. No way would she stay in the carriage with snoring Cambyses.

In the morning when the tide began receding back out to the sea. The water level lowered and left them a wet and soggy place to cross into Egypt. Crossing guards motioned them to start across. Water swirled around them and sloshed into the carriage.

Her guards were on each side of the carriage to keep it upright. They advanced so slowly that Nitocris thought they would not get to the other side before her wheels were washed away.

On the Egyptian side the soldiers motioned them to a guard station. They were herded into a waiting room in the small building. Several of Cambyses' guards who made it across were already there, their wounds being tended. Bedraggled others were still staggering in.

Nitocris gave her name as Ninana, fearing that if they recognized the name Nitocris as one of their own royalty, they would detain her. Cambyses had no such fears. He blustered forth about his royalty and the power of Persia.

They ignored his outbursts, questioned everyone else for a few hours, and eventually released all except Cambyses. While they were deciding what to do with him because he was a present threat to Assyrian-run Egypt, he and his guards slipped out, grabbed horses, and headed for Memphis on the Nile.

Nitocris discovered from a returning traveler that her best bet to get information about the ancient Egyptian Queen Nitocris would be in Thebes. She and her guards got directions to Thebes on the east side of the Nile. The road was rough but well-traveled. If questioned she could pose as a historian from Assyria and not as the queen from Babylonia. The local political scene was adversarial with heightened alerts about Babylonia and Persia. This was not good news for her or Cambyses.

With Cambyses out of her hair and out of her way, she found people who would guide her, and inns where she could stop and rest. Once again she experienced the erasing of that line between royalty and the commoners.

How she wished that could always be true. But she would hear her father's voice saying, *"you are a girl and cannot understand ruling empires and wars."* Still true she did not even care to understand that world.

Two of her guards, Ahmad and Karim, posed as her brothers so they could stay close. Nitocris was careful not to speak in the Babylonian, Akkadian, or Persian languages, but to speak as the Egyptians did. It was nearly the same as spoken in Arabia. She learned some of it from Nabonidus, so it was not very difficult. She also studied the picture writing that the Egyptians used.

They found a clean and well-built inn in Thebes. When she asked about the ancient Egyptian Queen Nitocris, an elderly looking woman overheard her.

"There is a place across the Nile from Thebes where the tomb of Queen Nitocris is located, but it is not well marked. My son works on the river and will ferry you across. From there you follow the road until you come to a statue of a Pharaoh's wife and son. Walk behind the statue and turn toward the hill, and you will find it."

Nitocris found her heart pounding with excitement. The woman's son came for them early in the morning. He docked his small barge on the riverbank. The two "brothers" walked to the riverbank with her.

"These are my brothers who are coming with me."

He nodded.

"Do not step into the water. There are snakes and crocodiles in it. Let me take your hand."

Nitocris shuddered at the thought of snakes and allowed herself to be assisted from the muddy bank onto the barge. He guided them to a bench where they could sit while they crossed the Nile. It looked like a very long way across the water and the sluggish currents tugged at the barge. But he was skillful and kept it moving steadily across to the opposite shore.

"Will you return for us?"

"I will wait right here for you. The robbers are far back in the desert hills and do not come this close to the river where soldiers wait for them. There will be no one else around but if someone should come, hide until they leave. I may move off the river bank out of reach, but I will l return when they go away."

She stepped gingerly onto the shore and they started down the narrow dirt and sand road. They came to the statue of the woman and the child. It looked very strange. The woman was tall and the child was disproportionately small. Another statue beside them was only the lower half of a man. The upper part was broken off and the pieces were scatter about.

They stepped around to the back and started toward the hill. At the foot of the hill was an arched opening. Scratched on the side of the opening was part of the name, Nitocris.

"I will go in alone. Please stay here. I will not be long."

They were concerned about snakes and adders that might be in there but decided not to frighten her. They stayed close, knives drawn.

"Call out if you need our assistance."

"I will."

She walked into the cool darkness of the cave and approached a stone sarcophagus. The slightest beam of light came from the opening of the cave. The tomb had no decoration and the sarcophagus was plain, but there was a saying etched into it. She spent some time trying to decipher the writing.

Worried, Ahmad came into the cave.

"Look at this inscription. I am trying to read it. She began drawing it."

He peered at the scratching and ran his fingers over it.

"I will remember it. Now we must go. There is much danger here."

The young man was waiting at the riverbank as he promised. Nitocris stepped gingerly through the mud. He reached for her hand and pulled her up onto the barge. Ahmad and Karim quickly jumped onto it and sat down beside her.

When they returned to Thebes, she asked the woman who told her about the tomb for a translation and a description of Queen Nitocris. Ahmad drew her a picture of it.

She smiled as if she already knew.

"It says 'I go where love awaits me.' She was said to be braver than all men of her time, the most beautiful of all the women, fair-skinned with red cheeks."

Nitocris repeated it silently over and over.

"I go where love awaits me. Did she mean in death? How can love await her in death? Perhaps that is the Egyptian belief. Everything is already dead in my life and I find no love or happiness. Four kings and a crown prince are dead, Daniel is gone and there is nothing for me anywhere. But I will keep this message in my heart. 'I go where love awaits me.'"

The next day the woman brought another message to the inn.

"Prince Cambyses of Persia was arrested in Memphis and escaped. We did not know he was in Egypt!"

Nitocris was shocked but tried not to show it.

"Tell me, grandmother. Why is this message so important?"

Chapter 43

DANGER AND ESCAPE

"Because Cambyses is Persian, Lady! Perhaps it means Persia will attack Egypt. News travels fast down the river. I thought you should be aware, too, since you are traveling. Where are you from?"

"From near Jerusalem."

"Oh, we know that Jerusalem was destroyed. Terrible! Are your people still there?"

"No. They are all dead."

The woman shook her head, turned away, and went about her business. Nitocris was relieved that she did not have to think up any more answers for this woman's questions.

Ahmad smiled.

"You did tell her the truth. We did come from Jerusalem."

"I dared not say Babylon. Babylonia is the greatest threat to these people now. I still do not understand why empires have to attack other empires and destroy their civilizations. Someone builds something beautiful and someone else has to tear it down. What if we all built only beauty and honored each other's beauty. I guess, as my father said, I am a girl and cannot understand these things."

"Your Highness, I think you understand in a higher way that they do not."

"Ahmad, please refer to me a Ninana until we get out of Egypt and danger."

"Yes. I will remember. It is hard not to see you as who you really are."

"Please try and also tell the others. Our lives will depend upon it."

There was that divide between royalty and commoners again. It was so ingrained that it could mean the death of all of them.

The guards retrieved the carriage and horses from a nearby stable. Fortunately it looked so bedraggled from the travel and crossing into Egypt, caked with mud and sand, emblems of Persia had fallen off in the water. It did not look even remotely like a royal carriage.

Supplied with food and water, they began the long trek north along the Nile Valley and followed the eastern delta toward the crossing out of Egypt.

Close to the crossing some men came out of the desert hills and stepped in front of the carriage.

"Cambyses!"

"Yes! Are you surprised to see me? I will need your carriage to get out of Egypt. I am being pursued. Get out!"

Nitocris became boiling angry.

"You do not need my carriage! You have gotten yourself into this mess and you need to find another way out. The crossing guards will spot you and then I will be in trouble."

She pulled out the sword the border guards had given her.

"You cannot have my carriage! Driver! Go to the border as fast as you can!"

"Yes, Your Highness!"

He laid the whip on their hindquarters of the horses and they leaped forward. Cambyses and his guards had to leap aside to keep from being run over.

"My father will hear of this! I will kill you!"

She did not look back. At the border they hired the usual guards to see them across to Gaza, waded through the waters of the receding Mediterranean, and galloped onto the sand from the desert crossing.

They galloped nearly all the way to Gaza before they stopped. The horses were sweating and foaming at their mouths. The driver jumped down, unharnessed them and led the into a stable for shade and water.

Nitocris and their other guards followed them into the stable.

"I hope the horses will be all right. I hate to abuse animals but our lives depended upon it. Cambyses could be right behind us."

"They will recover, Your Highness. Our stable hands will take good care of them. I understand. All of our lives were in danger. You have the courage of an Amazon warrior!"

Nitocris laughed.

"You are not the first one to say that including an actual Amazon Woman warrior. She challenged me to a mock dual which I lost."

Her guards with Ahmad and Karim, who posed as her brothers in Thebes, came into the stable.

"What do you wish us to do next, Your Highness. May we call you that now that we are out of Egypt?"

"Ninana, please. I wish to return to Babylon. I am sure Cambyses will go directly to Susa to report me or share more important matters about Egypt with King Cyrus. We can go back through Jerusalem so we will not encounter him on the way to Babylon."

"A very good plan. We will prepare to leave shortly. I am sure we can trade these horses for fresh ones. Do you wish to rest at an inn?"

"No, Ahmad, I will rest right here in the stable. It feels safer."

"The queen sleeps in a stall...that no one will believe, but it is most wise. We will stand guard as always."

Nitocris fell asleep immediately. A few hours went by and she awakened to the thundering sound of galloping, neighing horses. She jumped up and looked out of the door.

Cambyses and his guards were riding past at a swift pace, kicking up a lot of sand, but not stopping. Ahmad came from behind the stable and slipped in through the door.

"Your H...Ninana, I hid the carriage. We could stay here and give him a day's start so we will not encounter him on the road. Once we turn toward Jerusalem, we will be safe."

"He will likely continue on up the coast and take another route across Canaan into Babylonia and Susa. If the Assyrians catch him, they will kill him. Ahmad, perhaps it would be good to trade the carriage for a common wagon. We could pack more supplies and gather little attention as we travel."

"Yes, I will attend to that. Gaza is a seaport and finding what we need will be easy. May I escort you to an Inn?"

"Please. Remember to use my childhood name, Ninana, from now on. Royalty has always been a burden that I did not want, and now it puts us all in danger."

"Ninana. I will remember to use that name."

Chapter 44

GAZA SEAPORT

The inn was plain and spare. Ahmad and Ninana looked it over a little doubtfully, but the room was clean and a bed of sorts was welcoming.

"Karim has brought food and wine for this evening. Karim and I, your 'brothers', will be sleeping right outside of your door tonight."

The room was suddenly bright with the morning sun. Ninana got up and stepped out of the door. Karim and Ahmad were not there. She picked up her sword, tucked it into her robe, pulled on her sandals, hurried through the inn, and out into the street. Not seeing them she ran to the stable. The wagon was there but they were not.

A stable boy came in and motioned toward the docks. He made a sign of tied hands and being dragged. She ran down to the docks, the stable boy dashing ahead of her. He pointed to a ship that was being prepared to sail.

She boldly boarded the ship and was immediately confronted by a glaring captain. She drew herself up to her queenly height and stance and looked him in the eyes.

"I am Queen Nitocris of Babylonia and I understand you have my guards. Bring them to me at once!"

She fingered her sword in the fold of her robe. Shocked he motioned to the first mate to bring them out and untie them.

"Thank you Captain. I am sure this was an honest mistake."

"Ah...you will need to pay me for them. I have to buy others."

"It is Your Highness! And you did not buy them from me, you stole them in the night. I owe you nothing."

Ahmad and Karim moved beside her and they walked down the gangplank to the dock. Ninana drew her sword and turned to see if they were being followed. A pirate was close behind them. She swung the sword with both hands, cutting his arm. Ahmad pushed the surprised pirate off into the water.

The three ran back to the stable. The stable boy had the wagon packed and the horses harnessed. He seemed to know instinctively what to do. Ninana placed two gold pieces in his hand to thank him.

They climbed aboard the wagon and started off at a brisk pace toward the road to Jerusalem.

"Your H...Ninana, you amaze me every day. I thought we would not get off the ship alive and die at sea."

"Where could I go without you? I was ready to sink their ship! They have never met an Amazon Warrior Woman."

"Did you really meet the Amazons?"

"Yes. In fact my companion, Lishan, and I were kidnapped by them in the wilds near the Silk Road in China. Because I am tall and wield a sword like a mad woman, they thought I must be a cousin. So I became an honorary sister of the Amazons."

"Is it true that they are fierce fighters?"

"Oh, yes. It is true. They win all of their battles and everyone fears them."

She smiled with satisfaction. The words felt good coming from her mouth.

The road to Jerusalem was a welcome sight. She could relax. She could be Ninana riding in a common wagon as she did traveling to Babylon with Zaidu so many years ago. She could chat with Ahmad and Karim as if there were no social barrier. But she knew though it was hidden, it was always waiting to reappear. She knew they had heard her call herself Queen Nitocris loudly and forcefully on the ship in order to free them.

They were quiet most of the way to Jerusalem. It was a long hot bumpy ride in the wagon, not at all like the carriage. But she spent the time pondering the words on the sarcophagus of Queen Nitocris of Egypt.

"I go to where love awaits me."

They stopped mid-afternoon to rest in some shade. A few travelers went by but paid no attention to them. As the sun moved toward the west they started out again. It was night when they approached the dark ruins of Jerusalem. They camped a distance away in the hills to wait until morning light to go closer.

Morning came with the approach of Hananiah.

"Queen Nitocris! Is that you?"

"Yes, Hananiah. Please. May we come into your camp in Jerusalem? Are Azariah and Mishael still there?"

"We are all still here. Come with me. Did you get to Egypt? You must tell us about it!"

They entered an enclosure of building stones where there was a cluster of small dwellings not visible from the outside. Ahmad and Karim pulled the wagon into a hidden area and unharnessed the horses.

In the cool of the evening they shared their stories. She explained that Ahmad and Karim had been posing as her brothers in Egypt to stay close when they found the tomb of Queen Nitocris.

"Jerusalem is growing slowly. Sometimes a few from the Babylon Jewish settlement arrive. The young ones want to reclaim their heritage in Jerusalem. The old folks stay put, happy with the little city their princess built for them.

"They are pretty bedraggled and hungry when they get here. It is hard to know how they made it with little help. Perhaps some did not make it. There are enemies all along the way that do not like strangers traveling through their land.

"Where will you go, Your Highness?"

"First, I must tell you that I have reclaimed my childhood name, Ninana. Please call me that. I do not want to be known as royalty. It might have gotten us killed in Egypt since Babylonia has been an arch enemy of Egypt.

"I only used the name Queen Nitocris when it was necessary to face down a nasty ship's captain. Being royalty has its uses in dire situations. Sometimes it has been a blessing, but often a barrier, too.

"Cambyses, the Persian Prince, was in a lot of trouble there. He bragged about being royalty of Persia. Not a good idea. The Egyptians captured and jailed him. Somehow he escaped and tried to take my carriage from me to get back to Gaza. Before he could get to the carriage we galloped away and left him behind on the road. He shouted that he would kill me."

"He has not come by Jerusalem. I believe you are safe from him here."

Ahmad chuckled.

"More like he will be safe from...Ninana. She is a skilled fighter."

Chapter 45

HOLDING JERUSALEM

In the early morning a small group of men came near the camp from the hills and demanded in shouting voices that they all leave.

"This is not your land. It is ours and you do not belong here."

"This is Jerusalem and we are Jews. It is our city and our land, given to our father, Abraham, by God Almighty. Go back north to your people and leave us alone."

"You have until the noon sun to leave or we will drive you out."

Ninana, her "brothers" and their other guards were listening from behind some huge rocks.

"Who are these people? Where do they come from?"

A woman nearby moved closer to them to whisper.

"They are Syrophoenicians from Syria and the sea. They always make trouble for us, but we fight. This is still our city."

Ninana was in a quandary about whether revealing her royalty would help or make things worse. She decided to wait for Hananiah to come back into the camp.

Immediately the whole encampment was quietly moving farther back into the ruins of Jerusalem.

"It will be impossible for them to find us and drive us out. We have explored the ruins and know where to hide. No one can follow us in there."

"Hananiah, would it be helpful or not to reveal that you have royalty among you?"

"They are ignorant of such things and would not honor it. They will think we are creating a trick to scare them. Save that information should we need it later on. Hopefully they will think we are gone this time."

They determined not to be found in a group. Each one in the encampment went to their personally chosen hiding place. They were scattered throughout the Jerusalem wreckage and everyone was armed. With signals to each other in place they waited in complete silence.

Ninana and her guards hid in an area on the side of the front encampment where they could trap the attackers from behind. She was amazed at how organized everything was. They all moved silently and in place long before the noon sun.

As promised the Syrophoenicians arrived and shouted their presence, repeating the demand that everyone leave. They were met with silence.

"We know you are in there! Come out and surrender. We will let you leave quietly."

Again there was silence.

The attackers began climbing over the stones into the encampment. The place was vacant. All materials and equipment had been removed. There was nothing left.

More attackers poured into the encampment area. Ninana and her guards, Hananiah, Azariah, and Mishael pried a few building stones loose from above and they tumbled into the entrance of the encampment.

"It is a trap!"

Some of the attackers climbed farther into the ruins and found no one. Some who found a few of the Jews were quickly silenced. The only cries heard were those of the attacking men who shouted to encourage their fellows. When evening came the last of the Syrophoenicians were gone and the Jews came out of hiding.

Ninana, Karim, and Ahmad climbed down from their perch.

"Do you think they will be back?"

"One never knows, but Azariah and Mishael have followed them to discover their camp and watch their movements."

"They might be caught and killed!"

"Ninana, dear friend, we are the last of Daniel's generation and we are getting old. We are happy to sacrifice our lives to protect the younger ones who come after us to reclaim Jerusalem. We have nothing more to do in our lives except God's work in preserving the City of David for them."

Ninana thought about her own city and how she would have given her life to preserve it. She took a great risk going to King Cyrus and giving up her throne to save her city. He could have refused her, imprisoned her, or even executed her. But instead he gave her sanctuary and left her city intact. The whole memory brought tears to her eyes.

"My guards and I will stay here and fight for Jerusalem beside you."

"Your Highness, that is not necessary. You need not put your life in danger."

"Ninana. Please.

"Ninana. Forgive me."

"You know the story of how I went to King Cyrus to save Babylon including the Jewish community. He could have executed me right there. I built my city, I built your community there, and I rebuilt a village in China. I may not be able to rebuild another city, but I will defend the right of your people to do it. We will stay."

Azariah and Mishael returned with the news that the Syrophoenicians were attacked by Assyrians from their north side and went to fight that battle.

There was no sign of the Syrophoenicians the next day. The people gathered the following day after that to decide what to do.

Hananiah gathered the appointed elders to plan. Ninana sat in on the meeting, although she did not speak.

"We are at the north edge of Jerusalem where we arrived from Babylon. We must move farther in toward the temple mount behind what is left of its walls. There is nothing there now but relocating to there will make it harder for enemies to find and attack us. We are vulnerable here. Too exposed."

"How will newcomers from Babylon find us?"

"We can post someone to watch at the north side during the day. We can leave this camp open to draw them in. Then meet them and lead them back to us."

Everyone nodded in agreement. Ninana and her guards volunteered to keep the watch during the day.

"We are more likely to recognize travelers from Babylon. We can ask questions that enemies cannot answer, they will not get past us pretending to be from there."

Four strong young men volunteered to go back into the ruins to find a place for the community. Azariah would go with them.

"I am pretty lame, but I know the location of the Gihon spring that fed water through a tunnel for Jerusalem. It was built to help Jerusalem survive an attack."

Again it was agreed.

Ninana, Ahmad, and Karim went into the stones on one side of the old camp and the rest of the guards went to the other side. Ninana sat down on a rock partly shaded from the sun.

"Is this where love awaits me? In Jerusalem with Daniel's friends? If Daniel were here I would think so, but he is not."

At night they gathered at the old camp area for food and reports of the day's events. Ninana was concerned and turned to Mishael.

"Where is Azariah?"

"He wanted to rest there for the night. He was too lame, ill, and tired to return with us. We wanted to make a litter and carry him, but he refused to let us do that. Carrying him over the stones would be too difficult. He said to return the next morning with food. He had water there and that was good enough."

"Is there a path to where he is?"

"Not yet. We have to find an easier way tomorrow. Babylon was like this when we were taken there. It is most difficult and one can easily get lost in the rubble."

"Yes, Mishael, you are quite right. Without Zaidu's map and instructions I would have been lost many times."

The next morning several young men went back with Mishael to find a pathway that others could navigate. They took items to be used for levers to move stones and food for the day. When they got through to the Gihon spring, Azariah was laying right where they left him and he was gone.

They found a place to bury him near the temple mount and sang the appropriate prayers over him. They covered his face with his robe and carefully laid him to rest deep in place where his body would not be disturbed.

While the men worked on the area to place the community, Mishael went back to tell Hananiah. They wept together. Ninana joined them at the end of her day on the watch and wept with them.

"Perhaps this is not where I return to love, but to bury it. Oh, Queen Nitocris of Egypt, what did you mean? How am I to understand what you wrote? I have traveled so far and suffered so much to find you, only to find a riddle...a mystery."

Chapter 46

A NEW JERUSALEM

Once the pathway was established and somewhat passable, Ninana went to the new settlement to see if she could be of assistance. Hananiah went with her and they checked over the path at every point to be sure it was hidden and yet accessible to bring in people and supplies. Their gardens and sheep were secured in the hills so their food supply was assured.

There were other auxiliary paths to be constructed so there were alternative ways to come and go from the settlement. The dwellings were not even as good as the ones she had helped repair in China, but there were no monsoons here to threaten them.

Mostly they needed shade, food, water, and comfortable resting places. Some of the women gathered the tall grasses for the flooring and beds. They fashioned pots from the clay they could find by the spring, and from a few pots still intact that they found in the rubble.

The men found a few weapons beside skeletons. The women continued to scavenge whatever they could find among the piles of burned and split building stones. Small storage areas under houses were left largely untouched by the fires, and they began digging out passages to enter them.

Ninana could see that it was coming together. The Jews were survivors, able to make something out of seemingly nothing. She went back to her perch to continue the watch. Karim and Ahmad were there.

"Princess! We thought you might not come back until tomorrow or the next day."

They were usually alone when they called her that. She did not mind that they called her princess, just so long as it was not Your Highness or Queen.

"The people are doing a wonderful job creating the New Jerusalem and they do not really need me."

In the distance a small group of people were coming toward them. Karim signaled the guards on the other side of the encampment.

"Who do you think they are?"

"One of them has fallen and the others are trying to get the person up. We cannot not tell if they are men or women, but it is obvious they are not enemies."

The travelers could not call out for help. Their throats were so dry they could only whisper. They waved and the guards on the other side went out to help them.

"Babylon. From Babylon."

The guards carried a couple of them into the encampment and gave them water. Ninana climbed down from her perch to help them. Two were women and one was with child. They created a litter and carried her back through the paths to the new place. Women ran to help and settle her in one of the dwellings.

"The child will come soon. We must try to get a little food and goats' milk into her or she will die of exhaustion and starvation."

They sat with her all night dribbling a little watered milk and watery cooked grain into her mouth every so often. There was no sign of labor and the women prayed that it would not come until the young woman could survive the birth.

Their prayer was answered. It was a week before the labor began and the child, Joshua, was born.

"My name is Anna. I did not know I was with child before I began the journey here. Is this Jerusalem? Am I really here?"

Ninana put her arm around Anna and helped her sit up.

"Yes, you are really here. Jerusalem is surely being reborn. You and your child are the sign of that."

"I remember stories in Babylon! I was a little child, but I heard about the princess who built our homes. You are that princess, are you not?"

"Yes. My name is Ninana and we do not mention my royalty anymore. I am just Ninana, which is my childhood name."

"Ninana. Wonderful to meet you. Thank you for everything you have done. For my former home and for your guards who carried me here. You are forever in my prayers. Will you be staying here?"

"For now. My friends, Mishael and Hananiah, are here and I will be with them until the time comes for me to return to Babylon."

"Babylon is rather messy these days. The occupying soldiers from Persia do not keep it nice, just march through it and watch everyone. I think they have taken anything of value from the palace and temples. I do not know why they stay except for the stores of wine and King Cyrus decrees it."

"I know, Anna. I was there many months ago. It is very sad."

Ninana picked up little Joshua and rocked him in her arms. Belshazzar was a disaster, her lost pregnancy in India was heartbreaking, but Joshua seemed to heal all of that. He was the new world for many.

"Perhaps he is one step in my return to love. All of my past anguishes seem to be healing and disappearing, returning me to love."

She returned the baby to Anna's waiting arms.

"Thank you for coming here and having the first child born in the New Jerusalem. I am sensing a new beginning in so many ways."

The men who were creating the new settlement and the pathways had finished those tasks and were ready to return to the defense of their little community. The women had taken over the building of the community, the men now had arms to fend off an enemy, while some were tending the gardens and animals.

Hananiah sat with Ninana in the evening.

"You have given us protection, stability, and the opportunity to organize everything about the community. We are strong and growing. We have had two weddings which means we will grow families, too."

"I am so glad we returned to Jerusalem and all is going so well. I think it is soon time for us to return to Babylon. The spring is coming, a good time to travel."

"I did not mean that you should leave. I only meant..."

"I know, Hananiah. But I am happy that you and Mishael have a home in Jerusalem again."

"You made it possible for us to thrive in Babylon. You brought us to Persia after the siege of Babylon, you helped us create this New Jerusalem. You are still building cities, Princess."

Tears rolled down their cheeks as they embraced.

"We will remember and honor Daniel who taught me about a god of love in a city of hate. I have not forgotten his teachings. They live in me and his god is my god."

"When will you go?"

"I must confer with Ahmad and Karim, and the guards who are all from Persia. I am sure they are eager to return home. They have been so patient with my needs. The driver of my carriage will stay here or in Babylon since he nearly ran over Cambyses at the border of Egypt when Cambyses tried to take my carriage for his own escape. I am sure Cambyses has not forgotten and will order his execution...as well as mine."

"There is a woman who would like him to stay. He is welcome here if he wishes to remain with us...her."

"We can manage without him. I will tell him of your offer. I am sure he will accept."

Chapter 47

BABYLON FALLING

———— ⟨⟨ ⟩⟩ ————

Again the wagon was loaded, the guards were ready, and Ninana was climbing into the seat. It all looked so familiar. A long road stretched out before them up the west side of the Jordan Valley past the Sea of Galilee and Lake Hula toward Damascus. Then into the deserts toward the Euphrates River.

"Shall I be Ninana or shall I be Queen Nitocris again? Everything in my life was wrapped up in the rising of the new City of Babylon. I thought it would last forever. All my hopes and dreams have risen with it and are now falling. Shall I let my life fall with Babylon?

"I cannot return to Susa. Cambyses will not welcome me even if King Cyrus does. He will always be a danger to me worse than the lions or the fire.

"My mother is in Haran if she is still alive. But there would be nothing for me in Haran. Assyria is now the arch enemy of Persia and Babylonia. They are trying to take Egypt from Assyria. My life seems to be leading me to Babylon, my first love."

Damascus was not a friendly city to them. They pretended to be from Jerusalem.

Ninana had picked up some of the language of the Jews and was able to be convincing as they bought supplies and found lodging.

Ahmad hurried back from the marketplace.

"I do not speak their language, but I understand enough. There is talk that Cambyses came through Damascus and had to fight his way out. He and his guards killed many people and robbed the temples. There is still much anger."

"We were in Jerusalem a long time, so this probably is not recent. Cambyses must be in Susa now. He has been waiting to hear that King Cyrus has been killed in a battle. He wants to be on hand to be sure no one else tries to get the throne."

"True. It was when we left Gaza. But the anger and hatred will last for generations. Everyone hates the Persians."

Ninana knew this was true, even in China. The Amazons were constantly harassed by the Persians. The leader of the Amazons promised to kill King Cyrus, cut off his head, and stuff it into a sheep's bowel.

"We will be fortunate to get to Babylon, but I can go nowhere else from there. I will be hiding in my broken city. What will you do, Ahmad?"

Ahmad was thoughtful. When they went to dinner he told her his and Karim's decision.

"I think that Karim and I, and the other guards if they choose to stay with us, will go to the Jewish settlement in Babylon. Perhaps we can assist the people there in whatever way they might need. The younger men and I can even escort those who want to go to Jerusalem. This is the last journey I care to take. My bones would like me to settle down."

"You cannot settle down in Persia?"

"No. I have been in the military as a guard. I would immediately be conscripted into a militia or a battle. Once you are military you can never become a commoner."

"Yes, once you are royalty it is the same. It has been wonderful to be Ninana and pretend not to be royalty for a time. But it is always there ready to show up again, blessing or curse."

"Was Queen Nitocris of Egypt a blessing?"

"I have yet to understand what the message was on her sarcophagus. 'I go to where love awaits me.' According to Daniel's god and my god, love awaits us everywhere, even right here."

"So it is a blessing?"

"I keep watching for it and trying to be happy where I am now as Daniel always was."

"I wish I had known Daniel. But being with his three friends and the Jewish people, I have learned something of what you are saying."

Crossing the sand desert, high desert and swamps took weeks and seemed to be never ending.

"I am starting to wonder if Babylon is still there. Maybe we passed it."

"Even if everything passes away, I am sure your Ishtar Gate still stands strong. We have not passed it."

Approaching Babylon in the bright sun, it was still the city floating in the light. Regardless of how run down or neglected within the city, from a distance it was still the great shining City of Babylon.

"How good it is to see it one more time! My city is still beautiful. The blue and gold bricks still shine. The Ishtar Gate still towers over the walls. My own sarcophagus is up on top of it. Is that where I will end up? Is that a return to love? It makes me laugh to think of the superstitious merchants fearing to travel through the gate because my dead body will curse them."

"Do you wish to stop at the gate?"

Ninana thought for a few minutes.

"No, Ahmad, let us go by the side gate into the Jewish community. I am sure the inn I built close to the back gate and marketplace is still standing. Perhaps I can stay there."

"It is most likely a brothel, Princess. The residents of the community will surely offer you lodging where you will be safe."

Ahmad was correct. The Inn was a brothel and worse. The refuse in the streets had risen a quarter of the way up the walls of the buildings. The stench was sickening. It reminded her of the night she and Daniel ran through these very streets and out the back gate during the siege. It was even worse now.

What a relief it was to enter the Jewish quarter where the streets were clean and all was well kept.

"This was my dream for Babylon. Who could guess that only the Jewish quarter would be the fulfillment of my vision. All Mesopotamian cities are like this, but not the Jewish places. Daniel said that for them cleanliness is godlike."

They rolled into the center of the quarter and were greeted with music, food, and dancing. Sitting on a bench near the temple entrance were Zaidu and Arakhu. She jumped down from the carriage and ran to them.

"I cannot believe my eyes. I feared never to see you again!"

They got up and walked quickly to meet her.

"And we feared the same, Princess. Come, sit and tell us about your adventures. After you conquered China and the high seas, we should not have lost faith."

Ninana laughed.

"Add Egypt and Jerusalem to your list."

Chapter 48

ANOTHER ASPECT OF LOVE

"Princess Ninana! Princess Ninana!"

There were kisses on her cheeks, hugs, and blessings all around.

"You are the princess who gave us our city! You have helped save Jerusalem! Now come and tell us about Jerusalem! Who is there? What are they doing? Is the temple restored?"

Tables of food were set out and crowds sat round Ninana, Ahmad, and Karim to hear all they would say. The name Jerusalem was as sacred to them as Babylon was to Ninana.

After hours of regaling the residents with stories, Ninana was exhausted. It seemed such a long time since she had really slept. Her bones were aching from the jostling of the wagon.

"I am no longer the young princess, but a little older woman who gets tired and needs rest."

An elderly couple saw that she needed to sleep and took her to their home.

"We understand, Princess. We are older now too, and the body will not behave as it did when we were young. It is amazing that you have traveled all this way. Rest now and let us talk tomorrow or the day after."

A wonderful room and bed were provided for her. A grateful Ninana lay down and fell asleep immediately. The grandmother gently covered her. Ahmad and Karim stayed at the table far into the night and took turns answering their questions and describing the condition of Jerusalem.

Jacob and Abigail brought her breakfast on a tray, and some fresh clothing. She smiled at bathing in purified water from the Euphrates River. Her river, her Babylon, her people. They lovingly cared for her through many more days allowing her to be restored in mind and body.

"Ahmad, I would like to go to Yang Light of the Rising Sun, the building I built dedicated to Fu Ling Yang. Can you accompany me?"

"Yes, of course, Princess. I would not want you to go alone. Do you know the way?"

"Yes, I do know the way. I grew up on these streets and I built the buildings."

"Would you like to go now?"

They started off through the streets keeping to the main avenues to avoid the filth. It was a few miles to the building and people were gawking at them.

"I hope you have your sword handy, Princess."

"I have it. I hope I do not have to use it."

Two men approached them.

"Where are you going, Lady. I have not seen you before."

Ahmad stepped between them. Ninana drew herself up to her queenly stance.

"She cut the arm off the last man who attacked her. I suggest you go on your way."

The men hesitated, sneered, and walked away.

Ninana could see the walls of the palace in the distance. She pointed them out to Ahmad.

"Do you wish to go there, Princess?"

"No. There might be many dangers in there and nothing I care to see. The Chinese building is this way."

The architecture was unmistakable. It stood out and shone like the rising sun it was named for. Ninana stood quietly before it, taking in its beauty as it called up emotions of all it meant to her. Fu Ling Yang and Lishan, Shamhar, China, and her beloved Chaoxiang.

"Have caution, Princess. The lock has been broken. There will be people living in there."

Ninana's heart sank. Surely there would be much destruction and theft. There might be nothing left of its beauty and treasures.

Ahmad pushed the once ornate door open and stepped in. There were scurrying noises and someone mumbling.

"Probably rats and someone sleeping or dying."

Ninana stepped in behind him and lit a lantern that was still hanging in the entrance to the temple. She lit other lanterns and could see the sad condition of the temple. The one who was moaning came toward the light.

"Who are you?"

"I am Princess Ninana who designed and built this place. Who are you?"

"Praise all the gods, Princess Ninana! I am Dakuri, a former student of the architectural school. I was one who came to Babylon with you. You convinced me that my dreams were important."

Ninana was astonished.

"I do remember you, Dakuri!"

"When King Cyrus captured Babylon there was nothing for me to do except protect the place most precious to you. You were my inspiration and I accomplished many things. Now we are like prisoners, but free to roam the city. There is much peril in the streets. I have chosen to live here.

"Some things may have been stolen from this place, but I convinced those who approach that the place is haunted and protected by Chinese gods. So they stay away."

"Are you well, Dakuri? Do you not need help?"

"I am most likely dying of an illness that weakens my heart. I am pleased to die here rather than anywhere else. There is no help for my condition or my situation."

"I am sorry. Can I bring you food and something to ease your pain?"

"Yes, Princess. If you would have someone you trust to do that, it would ease my last days. Tell me, Princess, what of Shamhar and Lishan? Are they alive?"

"They went to China with Fu Ling Yang before King Cyrus besieged Babylon. They are safe and well."

A day later Ninana, Ahmad, and Karim returned to the Chinese building with food and something to ease his pain. They brought bedding to give him a comfortable place to sleep.

"Thank you. You are so kind. You were always kind to us and I have always blessed you in my thoughts."

"We will return after you have had some rest and see it there is anything else we can do for you."

Dakuri was gone when they returned. His heart had given out.

"Ahmad, is there a place in this building where we can bury him? I believe that somewhere there is a vault below the floor."

After much scratching and poking they found the edge of the opening in the floor. They stepped in carefully treading the stone steps. Ninana lit a lantern and brought it down. There was a sarcophagus along the wall. She went back up the steps to get Dakuri's bedding. They carefully wrapped Dakuri's body in the bedding and pried open the lid. They placed him in the sarcophagus, covered his face and replaced the lid. They sealed it with clay and pitch and replaced the flooring over it.

"May you rest, Dakuri. May God's love keep you forever."

Sadly they returned to the Jewish community for a feast, music and a night of rest.

Chapter 49

THE GOVERNOR OF BABYLON

Ninana dared not go back to Susa. It seemed there was nothing else to do but settle into the Jewish community in Babylon. There was an abandoned home in the center of the residential section. It was a little dilapidated, but Ahmad was on hand to help her shore up the walls and roof. She created a comfortable interior with a few donations from the community.

It was so strange to go from being a queen who had everything to a pauper who had nothing and depended upon donations from those who had little themselves.

Arakhu was close by.

"Princess, will you come and pray with me. Daniel has taught me."

"Where do you go to pray?"

"In the Jewish synagogue. We are always welcome there. We would like to visit Yang Light of the Rising Sun, but it is too dangerous. Since Dakuri is not there to scare robbers away with stories of the angry Chinese gods, it might be a problem."

Days and weeks went by peacefully until a messenger came to the Jewish community.

"We have a new governor of Babylon. It is Cambyses II, son of King Cyrus. He will take up residence in the palace. We have heard nothing further about what he intends to do."

Ninana froze.

"Cambyses is coming here. Will he find me and punish or even execute me?"

Ahmad came immediately to her side.

"We will hide you."

"Everyone knows I am here, Ahmad. Perhaps I need to find the place that Nabonidus created in northwest Arabia and go there. It should not be far."

"Zaidu, do you know where the settlement of Nabonidus is? Might it still be there?"

"Yes, Ahmad, I remember. I do not know if it is still in existence. Has Cambyses arrived in Babylon as yet?"

The messenger did not know the whereabouts of Cambyses.

Ninana, Ahmad, Zaidu, and Arakhu prepared to cross the Euphrates River immediately and travel into Arabia to find whatever might remain of Nabonidus' settlement.

That night they repaired the wagon they traded for in Gaza, hitched the horses to it, and loaded it with supplies, tents, and food. Before dawn they drove out of Babylon and far up the river to a shallow crossing to wait for light.

It was just before dawn. The horses struggled to get the wagon through the muddy water and onto the bank of the river. The three pushed the wagon as Ninana urged the horses forward. Even though it was unlikely that Cambyses was pursuing her, she kept glancing behind her.

"Where do we go from here?"

Zaidu squinted his eyes in the growing light.

"There will be a camel caravan road as we continue northwest. If we follow it we should come to a kind of settlement twenty miles from here. That might be where he was living."

"I cannot believe I am running away like this. It is so disheartening that my life has come to fleeing. I am a fighter, not one who runs from danger."

"How will you fight Cambyses?"

"There must be a way. I will have to pray about it. Surely God has an answer."

The caravan road came into view. There were a few tents and camels tethered near them.

"Should we stop and ask them about the village?"

Ahmad shook his head.

"I think we should continue without stopping. The village is over fifteen miles away yet. We will just follow the road for now."

Zaidu agreed.

"Let us not invite danger."

It was a familiar bumpy ride in the wagon. The heat of the day caused the hours to drag by. They came over the last sand dune and saw a village nestled under a few palm trees in an oasis.

"This could not be it. Nabonidus needed women and wine. There is nothing here."

Zaidu pulled his beard for a minute.

"You are right, Princess. We must go further. I am sure we will find it."

Past the next ridge there it was. The place that Nabonidus created. It looked like a desert palace of tents large and small in many colors. There were gardens of plants that Ninana surmised he stole from the hanging gardens, a well with watering systems, and people going about their business.

A man in flowing robes and a high turban came out to meet them.

"I am Mohamed, the chief of this community. Who are you and what do you want here?"

Ninana stepped forward and decided to take a big risk. It would not do to lie or try to deceive this man.

"I am Queen Nitocris of Babylon. King Nabonidus was my husband. I am here seeking refuge. King Cyrus captured Babylon, Nabonidus was killed, Cambyses II, son of Cyrus, now rules Babylon. I believe he will execute me if he finds me. These are my guards and my friends."

"Welcome! Please, all of you come with me to my tent."

They climbed down off the wagon and followed the man who designated himself as the chief. His serving girls seemed to come out of nowhere and served them wine and refreshments.

"Nabonidus appointed me as a chief because he did not care to rule the community, just the women and the wine. I begged him not to go to Babylon but he would not listen. He wanted new and younger women. I was not surprised when he did not return."

"How has this community survived?"

"It is a popular stop for camel caravans and travelers. You said that you are seeking refuge. Tell me what accommodations you require."

"I have returned to my childhood name, Ninana, releasing claims to royalty. I am the architect who designed the rebuilding of the City of Babylon. I had no other desire, not the throne or the power. All of my life I wished only to be an architect. Master Builder, Zaidu, here can attest to what I have said."

Ahmad went on to explain the incident with Cambyses in Egypt and the reason for the wagon, not a queen's carriage. The Chief nodded and smiled.

"We do not wish to disturb your community. Is there a way for us to be here and not disrupt or attract undue attention? We have tents and supplies. We can set up on the outskirts of the community and be as unobtrusive as possible."

"Perhaps. Create a story to be told for those who ask."

"Yes. Zaidu and Arakhu will stay with me as my brothers. I became ill while traveling and stopped here to rest and recover. Will that be satisfactory?"

"It sounds plausible. Others have done the same."

"Ahmad will return to Babylon and send word when Cambyses goes to attack Egypt. The Egyptians knew Persia wanted Egypt and imprisoned Cambyses. He escaped and now plans the attack.

"When he is away in battle, it will be safe for me to return to Babylon for a time."

"Then it is settled, Your Highness. Please accept our hospitality."

"Ninana, please."

"Ninana, of course"

Chapter 50

HAS LOVE FLED?

─────────────── ❧ ❧ ───────────────

Mohamed's community was very peaceful and prosperous. Ninana ventured to the marketplace daily to create the feeling that the world had not left her adrift in the desert.

Zaidu and Arakhu were content to sit beside their tent door. They were over a decade older than Ninana and age was curtailing their mobility. The rough wagon trip from Babylon and setting up their living spaces was all they could manage. She was sad to witness their decline but happy to have them with her.

Mohamed would stop by to visit with them occasionally and sit down with Zaidu.

"Are you doing well, my friend? Is there anything you need?"

"You are most kind and we are doing well, Chief Mohamed."

Mohamed desired to construct a few buildings for storage and a shelter for his Arabian horses. He came to Ninana for help in planning them.

"I understand that you can build. Nabonidus said something about your building talents."

"Yes and I am delighted to be of assistance! Tell me what the size should be and any interior spaces you need for special items."

They sat in Mohamed's tent next to a low table and spread out plans. He had not realized Ninana's ability to design not only sturdy buildings, but beautiful ones. They gracefully mirrored the landscape and blended with the colors of the desert. Nabonidus had not bothered to tell him about her part in the rebuilding of Babylon.

"How do you know these things? How do you see these designs that you use?"

"They come from within my mind. My name is Ninana, meaning I come from myself."

"Are you a sorceress?"

"No, I was just a young girl who loved to draw buildings. Zaidu built them as I drew them. You must come to see Babylon. I designed most of the city buildings, the walls and the Ishtar Gate."

"Ah, I have heard of the magnificent Ishtar Gate! It is your design then?"

"Yes. It is my masterpiece."

Zaidu agreed to supervise the construction, but he could do little else.

"There is too much pain in my back, probably from moving building stones."

"I am so sorry, Zaidu! You ruined your back because of my city."

"Oh, no, Princess. It is my city, too."

Mohamed immediately offered the services of a physician who lived in the community.

"He may be able to ease your pain so you can rest. He will come immediately."

The building materials were gathered and the buildings began to slowly rise. Soon Zaidu could no longer supervise. He was absent from the building site more and more.

"The builders are doing a good job and they no longer need me. I need to rest in my tent. My heart seems to be going too fast when I move around much."

A few days later Arakhu came to Ninana's tent.

"Princess, I bring sad news. Zaidu is gone. He died in the night. I did not hear him, just found him this morning. I will take him back to his beloved Babylon."

She burst into tears.

"I am so sorry. He has been with me since my childhood, taking me to Babylon in a supply wagon and on horseback. I cannot believe he is gone. I must go with you."

"But what about Cambyses? You would risk your life."

"Is there any word about him from Babylon?"

"None. But you must not go."

"What is my life worth without all of you? I cannot just sit here alone in a tent and wait to die."

Mohamed came to Zaidu's tent.

"What has happened? Can I be of assistance?"

"Our dear friend has died. Arakhu and I will take Zaidu back to Babylon. He built that city and he should be buried there. Can someone find our wagon and hitch the horses to it?"

"Your wagon has been safely stored with the horses in the stables you designed, Ninana."

"Thank you! We will prepare to leave tomorrow after we gather and pack our belongings."

"I will send guards with you. There could be trouble on the caravan road for two traveling alone."

"Mohamed, again you are most kind."

Mohamed's men brought out the wagon and hitched the horses. They helped Ninana and Arakhu load their belongings into it. Zaidu's body was covered with herbs and carefully wrapped.

"We will leave the tents for someone else to use. We will not need them."

"Perhaps you will return. You are always welcome among us. Allah's blessings upon you and keep you safe."

"And upon you, my friend Mohamed."

They approached the river far to the northwest of Babylon. The extra guards helped them across the river and then bid them farewell. Arakhu and Ninana were on their own praying to get into the side gate of the city unnoticed.

At dusk they rolled past the market into the Jewish part of the city. Everything was quiet.

"Do you know where Ahmad is, or Karim?"

People shook their heads. They traveled deeper into the center of the community where Ninana had lived. A few elderly people sitting by the well came to meet them.

"Princess! You have returned. Come with us. Ahmad has been very ill."

"We have brought the body of Zaidu to be buried here. Sadly he passed away in much pain."

"We will take care of him for you. Now go to Ahmad quickly."

Ninana's heart froze, afraid of what she would find. Ahmad was laying on a bed, very pale and thin. Karim was holding him in his arms. She sat down beside them and Ahmad opened his eyes.

"Princess! You are here. I wanted to come to you, but I could not. This illness has attacked me. I am weak. I will not last long. Cambyses has gone to Egypt. You are safe for now. Why are you here?"

"Zaidu died. Arakhu and I brought him home."

"Ah, I am sorry. Please bury me beside him and I will rest in peace."

"And I will be alone. Is this what my life has come to? My friends are leaving me and I have nowhere to go, no one to run to. I would go to where love awaits me, but where? How can it be?"

Chapter 51

A BOWL OF ASHES

Ninana had prospered in Arabia. Mohamed rewarded her handsomely for the buildings she designed and built. She hired a carriage and driver to take her through the streets of Babylon to the Ishtar Gate, past the palace, past the School of Architecture, past the financial district and marketplace. She covered her face with a veil and under it a cloth covering her nose. Karim insisted upon coming with her.

"Princess, what is it you are looking for?"

"I am looking for something of what inspired me from childhood to design this city, some glimmer of the purpose that I saw in it. What made me love it so much."

"There may be some good news. King Cyrus is sending more of his military to clean up the city. Those who are here are only occupiers, but the troops coming in will have a task, a very large task, to restore it."

"When are they to arrive? Do you know?"

"I hear they are on their way now. It will be another week before they arrive and another week to organize the cleanup. They will most likely chase the squatters out of the palace and other main buildings. They have been the ones making the mess, and also the residents dumping their refuse in the streets. The squatters and residents could be imprisoned or executed as part of the cleanup."

They went past the palace wall where Belshazzar was killed by his guards and to the western gate where she and Daniel had escaped so long ago.

"Driver, take us back to the Jewish community. I have seen enough. I do not want to be here when Cyrus' troops arrive."

The troops arrived with great fanfare. Proclamations were issued and notices tacked on the walls of all the main buildings. Huge holes were dug east of the city near the river for the refuse to be dumped and burned. Squatters were herded into detention camps outside of the city. Those who were able bodied were conscripted into the cleanup effort. The soldiers were loud and demanding. They arrested anyone dumping refuse or refusing their orders.

Babylon became a city of tramping soldiers, shouting supervisors, and wailing residents. The fire east of the city burned constantly. Only the prevailing breezes from west to east saved the Jewish community from the smoke and stench.

Ninana stayed in her home in the Jewish community. Karim brought her food and attended to everything she needed. She reminded everyone to refer to her as Ninana, and not Princess, for their own safety as well as hers. Better yet to forget she was there.

Month after month the cleanup continued and no one was safe on the streets. It went from one extreme to another. The occupiers sat around and did little, but the troops in charge cleanup constantly demanded work and obedience. The city was turned into a labor camp.

A small group of soldiers inspected the Jewish section of the city and left. They gave no indication of any further action to be taken. Still it was many weeks before the Jews began to breathe easily. They went about their business watchful but without fear.

The troops cleared all of the city's royal, commercial, and main areas, forcing the residents to clean up their own neighborhoods. The part of the city across the Euphrates River was mostly lesser temples, brothels, and walled private communities that stretched for miles southeast, south and northwest.

It seemed that now the troops were safeguarding the main buildings and streets, but rarely accosted people by asking for identification.

Ninana acquired a Jewish identity and name. She was Abigail, an orphan, whose family roots were in old Jerusalem. She hired a two-wheel carriage to take her to the Jewish market. It was many months before she ventured into Babylon proper again.

It had been a few years since she visited her Chinese building.

"Will I find it looted and destroyed? I am almost afraid to look."

Cautiously, she pushed the outer temple doors open. The lanterns were gone so she lit a torch on the wall. The flames created wavering shadows. She went to a second torch and lit it. Now the interior of the ancient Chinese temple was visible. The place smelled musty so she went to a small bowl in an alcove in the wall and lit the incense.

"The bowl is half full of recent ashes! Who would come here to light the incense?"

She walked around holding a torch thinking someone must be in the building. Searching through each room, she found no one. Any evidence of the squatters had been swept away by cleaners.

"There are no Chinese people in Babylon, unless...no, it could not be. Fu Ling Yang, Lishan, and Shamhar fled to China years ago. Then who?"

She emptied the bowl, polished it with the hem of her robe and replaced it. It would soon be evening. It was dangerous enough to be on the streets during the day. She hurried back to the Jewish section in the carriage and went to her home.

Several months later she again ventured into the city to the building, Yang Light of the Rising Sun. She tiptoed in, immediately lit a torch, and went to the alcove.

"Ashes! Someone has been lighting the incense. But who?"

She walked around looking for signs of someone entering, but not even the dust was disturbed. She lit the incense, extinguished the torch and left for home. The mystery was constantly on her mind day and night.

"Karim, something strange has been happening at the Chinese building. Someone is lighting the incense, but there are no signs of entry or someone living there. It is almost as if the ghost of my student Dakuri is letting me know he is still there."

"Ninana, you must not go there again. It might be a trap."

"But who would want to trap me? No one knows I am here. I use a different name when I am going to the market, my hair is graying a little and I cover my face."

Karim scowled.

"I do not believe in ghosts."

"I did not think I would either, but what could be the answer?"

One more time, Ninana went back to the Chinese building with a purpose in mind. Ninana thought about Chaoxiang's ring that she so carefully guarded all these years.

Entering the ancient temple, she removed the tile in the temple wall, took the jade and gold ring from its special container, and slipped it onto her finger. Tears came to her eyes.

"Should I take it with me this time? No, it is safer here."

Reluctantly, she put it back in the special container, placed it in the wall and put the tile carefully in place. There was the reassuring click that let her know it was secured. Sadly she got into the carriage to go home. A soldier stepped in front of the carriage. The driver stopped.

"Who are you and what are you doing here?"

"I am Abigail of the old city of Jerusalem. Someone told me of a Chinese building and I was curious, so I came to see it. I did not mean to disturb anyone. I am returning to the Jewish section."

He looked at her for several minutes and Ninana's skin began to crawl.

"Does he recognize me? How could he? He is Persian and far too young to know of me."

"Go. It would be unwise for you to return. Stay out of our city."

"His city? It is my city now and always!"

Chapter 52

CAMBYSES RETURNS

Ninana's days of traveling into the city came to an end with the threat of Cambyses returning Babylon.

"I wonder how long he will stay. I know he is not content to be a governor of a mere city. Probably only until his father is killed in a battle. He is always waiting for that message to come so he can be the king."

Karim rushed to Ninana's home.

"Princess, what will you do?"

"I am not sure, Karim. How can I stay in Babylon with Cambyses here? Perhaps I can go to Uruk. I was a child when I lived there. No one will recognize me now."

"Why not go back to Mohamed's community in Arabia?"

"I must know what is happening in Babylonia and in the City of Babylon. Something strange was happening in the Chinese building. Someone was lighting the incense. It felt like it was a message for me, but I do not know who sent it or what it means yet."

"It is a very long way to Uruk!"

"I know exactly how far it is. I traveled from there to Babylon and back many times with Zaidu while designing and building this city. Can you bring my wagon and horses to the side gate?"

"Yes, and I have stores of food. I will bring them too. I am going with you, Princess. It is always an adventure and I do not want to be left out."

Ninana laughed.

"I am always on an adventure. Yes, I guess that is what my life has been."

They left in the night when the moon would give them some light. Ninana knew that road well. It brought back many memories. After several days they arrived in Isin, the halfway point. Amazingly nothing much had changed there. They spent a night in an inn on the outskirts of the town. The next day they traded their tired horses for fresh ones and continued toward Uruk.

A troop of soldiers came galloping toward them in the direction of Babylon. Karim pulled the wagon far off the road and stopped.

"I will get out and pretend to fix a wheel. Hopefully they will not bother with us."

"They are Babylonian troops, not Cambyses' soldiers. I think we will be safe."

A few of the troops did stop and ask if they needed assistance.

"Thank you, officers, but I have just repaired the wheel and we will be on our way."

"Where are you coming from?"

"Isin. My cousins and I are going to Uruk for supplies."

"Oh, well, we will be on our way then. We are meeting Cambyses to join forces with him."

They galloped away to catch up with their company. Ninana's heart sank.

"I hope they do not report us when they get to Babylon."

"They seemed not to notice you."

They traveled on for another week and finally Uruk was in sight. Ninana recognized the skyline. The old palace and ziggurat were becoming visible through the summer haze. She remembered the streets and where the architectural school building was.

"If it is still there perhaps we can find a place to live nearby in the old residential section. The students all went to Babylon. I do not know if the school closed or continued with new students. I never inquired or even looked back after I got to Babylon."

There was still a long distance to cover getting into the middle of Uruk. Ninana struggled to remember the way to the architectural building because she only traveled to it from the palace.

"I see the palace, Karim. Go toward it and I may be able to find the other building from there."

"Who occupies a palace when everything is moved to Babylon?"

"I really do not know. Probably guards and visiting dignitaries.

Pull up by the back gate. If there are guards, they may not bother with the back gate. No one knows about it except the servants."

Karim nodded and drove around to the back gate. There was no one there.

"Why do you want to be here? I thought we were going to look for the architect school building."

"I want to see the room in the bottom level of the palace where I used to sketch my buildings. You can wait here for me. I will not be long."

"Are you sure this is wise? What should I say if someone comes by?"

"Tell them you are delivering supplies. This would be the delivery entrance."

Karim nodded and heaved a sigh.

"It is always an adventure…"

Ninana went through cobwebs and dust, through the deserted halls and down the long stairs to the level of her secret room. It had not been disturbed since they moved to Babylon. She eased the door open and lit a lamp. The walls were partly smoked, just as she had left them. Her sketches barely showed. She blew out the lamp, slipped back out and closed the door. Karim was relieved when at last she came out of the back gate of the palace.

"Did you find what you were looking for?"

"Yes. It was exactly as I left it. It reminds me that my childhood was real. I have been so many places, and as you said so many adventures, I just needed to find my roots again."

"Where to, Princess?"

"Go to the front of the palace and take the road that goes straight south and then west toward the hills. That is where the school building will be if it is still there."

Now the way looked familiar and Ninana could easily navigate the way. The building was still there. It looked empty and she wondered if it were being used. They stopped by the front door. She called out, but no answer came, just a few startled birds flying off the roof.

"The homes of the students were behind the building on the next street. Those places look empty, too. I guess we can just pick one and move in."

"I will check some of them. We want a place with a roof that will not fall in on our heads."

"It seems that the city is half deserted. I suppose that when we all moved to Babylon, there was no one coming to move in and fill up the places."

They chose a couple of homes placed far back from the school building and the street. They hoped no one would come by or notice them.

A squeaky elderly voice piped up from the door of one of the neighboring houses.

"Who are you? Should I call some soldiers. We do not want trouble here."

"We are Karim and Abigail. Just looking for a place to live for a while. We will cause no trouble."

"Well, good. My name is Mara."

Karim smiled his friendliest smile and bowed slightly.

"Thank you, Mara. If you need anything, we are happy to help."

She went back into her house.

"Now what?"

"I guess we should move our belongings into the larger house and find a stable for the horses and wagon."

"There is a stable close to where Master Jarem lived. He had a carriage and a horse. It is closer to the school. There might be a stable keeper there who would take care of the horses and store the wagon."

"I will go looking for this next adventure, Princess. I will return soon."

Mara brought them cooked food for their dinner.

"Please stay and eat with us, Mara."

"I am happy to stay, but then I must return to my house. It has some broken places in the walls and the vermin come in if I stay away too long."

"Oh, Mara, I am so sorry. Karim and I will come tomorrow and repair your house. We are quite skilled at fixing and rebuilding homes."

They worked on Mara's house for several days, finding materials from the abandoned homes in the neighborhood to use.

"Karim, remember to call me Abigail, not princess."

He laughed and promised to remember.

Mara became their only friend in Uruk. The population was decimated when everyone moved to the new Babylon. There were no children growing up here to take their place. Now there was little social life other than the market.

Chapter 53

REMEMBERING JOY

—— ❧ ❧ ——

After a few months, Karim and Ninana fell into a routine of going to the marketplace, exploring parts of the city, and climbing the ziggurat to watch the river flow by.

"Daniel said that God was his joy and if he forgot his joy, then he forgot God. There are so many things I have forgotten and mysteries I have not solved."

There was a small temple at the top of the ziggurat.

"I am going to use the temple to remember and to pray, Karim. Would you watch outside of the temple for me. I need to be alone but I need you close by, too. I do not know if I am lonely, in despair, or lost. I need to focus my mind as I used to focus on my drawings. I need to find some meaning in all of my life events. Is there still a purpose for my life?"

"I will be close by, Princess. I will pray to my gods that you are successful."

"Do you still have gods, Karim?"

"Oh, yes. I have a favorite Persian god that I turn my thoughts to. He is Mithra, God of the Rising Sun. He reminds me that the sun is always rising somewhere and so it should rise in my heart as well."

"That is beautiful!"

The temple was a bit musty but she could leave the door open and dust off a place on the seat. There was a small altar with an old bent candle in a holder, and a window in the wall to the east.

"I can face the rising sun. Light of the rising sun, Fu Ling Yang's name. Mithra, Karim's god. My god and Daniel's god. Joy. These will be my prayers."

Ninana and Karim went to the ziggurat every morning to watch the sun rise. Some of the loneliness and her feelings of despair began to ebb away. New thoughts began to come to mind.

"Material things decay, cities and empires rise and fall, people pass away, and yet I must go on. These things are not what I am. Five kings have died in my lifetime and I, Queen Nitocris, am still here. Oh, how good it feels to say that name with strength and assurance again! I am Queen Nitocris!"

The message was passed around in the marketplace that King Cyrus was killed in battle. Cambyses II was now king of Babylonia and Persia. He was preparing to attack the Assyrians and take Egypt from them.

"That is good news, Karim. Cambyses will be too busy to bother with me or even Babylon. He will appoint a governor for the city and go about his kingly battles."

"Do you think it will be safe for us to return?"

"Karim, I have learned that we are never safe in this world. But we are safe in our joy and our courage to live regardless of where we are. The sun is always rising!"

They retrieved their wagon and horses, packed it with supplies, and prepared to return to Babylon. Mara came out of her house to bid them farewell.

"I have something for you, Princess!".

Ninana was shocked at that word.

"Yes, I know who you are. I knew from the moment I saw you. I have something for you."

She pressed some gold pieces and jewelry into Ninana's hand and gave her the bronze scissors that she used to cut her hair so many years ago.

"I was a servant in the palace after everyone left and I found these in what must have been your apartment. Now I know why I have kept them. You have returned for a short time and I can give them back to you."

"But Mara, do you not need the gold pieces for yourself? You are welcome to keep them."

"The Goddess Nana cares for me as she has cared for you, Ninana. You have blessed me from the first day you arrived. Now I have all I need. Fare well."

With tears in their eyes they hugged each other. Then Ninana climbed into the wagon and they started down the road to the edge of the city and turned toward Babylon. They would stop in Isin for fresh horses, as she and Zaidu had done so long ago. She smiled as she remembered the fib she told him about riding a little horse and how he laughed.

In the few weeks it took to get to Babylon, she went over her memories with joy, treasuring each one. She told Karim about some of them and they laughed together.

She regaled him with stories of her father ignoring her.

"He made me work with more determination. He had blessed me even though I was thoroughly frustrated and angry. My mother taught me about being the queen regent. She protected me and never forced me to conform to women's ways.

"Then there was poor hapless Nabonidus who could not be a king, although it was handed to him on a golden platter. He gladly left me to my calling. King Cyrus patiently taught me about being a ruler and honored my accomplishments. He saved Daniel and me during the siege, and later Daniel's friends.

"Karim, the blessings are just overwhelming now that I follow the joy in my thinking. I retell the stories to myself in a whole different light, the light of the rising sun."

"I prayed that you would be successful in finding it. I am so pleased to hear your stories in joyful terms. Blessings are all around us if we but learn to see and embrace them."

They remembered how the Jews sang their prayers. Now they began to sing them together as they rode along.

They stopped in Isin to change horses and rest at the only inn. Part of the old inn was beginning to collapse.

"Karim, I can help them shore it up. It will not take much time or effort."

The elderly innkeeper was delighted and gratefully accepted their help. He showed them all that needed to be done. He was so happy that his inn was saved that he created a special meal for them. It was a joyful evening as they ate together.

"Princess, you never seem to stop building! Everywhere we go you find something to be built."

"Yes, and I did that in China, too."

The rest of the way she told him all about India and China.

"When I met you, Ahmad and I were just your guards. But you have taken us half way around the world and expanded our lives with your adventures. You are my blessing."

The sight of the walls of Babylon rising in the distance brought joy to her heart again.

"No one will ever own this city as I do. I am Queen Nitocris who designed and rebuilt a city. I am akin to Queen Samiramis who built the tunnel under the Euphrates, and to Egyptian Queen Nitocris whose name I share, and who was more powerful than all men,. Thank you, Daniel, for teaching me to follow my joy wherever I am, past and future."

Chapter 54

GOVERNOR ARAKHU

———— ❧ ————

The Ishtar Gate was in sight. What a joy to see it still shining as if floating above the ground. They were about to enter the gate when a guard stepped out in front of them.

"Stop, in the name of Governor Arakhu!"

Their mouths dropped open.

"What? Arakhu?"

"Who are you and what is your business here?"

"I am Queen Nitocris of Babylonia! This is my city. Please take me to the governor. He is my friend."

The guard stood frozen.

"Your pardon, Your Highness! But why do you ride in this lowly wagon?"

"My carriage broke down and this man kindly offered to bring me the rest of the way to Babylon. He is of the Persian Military Guard."

The guard recovered his composure quickly and saluted Karim.

"Please. Your Highness, enter and welcome. My guards will escort you to the palace. The Governor will be notified immediately."

Nitocris and Karim were amazed at how clean the streets were. It looked much like the day everyone moved into the rebuilt Babylon years ago. The palace sparkled in the sun as they approached it.

"Are we dreaming, Karim? Can this be happening? The city has recovered its glory long hidden under the dirt and trash."

"It is not a dream, Your Highness. It is your lifelong dedication to your vision that could not be destroyed. You are Babylon and neither can you be destroyed. I have seen that with my own eyes."

The guards saw to the wagon and horses. Queen Nitocris and Persian Military Guard Karim walked up the long steps to the palace. Governor Arakhu came to the top of the steps to greet them.

"What a triumphant reunion! Your Highness, welcome to your city and your palace. Karim, my friend, you have done well to be her friend and keep her safe. I am overwhelmed with joy! Come in with me. Your quarters and fresh clothing are being prepared for you at this moment."

"Governor, you must tell me how this came about. I left when the city was a locked down labor camp, and now you are the governor."

"I went to Cambyses' envoy with my military captains' credentials and asked if I could be of assistance to the great King Cambyses. Though I am older and a bit frail, I was quickly accepted. Cambyses had forgotten or did not know of my friendship with you. At least there was no mention of it. Where did you go?"

"I did not wish to go back to Arabia. I could not desert my Babylonian empire again as Nabonidus did. We went to Uruk. There I had much time to recover my strength and regain my joy thanks to Daniel's teachings. When we heard that King Cyrus was killed, I knew Cambyses would not be bothered with Babylon anymore. He was eager for the larger battles that he knew awaited him.

"So I am no longer hiding. Queen Nitocris is here to stay. You are now my governor thanks to all the events that led up to now. I am honored to have you with me now and always."

She moved into her mother's apartments. The servants cleaned it thoroughly for her. They were now fit for a queen again and she felt most comfortable there. Karim retired to the palace guards' quarters and continued to accompany her wherever she went.

Arakhu and Nitocris set about looking over plans for the governing of Babylon.

"Much still needs to be done. All of Cyrus' troops were taken to join Cambyses army. We have little security."

Nitocris began plans to recover what was left of the Babylonian military.

"I will send word out by envoys among the population for those soldiers who were alienated by Nabonidus and Belshazzar over the years to return."

Surprisingly, many returned with their sons who had come of age. They were proud to be known as the Babylonian Army again.

Arakhu and Nitocris set the first task which was to police the city so that it did not deteriorate, return to the debauchery, and the pigsty that it was. The people had to feel safe so they could create prosperity and be proud of their city.

The population was invited to neighborhood meetings to discuss the running of the city. They were shocked that anyone cared about them. They were hesitant to show up, but the soldiers went from door to door and kindly invited them.

The meetings encouraged pride in their city and in being Babylonians, regardless of the Persian takeover. The siege mentality faded away, brothels were few, and people were again coming out into the streets and markets.

When Queen Nitocris went out in her carriage, she had Karim beside her, a driver, and guards behind the carriage. It was still important to maintain the image and respect for royalty.

"Karim, I wish to go to the Chinese building, Yang Light of the Rising Sun."

"You want to find out who was burning the incense?"

"That is part of it. I want to know what condition the inside of the building is. It needs to be cleaned and some of the hangings that are left to be restored. I am sure it needs a lot of work. I was batting away cobwebs and stepping over pieces on the floor the last time I was there."

She did not mention Chaoxiang's ring. She would get that when she was alone in the old temple at the entrance and take it to the palace. Queen Nitocris of Babylonia could wear the jade ring and the bracelet now. The bracelet was purchased her first week in China. The ring was made out of love for a queen. They would no longer be in danger from the vagaries of her travels and escapes.

The doors swung open easily which signified that some restoration may have already been done. However, as they walked inside and lit the torches, nothing else had been touched. They walked around, lit more torches, and pulled back the coverings on the horizontal narrow windows close to the ceiling.

"Karim, I thought the place would be empty, that people would have taken everything. But much is still here!"

"I will send an officer for a cleaning crew. Be back in a few minutes."

It was the perfect time to get the ring and bracelet from behind the tile. She pulled the tile away, picked out the special box and bracelet, and replaced the tile. She put them in a special pocket on the inside of her robe and waited for Karim.

The palace cleaning crew came immediately and Karim came back with them.

"I will stay until you are ready to leave, Your Highness."

Nitocris showed them around the rooms and the temple. They were fascinated and a little frightened.

"Pardon, Your Highness, but we heard the rumors that the Chinese gods haunt this place. There are many strange things here."

"Please, people, do not be frightened. I built this building, we blessed it, and I assure you there are no gods haunting it. That is a story someone made up to scare thieves away."

The head of the crew apologized to Nitocris.

"Your Highness, we are sorry for the foolishness of some of our workers."

"I understand. I will stay here with you. You may ask me any questions and I will help you."

Actually, Nitocris enjoyed spending time in the building. She was delighted to have a reason to be there and in some way to be part of it again.

"Is there anywhere else you wish to go, Your Highness?"

"Yes, I desire to see the architectural school building. I wonder what has happened to it. I want to know if it has any students or if there are classes being held."

Nitocris was almost afraid to look, but relieved. The streets around it were clean and there was a carriage parked in front, almost like Master Jarem's carriage. It brought back a flood of memories.

They went to the door and walked in. There were a dozen or so elderly people sitting at the drafting tables. No one looked up. Tears came to her eyes and they quietly left.

"They are probably students from before Cyrus took the city. There are living quarters in the building and I hope they are occupied by more students as time goes on. Surely one of those students we saw could be the head of the school. I will speak with Arakhu about it."

Chapter 55

LOVE STILL AWAITS ME

―――――― ❦ ――――――

Nitocris sat alone in her mother's rooms contemplating all that had just happened.

"I have returned to the throne, but is this what the Egyptian Queen had in mind in sharing her inscription? Might she have left it for someone else to interpret for their own life? What is the love that I pursue? Where is it?"

She walked to the windows and looked out over Babylon. It still shone in the moonlight. Beautiful and cold. What made it warm was Jarem, Zaidu, Daniel, the students, and the Jews who welcomed her. She stood on their willing and capable shoulders to achieve her purpose, which was finite and seemed to be ending. Many of them were now gone.

"I had a life with people in it, some good and a few bad. But now I have no people, or just a few, but I do not belong. I have loved giving, but now people keep their distance. I felt so much joy coming back here and now the line between royalty and commoners has raised its ugly head again.

"Where was I happiest today? In the building of Yang. What was so precious about it today? Retrieving the ring, given in love. Oh my God and God of

Daniel, can I give up all I have accomplished here, leave it again never to return?"

She ran from her apartment, out of the palace, and started for the Chinese building on foot. Karim saw her leave and ran after her.

"Your Highness! Where are you going?"

She stopped and waited for him.

"Oh, Karim, I have a huge decision to make and I am afraid that I have already made it. These many months in my mother's apartment has brought me back to the inscription on Egyptian Queen Nitocris' sarcophagus. 'I go to where love awaits me.' My happiest hours are the ones I spend in the Chinese building. I was going there tonight to just sit there in the temple and pray."

Karim signaled for the carriage and he drove her there. The door of the building was open and someone was inside. She jumped down from the carriage and rushed in...hoping to catch whoever was lighting the incense.

A Chinese man stepped into the dim light and bowed.

"Yes, it is I, Fu Ling Yang, who has caused the incense to be burned. I did not do it myself but commissioned someone to do it. I am getting a little too old to rush back and forth over the land and sea. But the gods told me you would be here now, so I came."

Nitocris burst into tears and embraced him.

"Ninana, I know your loneliness and I know that love awaits you. Your life is no longer here. You have done all you can. You have given your all, but you must not give up your love. Will you come with me?"

She looked at Karim and back at Fu Ling Yang. Karim took her hand.

"Fu Ling Yang is right. It is time to find the fulfillment your heart desires. Follow your joy, your god, and find the greatest gift that life can offer...love."

Another person came quietly out of the darkness of the other rooms, Lishan.

"I packed your belongings and took you with me once before. Shall I do it again?"

Tears turned to laughter as they embraced.

"Yes, please do it dear Lishan."

"We will leave this very hour. I have a carriage that will take us to the Port of Ur and the ship that awaits us."

Nitocris could hardly believe her ears, hardly believe what was happening so quickly...again. It was as if life was constantly picking her up and taking her somewhere else, and now this.

Karim and Lishan went to the palace and came back not only with her belongings, but with Arakhu.

"I could not let you leave without saying goodbye. You have done so much for me and for Babylon. Karim and I can handle it from now on. Just as I gave up the military to be with Daniel and his teaching, so you must go in peace and follow your joy. If you have forgotten joy, then you have forgotten your god."

She hugged him and kissed his cheeks.

"Each one of you has taught me something about love. I will remember you with love."

Karim and Arakhu helped the three into the carriage and tearfully bid them farewell. The carriage rolled out of the Ishtar Gate for the last time.

Ninana left Queen Nitocris, her royal identity, in the coffin overhead in the top of the gate.

Word went throughout the city that someone had kidnapped the queen! The military guard rushed to the palace. Governor Arakhu met them on the steps.

"I fear she has passed away in the night and her body is now in her coffin at the top of the Ishtar Gate, as she wished. Always thank her when you pass through the gate. Remember that she built Babylon, she was Babylon, and she will remain at the top of her gate, her most treasured accomplishment. It will forever be a symbol of the greatness of Babylon to the world."

Ninana felt the peace that passes all understanding flow through her. Free from all of her royal duties, the weight of Babylonia no longer on her shoulders, she was tearful and at the same time light and joyful.

How good it was to see that Fu Ling Yang, though older, was not frail. He seemed to be vigorous as ever and his eyes always twinkling. Lishan was glowing and indeed a powerful woman in her own right.

"Do you and Shamhar have children, Lishan?"

"No, we do not. We decided to wait for you to come home to China."

"But how did you know I would come back?"

"I knew that love would not let you go but draw you back."

Ninana looked at her in amazement. But now you will have children? I pray it is not too late."

"We will see what the god's have in mind."

They looked at each other and burst out laughing.

"Oh, how good it is to laugh freely with such wonderful friends. I do not remember when the last time was that I felt this way. It was so long ago."

For the first time Ninana noticed that Fu Ling Yang had tears in the crinkled corners of his eyes.

"I feared I would not find you or that you were dead. Some said you fled to Persia. But I sailed to the Sea Port of UR when the gods told me you had returned. I am amazed at how favored we have always been."

"Yes, Master, I fled to Persia, then to Babylon, then to Jerusalem, then to Egypt and came back through all of those places again. I fled to Uruk to avoid being murdered by Cambyses. When he became king, he went to battle with Assyria and I was free to return as Queen Nitocris and rule Babylonia.

"I know of one god that favors me always, the god of Daniel. I met Daniel when I was young and still designing Babylon. He told me that to follow God was to follow his joy. And if he forgot joy, then he forgot God. So I hope I have learned to remember joy."

Chapter 56

THE DRIVING STORM

———————— ❧ ❧ ————————

They had so many stories to tell, to catch up with each other's lives. After many days of travel the port was in sight. The distance to the Port of Ur somehow did not seem as long as it had in the past. Eagerly Ninana walked down the dock to the familiar Chinese ship. Shamhar met her halfway and they embraced.

She turned to look back at Fu Ling Yang and Lishan. They were standing still.

"Is the ship not ready for us to board?"

"We have a surprise for you. Wait for a moment."

She turned to the ship again and saw Chaoxiang coming down the gangplank. She was so stunned that she could not move or breathe. He ran and caught her in his arms just as she was about to collapse.

"They could not keep me in China, Ninana. I have waited so long with hope and then without hope. When I knew they were coming to find you I threatened to get my own ship and follow them. So they relented and allowed me to come with them."

She leaned against his body, tears streaming down her cheeks. Words would not come. He picked her up and carried her off the dock toward the hotel.

"I think I can walk. You have waited for me as Queen Nitocris wrote on her tomb."

He set her on her feet.

"Who or what are you speaking about?"

"Chaoxiang! You speak my language!"

"Yes, I spent the time learning from Lishan should I ever see you again."

"The original Egyptian Queen Nitocris is a long story and I hope we have enough time or the rest of our lives to tell it to you."

"I will not let you go ever again. So you may tell me...all of it."

"I lost your child..."

"I know."

The five of them went to the hotel for dinner and to reserve rooms for the night.

"The ship will be ready tomorrow. Shamhar and I will see to the progress. We will sail at dawn when the tides go out."

Fu Ling Yang seemed never to age. He was as spry as ever, even though he said long journeys were a challenge.

Much as Lishan wanted to stay with Ninana, she knew they needed time alone.

"Master, I will go with you. I will see to the cleanliness of the staterooms."

She turned to Ninana and Chaoxiang.

"We have built small compartments on board so we can have privacy from the crew and a room for meals and gatherings. Shamhar and I will come for you tomorrow when all is in readiness."

Ninana embraced Lishan.

"I am so very happy that we are all together again. It has been a long journey and I never expected to be coming back to China. And thank you for teaching Chaoxiang my language! What a wonderful surprise."

"That was his way of honoring his love for you."

Ninana gazed at Chaoxiang over dinner. Other than a few white streaks in his hair, like Fu Ling Yang, he looked the much the same as when she left China.

They delighted just in being in each other's presence. They went up to their room and lay down together touching and talking.

"My love, I hope I am too old to conceive another child."

"We will see if the gods have that in mind…"

At breakfast the ship's captain came to the hotel dining room.

"Your pardon, Master. There is a storm brewing in the Arabian Sea. It is said to be moving away from us. Perhaps we should delay sailing another day if you agree."

Fu Ling Yang thought for a few minutes.

"We can sail and if the storm comes our way we can find a port on the coast of India. Does that seem reasonable?"

"I agree. We will pray to the sea gods for calm and prepare to sail."

Bowing, the captain left the dining room. They all got up and followed him to the ship. Shamhar and Chaoxiang trotted down the dock to the ship and boarded. Fu Ling Yang, Lishan, and Ninana walked slowly enjoying the cooler morning air. It would soon be quite hot.

The sail through the Makran Sea was quiet. They passed through the strait and out toward the Arabian Sea. The five sat together on deck regaling each other with stories of their adventures.

Shamhar was amazed that his teacher made it all the way to Egypt.

"What drew you to Egypt? It is such a long way and dangerous."

"My name, Nitocris. It is an Egyptian name. My father invaded Egypt and probably heard it there. An Egyptian princess named Nitocris lived almost one hundred years earlier. Then there was the one I was most interested in, Queen Nitocris of two thousand years ago. I wanted to find the tomb of that queen and learn what I could about her. She was said to be smarter and more powerful than all the men and would not put up with their foolishness."

"Ha! Did you find it?"

"Yes. I was not sure what I would find when I got there. The tomb was very plain and nearly ruined. But there was an inscription on the sarcophagus. When translated for me it said, 'I go to where love awaits me.' It was puzzling. I did not know what it meant, but it stuck in my mind and seemed to draw me. I looked everywhere in my travels to find its meaning. I finally found it here."

Chaoxiang moved closer to her and she leaned into his shoulder.

"Master Fu Ling Yang, do you think the caption of the ship would marry us? Is it not customary that a ship's captain has the power to do that?"

"Yes, it is, Ninana. But it is rare since women do not often travel on ships. Chaoxiang, if this is agreeable to you, will you accompany me to the captain's quarters?"

"It is agreeable. Ninana Nitocris must accompany us. Queen Nitocris was said to be more powerful than all men, so this Nitocris will please join us."

They all laughed.

The captain was a little flustered.

"Yes, Master Fu Ling Yang. But I am not sure I remember how this must be done!"

"I know and I will help you."

While they planned the ceremony, Shamhar and Lishan did what they could to have the right elements for a Chinese wedding. This was not the first time Ninana and Lishan planned a Chinese wedding and they had great fun finding items to represent the elements.

Ninana found some incense.

"I wish we could be in the temple of Yang of the Rising Sun for this. We will just have to close our eyes and imagine it."

In a short and moving ceremony Chaoxiang and head of the Architectural School of Guangzhou and Ninana Nitocris, head of the Architectural School in Babylon were married as they sailed into the Arabian Sea.

The captain's first mate came to Fu Ling Yang looking for the captain.

"Master! The storm is stalled in the middle of the sea and could come our way. The wind is changing in the wrong direction."

The captain heard him and came out onto the deck.

"Sail closer to the shoreline. We may have to dock somewhere if it comes this way."

Chaoxiang and Shamhar followed him to be of assistance. Ninana and Lishan went into a stateroom to secure their belongings should they need to leave the ship. Fu Ling Yang watched from the prow of the ship.

The sailors immediately turned the ship toward the coast. The sky to the south was darkening and waves were getting higher. They turned the sails to the wind to increase their speed. Soon the captain ordered them to lower the sails.

"The wind will tip us over. It is getting far too strong! Break out the oars! We will head for the Port of Debal on the Indus River."

Chapter 57

SEA CLIFFS, ROCKS, AND SAND

High waves washed over the docks and walkways. Docking was impossible. Other ships escaping the storm clogged the harbor. Some were coming loose from their moorings and blowing into each other.

They sailed along the shoreline but not too close. The sandy beach disappeared under the water and soon they were facing piles of rocks and high sea cliffs.

The captain shouted at the oarsmen.

"We are too close to the shore! Turn starboard! Starboard now!"

Even without the sails the wind was blowing them toward the rocks and the soon oars had little effect. The ship was passing the rocks and drifting toward the sea cliffs. A rock under the water caught the bottom of the ship and ripped a hole in it.

Shamhar and Chaoxiang scrambled to the stateroom where Lishan and Ninana were holding on to whatever they could.

"Grab the belongings. We must abandon the ship. It is listing and may turn over!"

The ship was snagged and afloat long enough for everyone to climb off onto the rocks. They made a human chain over the wet rocks to pull everyone to the shore. Soaked and bedraggled they scrambled up into a shallow cave in the cliffs to wait out the storm.

It seemed hours until the storm passed and then suddenly the sun shone as if nothing had happened. The captain and his first mate slid down out of the cave and went to find a way to the port. Much of the beach was washed away and what was left was not stable.

Parts of the ship were still laying on the rocks. The sailors climbed back to them to salvage what they could of the equipment. They hauled oars, boards, ropes, and sails onto the shore until the rest of the ship slowly sank into the surf and disappeared.

Ninana helped pull some of the items to the shore.

"What will we do with these things?"

The captain came tramping back through the debris.

"We will sell or trade them. Then decide what we need to do. Certainly we no longer have a ship. Our freighters will not know anything happened to us because we are ahead of them and far out of our usual shipping channel."

Fu Ling Yang was his usual undaunted self.

"I will go to Debal and look for a merchant that I know. They come down the Silk Road on the Indus River bringing trade to the sea. He has his own storage building here."

He picked up a piece of an oar for a walking stick and started briskly toward the port buildings. Ninana, Chaoxiang, Lishan, and Shamhar came out of the cave with their belongings. Ninana hurried to Fu Ling Yang's side.

"We will go with you. There must be a hotel where we can rest and plan what we will do next."

Chaoxiang took her arm and Shamhar Lishan's, and their bundles, as they hiked over the debris. They hesitated, looking back to where the ship sank.

"I am sure the captain and his crew can do the salvage work without us getting in their way."

Fu Ling Yang smiled, the familiar crinkle in the corners of his eyes appeared.

"I am happy to have such a capable family with me. Sometimes I forget you are not children. And you, Ninana, have climbed over the wreckage of Babylon all your young life."

The waves began quieting down so they could walk along the shore. The boats in the seaport were wrecked, but the seaport seemed to be intact and undamaged. Fu Ling Yang led them to the storage building. Its doors were open. People inside were moving the contents about.

Xiang Qing came running to them.

"Fu Ling Yang! Is that you? Was your shipwrecked in this storm?"

"Ah so it was, my friend. We did not make it into the port and were fortunate to get off before it sank."

"Fortune always favors you, Fu Ling Yang! Come in. How can I help you?"

"These are my royal family, Ninana, Chaoxiang, Lishan, and Shamhar."

"Ah, I recognize you, Lishan, even though you were just a child then. Welcome."

Lishan smiled and silently bowed.

"Our ship's captain and his crew will be along shortly. They are salvaging what they can from the wreckage. They hope to sell some of the equipment here at the port."

"I will send for people to help them. I am sure a sale can be arranged quickly. Many ships have been dashed here and there will be much trading and repair work."

Xiang Qing sent a worker to the hotel to have rooms and food prepared.

The next day they all gathered in the dining room at the hotel to plan what to do. The ship's captain and crew decided to stay at the port and find passage on another ship perhaps to India if not all the way to Guangzhou.

"Will you go with us, Master?"

"It would be difficult us to travel that way. Being royalty we could be kidnapped, shipwrecked again, or worse.

"I have an idea. It may sound crazy, but I am a sister/cousin of the Amazon Warrior Women. If we go up the river to Scythia, they may help us get to the Silk Road. We might join a caravan to travel home. The danger would be no more than traveling by sea and at least we would not drown."

Xiang Qing entered their conversation with great interest.

"There is danger either way. I can get you passage on a river boat to take you safely to Scythia. My people there can assist you in making the connections you need. I will hire trustworthy guards to go with you and see you through the Khyber Pass."

Ninana looked around at all of them. They all nodded. Fu Ling Yang was worried, but agreed this might be the best way.

"Ninana, you have all the gods and goddesses watching over you wherever you go. You have been in a war, traveled to Egypt and back, escaped

Cambyses, returned as the queen, and now with us coming home to China. We will go forward and have one more great adventure and this time we are together."

Chaoxiang, Lishan, and Shamhar lifted cups of wine and chimed in together.

"One more great adventure together!"

The next day they bid farewell to the captain and seamen. The captain raised a cup of rice wine and announced to them,

"We will see you in Guangzhou. Pray to the gods that we all arrive safely and are reunited."

"In Guangzhou!"

Fu Ling Yang turned to Xiang Qing.

"Thank you for your help my friend. If we do not meet again, know you are forever in our prayers."

The guards stepped up beside them ready to go.

Chapter 58

THE INDUS RIVER

———————— ❦ ————————

The accommodations on board the river boat were very comfortable. Xiang Qing had chosen well. They could look forward to many days of peaceful sailing up the river. The river water coming from the mountains was cool until it rolled into the hot river basin and met the sea. It was an increasing relief from the heat of the day as they neared the snowy mountains. Time to rest and recover.

Ninana turned to Chaoxiang smiling.

"My husband! This is the first opportunity I have had to think what those words mean. This is the first time I have said that with pride, the first time I have chosen rather than be forced to marry. I have gone where love awaits me. I looked everywhere to find what that is. Now the search is over and I am not sure what to do."

They both laughed.

"All the stories you have told me about your life could not be done by a lesser woman! I do not think there is a time when you did not know what to do! You are always sure footed, ready to act, ready to solve huge problems. You are more like that Egyptian Queen that you might think."

"No one sees the butterflies flitting around in my stomach."

"Go to where love awaits you? How can you be sure it was me? I might have married or died in China."

"This was the inscription scratched on the sarcophagus of the ancient Queen Nitocris, whose name I share. I have been looking for its meaning since I left Egypt. I am happy you are not married or dead!"

"I am happy about that, too! My family wanted me to marry, but I was devoted to my architecture and the school. They were about to arrange a marriage for me when they died of a fever. My relatives were very elderly and died with that wish on their lips. They can all be happy that their dying wish is finally fulfilled. But marriage has been so far from my mind. Now I am not sure what to do next."

They began laughing. Lishan and Shamhar joined them with some rice wine to share.

"May we join you? What is your laughter about?"

He was not embarrassed to tell them. Chaoxiang had worked with them at the school in the years after they returned to China.

"I have never been married and Ninana has been a widow for many years. Her marriage was not of her choosing. Now we are married, happy to have chosen each other, and we are not sure what comes next."

Ninana could hardly stop laughing.

"Yes, tell us what comes next...I mean...in our future...being married."

The captain of the river boat approached them.

"We are approaching the mountains where the river has its origin. The air will be significantly cooler and there will be strong winds. Use caution walking the decks in the wind."

Fu Ling Yang acknowledged the captain and turned to join the four who were still experiencing the merriment of their conversation.

"My dear family, the current will be stronger now and the water colder. You may want to use the heavy robes Master Xiang Qing supplied for us. The breezes that come down from the mountains are cold and blustery. Walking on the deck can be hazardous and slippery."

They saluted him with their wine cups.

"So now may I ask the source of your merriment and laughter?"

Lishan handed him a cup of rice wine and patted the seat beside her.

"We are discussing what comes next after the wedding. What should the future hold? Have you some wisdom for us?"

"I know nothing more about my own future and what it holds. How might I know yours? Let me think on this."

They refilled their cups of rice wine and reached for fruit and cakes.

"The future starts in your heart and mind. The strongest energy source is the heart where love resides. You weave your thoughts around that love and ask the gods to show you where it will lead. You must listen very carefully. Still your minds and ask the heart what it wants to tell you.

"Remember, Ninana, when we went to the shop where the man made a special container for your ring? What do you remember it?"

Ninana fingered Chaoxiang's ring on her finger, thankful it has not been lost in the sea.

"He seemed very focused on my energy. He measured that energy on special papers and then dismissed us. The container could be opened only by me . My energy would match it. It would recognize me and open."

"Yes, very good. You were so mystified."

"I was completely unable to comprehend. But then I was mystified many times in my experiences in China. The philosophies, the mysteries, the symbolic dances, and stories. Even the raising of silkworms which I do not care to do."

She shivered.

"Are you cold, my love?"

"No, I just cannot be comfortable with worms that remind me of snakes like the one I nearly stepped on when we were rebuilding Babylon. It always makes me shiver."

Fu Ling Yang smiled with his crinkly eyes nearly closing.

"But do you understand how the loving care of the people eventually transforms them into beautiful garments? It matters not how they appear, but the transformation that is possible. We are growing older and may not look so beautiful as time goes on, but the power of transformation remains within us and shines out forever."

Lishan put her hand on Ninana's arm.

"I am Chinese and Shamhar is not. It is hard for us to advise you because we are opposites. I know how to be the Chinese wife and Shamhar knows how to be the architect. You, Ninana, a royal woman architect from Babylon. Chaoxiang is a Chinese man and architect. There will be differences."

Fu Ling Yang nodded with his eyes closed, and then continued.

"Yes, my family, there will be differences. Differences can be good if you come from your heart. This is part of your new adventure. You are all highly educated and accomplished. When you share your differences everyone becomes new. You educate each other and expand your world. This is your future and only you can determine what it will be day by day."

They nodded in agreement and became thoughtful as the rice wine began to take hold. They napped for a while until the bell was rung announcing that dinner was ready and about to be served.

Chapter 59

THE KHYBER PASS

———— ❧ ———

A spur of the Silk Road came through valleys and over a mountain pass. It ended in a market area down by the river. The river dock seemed tiny compared to the ones on seaports she was used to seeing.

Ninana gazed up at the high snowy mountain peaks.

"Babylonia is flat! I have not seen snow or mountains this high. How do we cross them?"

Fu Ling Yang was standing at the rail beside her, Chaoxiang on the other side of her. Fu Ling Yang had seen these mountains many times.

"There are passes through the mountains and valleys between them. The Silk Road travels through the Khyber Pass to meet the main road farther north. We will travel by horseback and have pack animals for our belongings.

"Our guides are known as sherpas. They are skilled in traveling the heights as well as assisting our guards in defense during attacks. The altitude of the pass measures over three thousand feet above the level of the sea and is over thirty miles long."

Chaoxiang turned from the rail of the boat while watching the approach to the dock.

"How will we travel?"

Fu Ling Yang smiled. He knew Chaoxiang's concern.

"Horses, donkeys, mules, camels and whatever else is recommended."

"Well, I have not ridden a horse. I am sure it cannot be too difficult."

Ninana laughed.

"I remember my first experience riding a horse. True, the riding was not difficult, but getting off and trying to walk when we finally stopped was painful. Zaidu had to pull me off the horse the second day of constant travel and carry me to a place to sit. It was a while before my legs would work properly."

"Perhaps I could just walk…"

"Walking thirty rough miles over passes and through valleys would be worse!"

"Do you think it might have been better to take our chances on the sea?"

Ninana slipped her arm around him.

"We will know that if our sailors make it home to Guangzhou. And if they do not, sadly we will have that answer too."

Lishan and Shamhar met them at the rail as the boat docked. She was concerned. Someone called out from the dock.

"Master Fu Ling Yang! Master Xiang Qing has ordered your arrangements for travel and lodgings. He gave them to your riverboat captain and they were given to us. We will take you to a hotel while they are finalized."

The men didn't look right. Lishan felt there was something very wrong. They looked anxious and shifty. She turned to the riverboat captain.

"Is this true, Captain? Do you know these men? Did you give them a message from Xiang Qing?"

He called his first officer to him.

"Are these the men you gave the message to?"

He looked at the men.

"No, they are not. Please keep our passengers on board!"

He ran down onto the dock with two of the sailors and grabbed them. They struggled to get away and the sailors immediately killed them. Xiang Qing's orders were tucked in one of the men's robes.

"We will go to find the man I contacted. He may well be dead, but we will look for him anyway."

The went into the market looking for him. Not finding him they went toward the hotel. A stable boy ran to them.

"Come! There is someone in the stable badly hurt."

They ran to the stable with him. It was their man lying in the stall alive and groaning. They carried him to a hotel room and found a physician to attend him.

One guard went back to the boat to summon everyone to disembark and gathered at the hotel.

Fu Ling Yang met with the riverboat captain and sailors before they went back to the boat.

"Our thanks and gratitude for your help, Captain. I will read Xiang Qing's orders, make the connections, and carry on from here. Your efforts to help royalty will be rewarded."

They stayed with their guards at the small hotel for the week until the man was recovered enough to help Fu Ling Yang find the right connections.

Chaoxiang, Shamhar, Ninana, and Lishan wandered through the marketplaces, walked along the river, and talked about ideas for their future. Fu Ling Yang had given them much to ponder.

A small caravan was put together with a mule team, wagon, pack animals and horses. There were sherpas, guards, and some workmen.

Ninana gazed up at the mountains and the pass.

"What do we need workmen for? What will they do?"

"They will be needed to clear the road through the pass. Sometimes it is filled with snow or there are avalanches. But none of them are likely this time of year."

Fu Ling Yang gave them all mittens, heavy robes, hoods, face coverings and fur lined boots. They had not seen this kind of clothing before. Ninana turned them over and over examining each one.

"We will look like the sherpas. They wear these things."

"It will be very cold through the pass since it is high above the level of the sea. The higher the mountains the colder is the air. There are cold winds that can blow night and day. We must not let our skin be exposed to the cold or it will become gray and die. The sherpas know this. We will follow their advice and put these things on when they tell us it is time."

"How can the mountains be cold in this desert land? The valleys and deserts are very hot."

"Yes, Ninana, they are. That is because they are low like the level of the sea. But the air high in the mountains and higher beyond our senses is always very cold. You have seen the mountains above the Indus River. They are never warm even though the sun shines there and the snow stays up there forever. The valley floors never change their heat."

It was not far before the road grew step and rocky. They could feel the chill blowing down from the heights and beginning to touch them. Chaoxiang and Ninana preferred to walk until their breath became labored. Lishan ran to them.

"Please, you must ride in the wagons or on an animal. The air is thinner the higher we go and it becomes hard to breathe. You must rest or it will make you sick."

Ninana and Chaoxiang looked at each other and nodded their agreement. Chaoxiang rubbed the pains beginning in his chest.

"I have never felt this before. My heart is pounding and my breathing is painful."

Shamhar came to him immediately and helped him into a wagon. A Sherpa came back to check on him and brought a potion for him to drink. Fu Ling Yang was beside them.

"It will help with the sickness. You are not accustomed to the heights. Sherpas do not get this sickness because they live in the heights and their bodies are acclimated to it."

Ninana was a little frightened for Chaoxiang.

"Lishan, why do I not experience this? Why not everyone? And Shamhar?"

"I will ask a Sherpa. They always know these things."

Ninana picked up a heavy robe and tucked it in around Chaoxiang. He soon fell asleep.

"The Sherpa said that women are not very affected. Shamhar is younger than Chaoxiang."

That surprised Ninana. She had not thought of the difference in their ages.

"Of course. Shamhar was her young student. Chaoxiang and Fu Ling Yang were older and had been friends for years. Why did I not think of that?"

Chapter 60

CHALLENGE IN THE DESERT

It was good to come down from the heights. The air was warm and they could take off the heavy apparel. Much to Ninana's relief, Chaoxiang was feeling much himself again. The Sherpas collected the heavy coverings and boots and packed them in the wagons.

"Are we taking those with us?"

Fu Ling Yang smiled and picked up his walking stick that the Sherpas has given to him.

"Yes, there are more mountains before we get to Guangzhou. They will not be as high as those that produce the source of the Indus River, but we will have cold nights. We will be glad to have them. And my walking stick. The Sherpas gave it to me. They told me an old man should have one."

Ninana burst out laughing.

"An old man? I never thought of you as an old man!"

"I pay no attention to years. I just live joyfully and see myself as young."

"And Chaoxiang?"

"Ah so, he is like my son as you and Lishan are like my daughters. And now Shamhar is added to my family. You are my only children. My wife and child died in childbirth a very long time ago. Then I began to travel the Silk Road as a merchant and never returned to my former way of life."

"Did you love her? I am sorry. I should not have…"

"It is all right, Ninana. We were very young. Our marriage was arranged. We had no chance to mature into love. But we were kind and gentle."

They traveled through rough, rocky hills and dry stony valleys. Nothing could grow in the land except for a few sparsely watered areas. They stopped in Kapisa where the Sherpas left them and returned to the Khyber Pass.

Fu Ling Yang traced a map in the dirt of where the Silk Road would go.

"It is thousands of miles and many months of travel. If the gods are with us we will arrive safely in Guangzhou. It is a perilous journey."

Ninana and Chaoxiang walked through the market and met a group of strangely familiar people. Ninana recognized them.

"These are Persians! What are they doing here? We must go back to our camp."

She started to cover her face but too late. A man approached her.

"You look like the Queen of Babylonia."

She turned away covering her face and her ring.

"You look like Queen Nitocris of Babylonia!"

Chaoxiang pushed the man back and ushered Ninana away. She fingered the dao sword under her robe.

The man did not pursue them.

"We must tell the others. We are in much danger. They might be Cambyses' people. Could they be looking for me? Is Cambyses pursuing me? How could he know where I am? I left Queen Nitocris in her tomb at the top of the Ishtar Gate."

Fu Ling Yang saw them coming and hurried to met them.

"Is something wrong? Has something happened?"

"Cambyses! Someone in the market recognized me as Queen Nitocris of Babylonia."

"I did you answer him?"

"I said nothing. Chaoxiang put his arm around me and we hurried away without responding. I thought announcing that the queen had died and was in her tomb would be enough to keep us safe.

"Someone in Babylon was a spy from Persia. That is the only way anyone could know the truth. They may have followed us to the Port of Dabel. Surely they were not on the sea in the storm. They must have known me and knew I would travel the Silk Road. They could easily come from Persia and meet us here. What can we do?"

Drawing a jian from his robe, Chaoxiang turned to go back to the market.

"I will find them before they can notify others."

Ninana wanted to object, but Fu Ling Yang stopped her.

"He is a skilled fighter. Trust him. He pulled you from the jaws of the sea and these people will be no match for him."

Ninana caught her breath. She had not thought of Chaoxiang as a warrior.

"I will go help him. I am a warrior."

"Let him do it this time, Ninana. I know you would take on the entire population of Persia for him, for us, and everyone you care about."

Eventually Chaoxiang returned to their camp with blood on his sword.

"I caught those two, but they have a small camp in the mountains nearby. I climbed to a high point and saw it. When they do not return to their camp, others will come looking for them. I quickly buried them under some rocks and sand, but they might still be found."

"How many are in the camp?"

"Perhaps twenty or more. I could not get closer."

Fu Ling Yang squatted on the ground beside a map he scratched in the dirt.

"We must leave the Silk Road for now. We will go straight north, follow the foothills to the Amu Daria River and follow it to the Silk Road and Yarkand."

Ninana looked helplessly at the map.

"Would it be better to fight them here?"

"We do not know how many there are. I know these places well because I have traveled here for many years. There are merchants in Yarkand who will assist us to find a camel caravan from there. We have a very long way to go."

"I am so sorry to bring this danger to you, all the people I love. I should have stayed in Babylon and continued to be the queen. I commanded an army there…"

She collapsed into Chaoxiang's arms and let the tears flow.

"My love, we will live together and we will die together, however that turns out and at what time the gods decree."

In the comfort of his arms she began to hear Daniel's words in her mind.

"No one forces me, Princess. I joyfully and willingly go where my God leads me."

"Oh, Daniel! I have not forgotten you, but I forgot to follow my joy. Your god and my god. My joy is here and now. Our god is here and now. How could I forget. But you said I would forget from time to time because I came late to the teachings of God."

Chapter 61

ESCAPE INTO THE WILDERNESS

There were no roads. No paths of any kind. The seven of them battled their way through rocks, watching for vermin, spiders, and snakes. They were on foot and led the pack animals. It was safer to stay high in the foothills even though it might have been easier to follow the lower valleys. They put on the heavy footwear to protect their feet. The guards occasionally went to a high point to look back over their trail to see if anyone followed them.

The guards volunteered to go into the city first and ask in the market if there were Persians. Fu Ling Yang agreed.

"Be aware that they will be traveling fast on horses and will likely be there already. Do not mention any names. Many people on the Silk Road know me or know my name. I will go into the city to find my market contacts after you return."

"They will travel on the Silk Road and try to catch us when we return to it in Yarkand. We can stay just outside of the city."

Shamhar and Chaoxiang went a little ahead to look for passageways through the terrain.

Fu Ling Yang was consulting a small instrument.

"What is that, Master?"

"Ah, it is something that tells me if we are going the right direction."

"How does it do that? More of the energy mysteries like my ring box?"

"Yes, something like that. It is called magnetic and always points north. I traded for it with a merchant from the north. I can navigate by the stars unless it is day, cloudy, or the dust storms kick up. This instrument never fails."

"Please tell me how to navigate by the stars."

They sat on the hillsides in the evenings while he charted the stars for her, scratching the patterns in the dirt with a stick. When it became darker he pointed them out in the sky.

Ninana became an avid student of the skies and Chaoxiang was interested as well. He could sense the same drive to learn that she exhibited at his school of architecture.

"It seems that whatever you do, you become masterful at it."

She smiled and shook her head.

"I have not mastered the art of sword fighting. I can defeat an ordinary untrained brigand, but not the Amazon Warrior Women. I have much to learn."

Approaching Yarkand, the guards went ahead. They did not return. Fu Ling Yang was sure they had been killed.

"That must mean there are many Persians in Yarkand looking for us. We cannot go in."

There was a rumble of horses' hooves. They were about to hide, but Ninana drew her jian and stood firm.

On the horses were Amazon Warrior women and the wounded guards.

"Do these belong to you? They were greatly outnumbered. There were more than thirty.

Lishan stepped up to translate.

"I know you! Is Ninana our sister/cousin warrior with you?"

"I am here!"

"I am Polydora, Queen of the Amazons, descendant of the great warrior queen, Penthesilea. These are my sister warriors."

"I remember you, my sister/cousin. I am honored to be in your presence again."

Chaoxiang and Shamhar rushed to take the battered guards from the horses and carry them to a blanket.

"Ninana, our sister/cousin, what is your business here? Do you need assistance?"

They dismounted and sat down with Ninana, Fu Ling Yang, and Lishan. Lishan introduced the men.

"These men are our husbands, Shamhar and Chaoxiang. Fu Ling Yang is our royal father from Guangzhou."

The warrior women listened with interest at all Ninana told them.

"We hate the Persians. They insist upon attacking us. We defeated them and killed King Cyrus. He was warned. We will also kill Cambyses and his brigands if they interfere with us."

"They killed King Cyrus as they promised! It does not matter now. It was wise that I never mentioned knowing Cyrus."

"We are returning to Guangzhou."

"It seems we have met before when you were returning to Guangzhou."

"That is true. We were much closer to Guangzhou then. Now we are thousands of miles away. We were returning by sea, but our ship was sunk in a storm."

"It seems horses are safer than ships. We are willing to escort you to the place we last met. Then we must turn back."

"Your assistance is accepted and very much appreciated."

"We will trade your pack animals for horses so our travel will be faster. We will come for you at dawn and with extra horses."

They mounted their horses, turned, and galloped away.

The guards were not too badly hurt. Fu Ling Yang insisted they go into Yarkand to recover and return to the Port of Debal to Xiang Qing. He gave them a royal seal to pay their passage.

Chaoxiang and Shamhar came back from getting the guards to Yarkand.

"So, Shamhar, it appears we will be riding horses. I still would rather walk, but I am sure I could not keep up."

"The Amazons are disdainful of men in general. It would be good not to show weakness or any challenge to their leadership. Follow Lishan's lead. That is our best chance of getting home...alive."

As always the Amazons arrived in full gallop and stopped abruptly kicking up sand. Lishan made sure everything was ready. The horses were packed and they mounted the other ones.

They passed Yarkand and headed for the southern spur of the Silk Road. The flat desert lay before them and they traveled fast. The horses seemed tireless. When they stopped for water, food, and rest, the five were more than ready.

Chaoxiang tried his best not to show how stiff and sore he was, but Ninana knew. She tried not to smile.

Chapter 62

AMAZON SISTER/COUSIN

Polydora invited Ninana and Lishan to sit with her when they stopped. Lishan was very busy translating and enjoying the interaction.

"Who are these men with you? Husbands and father. Why do you need men? I want to know why women need men, aside from making babies."

Ninana took a deep breath.

"I have not needed a man or men until I discovered that I was missing love in my life. I am too old to have babies, getting to old to fight, old to be the queen of Babylonia, too old for war. I have accomplished all of this. What I want is love. Someone to love me and live the rest of my life with me. If Cambyses catches up with me he will kill me and I will lose my chance at a life of love."

Polydora sat silently for a while.

"I cannot say that I understand your desire for love, but I do understand that Cambyses needs to die and I will not let him kill you, my sister/cousin. So, you love this man, Chaoxiang? Why?"

"We were both at the top of our professions as architects. We both conducted architectural schools, but in different countries. We understood each other's professional passion and that somehow turned into love for each other. We were married on the ship before a storm came and it sank."

Polydora gasped and burst out laughing and laughing.

"I told you horses were more reliable than ships! Did you conclude the ceremony before it sank?"

And she laughed some more.

"I like your stories! You must tell me more of them. Now, who is Queen Nitocris?"

"She is an ancient Egyptian queen. I also have her name."

"Are you a queen?"

"I was Queen Nitocris of Babylonia, until King Cyrus attacked and took the city and the empire. He promised to save the City of Babylon because I designed and built it and I begged him to. He would not save my throne. So I am no longer the queen. My city was saved but now it is in the hands of Cambyses."

"Does he want to kill you because you were a queen?"

"No. Because we were escaping from Egypt when he bragged that he was the Prince of Persia and would take Egypt from Assyria. They imprisoned him but he escaped. I was in Egypt to find out about Queen Nitocris. When I was crossing the waterway back to Gaza, he tried to grab my carriage. I would have been trapped in Egypt. They hate Babylonians, too. I ran over him with the carriage and escaped without him to Gaza. His pride is very important to him. He would kill me for it."

"You ran over him! You are amazing. A true sister/cousin. Now tell me what I can do for you. Is there anything you want besides love?"

"Yes, I want my sisters to teach me to fight with the dao and jian swords. The last time I sparred with one of you, my sisters, I was not very good. She easily flipped the sword from my hand."

"Yes, I seem to remember that. You were holding it wrong. We will teach you. Then what will you do?"

"If Cambyses gets past you, I will kill him myself."

"Do you think he can get by us?"

"No, I do not."

"Good. We will get started."

Ninana spent down times practicing with the swords. She spent evenings with Fu Ling Yang studying the stars. Shamhar and Chaoxiang went hunting in the hills for game to help feed everyone.

They moved on to the village of Cherchen where the Amazons were known and respected. It was on the Tarim River that came down from the mountains and rushed north into the desert. It was a pleasant place to rest from the desert sand, wind, and travel.

Ninana, Chaoxiang, Lishan, and Shamhar spent time over wine and bread, talking about their travels, how close they might be to Xian,6

. and the road home through China.

"Mongols! Mongols!"

The merchants were shouting. They shut down their shops and hid. The Amazons crept out into the market area to see the Mongols rushing in on their short Mongolian ponies. Ninana saw them, too, and ran to help the Amazons. She drew her jian double edged sword and swung at the closest one. He dropped from his pony and lay bleeding on the ground. Next thing she knew, Chaoxiang was beside her, his sworn drawn and cutting down one that was coming from behind them.

The battle was short. They and the Amazons dispatched all of the raiders. Lishan and Shamhar gathered up their shaggy ponies and put them in a corral. The merchants came out of hiding and cheered.

Polydora came to Ninana and Chaoxiang.

"Good work. Chaoxiang, I did not know you were a swordsman. I see some of why she loves you. We are going to ride out a way to see if there are more. They tend to have a few in hiding in the hills waiting to help them carry away the spoils. Would you guard the town until we get back?"

"It will be an honor, Polydora."

"So now we are guards! Another adventure."

Chaoxiang and Ninana laughed as they stood on guard for the rest of the day. The Amazons returned at dusk.

"It was as we thought. There were eight of them hiding. We got them all. When word gets out they will not bother this town again. We will leave tomorrow to meet a camel caravan."

Chapter 63

XIAN CITY

Ninana was most puzzled. She glanced at Fu Ling Yang. He nodded. Polydora nodded in return.

"A camel caravan, Polydora?"

"Yes. It will be safer for you. You will not be so exposed as we get closer to China. This close to China it is known that you are all royalty. My warriors and I will be traveling through the mountains as a shortcut and will meet you on the Silk Road again southeast of Xian. We will assure your safe passage with the head of the caravan. He owes us for our defense of this caravans many times. We will trade your horses for camels."

Ninana turned to Chaoxiang with a big smile on her face.

"Now you can learn to ride a camel, my love. What an education and a lot of experience you are getting! Another adventure!"

Fu Ling Yang chuckled at him.

"You insisted upon coming on the ship with us, my friend. Now look at what is happening. The adventures never end."

"I have come to expect it. Marriage and shipwreck. But I did not think of camels!"

"They are more comfortable than horses but much slower. Camel caravans travel slowly."

Shamhar and Lishan were excited at the prospect of actually traveling with a caravan.

"We saw camel caravans at the western end of the Silk Road on our journey after our wedding. We were always sorry we had to leave so quickly because of trouble that was brewing. Our guards insisted we leave before dawn."

They rode to the caravan where the captain was waiting for them. Their camels were ready and the pullers were about to shout at their lines of camels to get them started.

The captain gave them flowing abayas to wear which would shade them from the sun in the day and keep them warm at night.

Chaoxiang was doubtful but walked courageously to the camel. Ninana came trotting up behind him.

"Wait. I am going to ride behind you."

"On the same camel?"

"Yes. I want to be able to talk to you. If we are on two camels we will be separated for weeks."

The captain gave them instructions on how mount and lean when the camel was getting up on its legs. Some elderly men were sitting atop the cargo of the pack camels. They were former camel pullers who became to old to pull the camels, but had no home other than the caravans. The men walking were guards and if necessary, those on the pack camels would also defend the caravan in case of an attack.

Lishan decided to ride with Shamhar, too. Fu Ling Yang was happy to ride alone with his thoughts and meditations. Chaoxiang managed to mount the camel easily. He hadn't expected it to kneel down.

"Ninana, these are the most ungainly creatures and they make terrible noises."

"Yes, but their stride is quite graceful and easy, not like trotting horses."

When they were all safely mounted, Polydora gathered the horses, waved farewell, and galloped away with the warriors. All the camel pullers shouted and pulled the first camel in their strings. They moved forward and the rest grudgingly followed.

The rocking of the camel's gait soon lulled them to sleep. Ninana laid her head on Chaoxiang's back, her arms around him, and drifted into a nap. The huge camel saddle held them securely so they would not fall off.

They slept, they ate, and they talked through the weeks it took to reach Xian. They were close to China, but there was still nearly a thousand miles to go after Xian. Ninana thought of all that she left behind her as she rode.

"The Persians are far behind. Cambyses will not pursue me any longer. The City of Babylon will survive and live on. My work there will be a sign to the ages of the glory of Babylon. It seems that I have left Daniel far behind, and yet he is still very much with me. Without him I would not have thought to follow joy. I would not have realized that my love of our people was right. It has been a long road but it has been my heart, our god, that has seen me through everything. Fu Ling Yang has brought all four of us together. I have come to where love awaits me. I find that it is not a destination, but a continuing journey. It is a great adventure."

Xian was a capitol city and a busy place with caravans and merchants everywhere. They were camped up and down the river banks and there was hardly room for more. The royal family dismounted from their camels for the last time. They looked around a little bewildered.

"Master Fu Ling Yang, what do we do now? I thought the Amazons would meet us here to help us continue our journey."

"I think we can trust Polydora. We will wait."

They waited until evening, gathered their belongings, and started for Xian. It was a long hot hike into the markets. Everyone copied Fu Ling Yang and picked up something to use for walking sticks.

They trudged past caravan after caravan. The sand was hot and the smells overwhelming. They kept their faces covered even though it was hard to breathe. Chaoxiang tripped and fell to his knees. Shamhar pulled him up onto his feet. Ninana was jarred.

"Are you all right? Are you hurt?"

"I am just a bit dizzy and lost my footing."

"We will rest here for a little while."

Fu Ling Yang drew something from his robe and put it in Chaoxiang's mouth.

"What is that?"

"It will save your life as it has saved mine at times. It seems we give the impression that we live forever. Yes, we do. Illness and decline between life and death do not exist for us. We live fully until we actually leave the body."

Ninana took Lishan aside.

"What does he mean? How old are the master and Chaoxiang?"

Lishan burst out laughing.

"Do not worry. They are not ancient. But we have long lives because we meditate and appreciate everything. Most people live in their outsides, thinking only of the physical world. We live from the inside out, contemplating our true nature. There are mysteries to be discovered about that nature that we can find only with contemplation."

"Can you teach me how to do that?"

"You have searched yourself, Ninana, according to your experiences in the world. That is a good start. Come and sit down with me."

Chapter 64

TOUCHING THE ETERNAL

"When you were in China, we went to the school of philosophy and the school of magic and mystery. I took you to the mystery school where there are seers, magicians, and art depicting the mysteries. There are books explaining them for the student of the mysteries."

"I remember. It was quiet, dark, and there were rooms we were not permitted to enter. Some explanations were as much a mystery to me as the place."

"Master Fu Ling Yang has always been a student of the mysteries. He is now a grand master of them and has access to all areas of the school and its libraries."

Ninana was shocked.

"But he never said anything about it!"

"What about the box that contains your ring? The box that only opens for you."

"Oh, yes. Well, I was new to China and did not know enough to even ask questions. I just followed him to the shop and tried to understand what was being done. I had no idea…"

"The shop keeper is a student of the mysteries as well. Do you still have the ring?"

"Yes, of course. I keep it hidden in the box unless it is safe for me to wear it."

She touched her robe to reassure herself it was there.

"Actually, Ninana, it cannot leave you. And the ring is blessed with your same vibration. It will always find its way back to you, should it be lost or stolen."

"But I have left it behind for safety so many times. It stayed in the Chinese temple in Babylon for years."

"Your faith in it needed to grow. It was keeping you safe. The vibration, the blessing, is not just one way. You have been connected to it all the time."

"Lishan, are you a student as well?"

"I am a novice. Master teaches me and when we are in Guangzhou I attend classes. I am not a practitioner of the arts, but I am somewhat knowledgeable about them."

"And Chaoxiang?"

"He is not a student of the mysteries. However, he is knowledgeable according to how it affects the architecture of buildings. Many rituals are performed to determine the correct geometric calculations."

"Was this done for all of the plans I saw when I was there?"

"Oh, yes. It is called the mantic way. It is applied to everything in daily life. To archaeological work for thousands of years and has inspired a deeper understanding about the impact of mantic on politics, philosophy, religions, and divination. Everything is involved. Everything is connected. Just as you and your ring are connected. Nothing is separate."

"Did Chaoxiang know this about the ring?"

"Yes. It was subject to all mystical blessings and practical calculations."

Ninana thought her head was beginning to spin.

"Chaoxiang knew when he gave me the ring!"

"He gave you the most precious thing he had. He was saving it for love and you came into his life. You were the love."

"I go to where love awaits me. Queen Nitocris of Egypt knew her message was universal and would bless whoever read it and pursued love. Daniel's god, now my god, is truly everywhere present, in and through everything for all time."

The market was crowded and becoming more so as the sun went down and torches were lit. Shop owners and their families were gathered at the back part for a meal and prayers. Music being played softened and the whole atmosphere changed. A hotel owner sought them out.

"I have rooms prepared for royalty. Polydora told us you were coming. She and her warriors will return soon. Please, follow me..."

Fu Ling Yang greeted the hotel owner in words that only the two of them would understand. He motioned for everyone to follow. It was so good to sit down at a table for dinner and be served wonderful food. After months on a camel caravan, the beds were heavenly.

After the conversation with Lishan about her ring, Ninana felt an extra closeness to Chaoxiang. He put his arms around her. She snuggled next to him with a contentment as delicious as the first time in the tea house.

"Has the god of birth and life visited you yet?"

"No, and I pray to my god that does not happen!"

"We will see which god is in charge tonight."

"Your god is in China. Mine is everywhere all the time."

"But we *are* in China...

"Oh no...when did we cross into China?"

"While you were sleeping on the camel behind me."

Chapter 65

POLYDORA'S PROMISE

———— ❦ ————

Many weeks went by in Xian as they waited for Polydora and her warriors. Fu Ling Yang purchased a carriage and horses.

"We will travel in more comfortable accommodations. It is still a very long journey. We should arrive in Guangzhou as befits royalty.

Chaoxiang was most concerned. Things were not coming together as quickly as he felt they should.

"If the Amazons do not come for us, will we need to hire guards? Are we not exposed to danger here without the captain and caravan, Master?"

"We will wait for Polydora. She will keep her promise to meet us. We are secure here as anywhere. Whatever might be delaying her, the warriors will overcome it"

They turned to find other pursuits to fill their time. The marketplace was being expanded with new buildings. Ninana began to laugh with joy.

"Well, we can build a building!"

Chaoxiang, Ninana, and Shamhar went to the master builder to offer their assistance. He was completely amazed that such talented people, architects, would help him in designing and construction. Lishan was happy to help with translating.

Ninana was delighted to work on buildings with the Chinese curved corners on the roofs. This was the first time she actually had her hands on the construction of them.

"This reminds me of my early times of climbing around building stones and materials in Babylon. I almost forgot what a joy it is!"

They created designs for the walls and ornate edges on the doors. Lishan made lanterns and dragons to float around it. Soon people in the market were coming by to watch the work.

Lishan set up a small stand to sell dragons and lanterns. It became a popular place for shoppers and those who wanted to watch her at work.

Fu Ling Yang was a frequent visitor. He enjoyed seeing the true Chinese art that went into the construction.

"You are all having such an enjoyable time, I may not be able to entice you to come back to Guangzhou!"

"Yes, Master. But I have a feeling that something has happened to Polydora and her warriors. I keep having a dark feeling about them."

"How long have you had this feeling, Ninana?"

"For over a week. I know they will return, but somehow I think they need our help, as absurd as that sounds."

"It is not absurd, Princess. Let us go to a quiet place at the hotel and meditate on this. There are forces that can aid us if we will ask, become still, and listen."

They found a private place, burned incense, and invoked a higher presence. Ninana silently prayed to her god and Daniel's god for guidance. Fu Ling Yang moved into a trance-like state.

"They have been attacked not far from here. I sense it is to the south in the hills."

Ninana agreed. They prepared to leave the hotel, go to the market to tell Chaoxiang, Shamhar and Lishan.

"We will go with you."

"Lishan, would you rather stay here and tend your stand? The master builder will watch over you."

"Yes. I am not much of a sword fighter, but I can hold the higher consciousness for you."

They rented horses from the stable and rode into the hills. At the top of a hill Fu Ling Yang held up his hand and stopped. He dismounted and put his ear to the ground. He remounted and pointed in a direction, putting his index finger to his mouth. They kept silent, walked their horses, withdrew their jians from their robes.

A few Amazons burst forth from an arroyo and stopped when they saw Ninana.

"We are here to help! What has happened?"

"Traps were set for us and we rode into them. The horses scattered and some of our warriors are injured. Just brigands but clever and well-armed."

Ninana and Fu Ling Yang went with them to tend the injured. Chaoxiang and Shamhar rode away to gather their horses.

Polydora was sitting on the ground among the injured.

"Do not worry Ninana, it is not mortal. Just a broken bone in my foot. I promised we would come back and now you will have to carry me back."

Ninana was so relieved that she laughed and hugged Polydora.

"So happy you are alive! We will be glad to carry you to Xian."

Shamhar and Chaoxiang brought back the horses they could find and went to the market in Xian to get materials to make litters to carry those who could not walk.

Fu Ling Yang examined Polydora's foot.

"You will not drag me on a litter. I will crawl first."

"I can bind that for you and you will be able to walk but carefully."

He expertly bound her foot and helped her onto a horse.

"I have ridden with many men, but none as kind and gentle as you."

He placed his hands together and bowed and went to assist the others.

Chapter 66

THE YELLOW RIVER

―――――――――― ❧ ⚘ ――――――――――

The carriage was a welcome comfort. They could be together and talk or sleep. They all took turns driving the horses.

"Why did you decide to get a carriage, Master? Was there another reason beside our being royalty?"

"Yes. We are coming down to the level of the sea. The Yellow River tells us we are out of the mountains and the travel will be easier. Our bodies will acclimate to the lower elevations and our hearts will not have to work so hard. We have lived in Guangzhou at sea level and traveled on the seas. The mountains are a challenge for us. Sherpas live in the mountains so have no problem with altitude."

Ninana looked at Chaoxiang with concern. She remembered his illness on the Khyber Pass and in the desert. He glanced back at her.

"I am well, my love. Please do not worry."

She smiled and moved closer to him. She looked to the side so he would not see the tear in her eye. When she glanced at Fu Ling Yang, he was asleep. She could not remember ever seeing him sleep. His eyes were always watchful and kindly at the same time. What wisdom and mystery lay behind those eyes!

The Amazons rode a distance from the carriage to watch for brigands and any other trouble. Ninana stood in the carriage and looked around.

"Who would attack the Amazons here?"

"Wild and untrained local renegades attack the towns and villages but they never bother the Amazons. They are no match for the women warriors. The Amazons will take us as far as the village you helped repair. They sent a message to Guangzhou to have the military meet us there. They know where it is."

"I remember it well. It will be good to see the villagers again. I want to know how they are doing with the upkeep of their homes. And if they need any help."

Fu Ling Yang smiled with those crinkles in the corner of his eyes.

"Princess, you are always looking to build something. Your calling is very strong!"

Crossing the river south of Suzhou, there were war yells and the pounding of horses hooves. Ninana put her ring into the box in her robe. Everyone in the carriage drew their jians. Shamhar leaned out of the carriage.

"Those shouts are women. The Amazons must be chasing brigands. They will not survive the onslaught of the Amazons. There will be one less gang on our road. They take no prisoners. Leave no one alive."

Lishan shared what she remembered.

"The attack of the brigands by the Amazons was at night. Some of the village boys escaped and hid. They returned home while Ninana and I were there. They set to work helping the villagers with the repairs of their dwellings."

Shamhar put his arm around her shoulders.

"You must tell me more about that story."

"We will go there and I will show you."

She pulled his hand to her cheek and smiled.

"I noticed you were not well this morning. Is there something else you have to tell me, Lishan?"

This got Ninana's attention immediately, but she said nothing. If there was news, it was Lishan's news to tell. If Fu Ling Yang heard her, he did not let on. At that moment Polydora rode up to the carriage.

"Everyone all right?"

"Yes! We were ready for battle, but we knew you would be victorious. Just want you to know you have back up. How is your foot?"

"It still aches at night."

"Come here and sit in the carriage. I will re-bind it for you."

She was about to protest, but instead obeyed. This was probably the first time she ever obeyed any man in her life. But Fu Ling Yang was different. She came to realize that he was a higher order of being, higher than any queen or king.

Ninana made room for her in the carriage and helped Fu Ling Yang bind her foot. Polydora stood up on the foot.

"That is so much better! You are a healer."

Ninana hugged her. She went to her horse, turned, put her hands together and bowed.

The weeks and miles continued to stretch out before them. Sometimes they stopped to walk and led the horses. The mountains and deserts had turned into foothills with dry grasses and small trees. Polydora and her warriors checked on them from time to time.

"We are getting closer to the village. We will soon leave the Silk Road to take you there. Then we will go. The military from Guangzhou will come to meet you or will already be there. We will not want to engage with them since we are considered enemies...of a sort."

"We will be sure to correct that perception when we have told them how you protected us all these months."

"Please, Master, do not tell them that we have been with you. We do not want them hunting us down to thank us. Your safety is thanks enough."

Chapter 67

RETURN TO THE VILLAGE

—————— ❧ ❧ ——————

The way began to look familiar to Ninana and Lishan. This was the way they came when they were picked up by the Amazons in the foothills and taken to their camp.

"We are still several days travel away from the village. I may not correctly remember the time it took to reach the Amazon camp. It was hard to figure it on horseback."

Lishan glanced at Shamhar who was worried about her.

"Well at least we are in a carriage this time. It will be a smoother ride."

Polydora and a few of her warriors guided them off the Silk Road and in the direction of the village.

"We will watch you from a distance. You may not see us, but we will be there. When you are in sight of the village we will be gone. Your military should be there to welcome you."

"If we do not see you again, Polydora, know that I consider you my true sister in spirit and will hold you in my prayers always."

"Much happiness and safety to you my sisters, Ninana and Lishan."

She turned her horse and they galloped away.

The village was in sight. The Guangzhou military guard were waiting at the well in the village.

Shamhar looked around shading his eyes.

"There are no village people."

"Of course there are no village people, my love. They are afraid of the military and are hiding in their homes. We should ask the military to retreat into the hills and wait for us."

They pulled their carriage up to the village well. Fu Ling Yang stepped down and went to the captain. He spoke to him quietly and they bowed. He signaled the military men to retreat.

Ninana and Lishan jumped down from the carriage and ran to the well. They started calling for the people. Lishan called in their language that they were the ones who helped rebuild their village. A few at a time came out of their homes.

Then someone recognized Ninana and Lishan, and came running, shouting to the others. Soon most of the villagers were at the well, many women hugging them and crying. They begged Lishan and Ninana to come to their homes.

Lishan explained to the others.

"They want us to see their decorations and new rooms. They have lanterns and dragons! Their sons brought them from a visit to Guangzhou. They want us to stay the night. We stayed with them once. I am sure we will be comfortable to do it again."

They could hardly refuse. But now there were five instead of two. Fu Ling Yang spoke to the officials of the village and accepted their invitation to stay in their homes.

"I am glad it is just one night. I have not spent a night away from Chaoxiang since we were reunited and then married."

"It will be like old times when you and I slept together on your first trip to China."

They both giggled and went to the home of a woman who had led them out to the Silk Road. They were surprised she was still alive.

"I thought she was quite old when we were here before."

"They are referred to as the grandmothers and have had a very hard life. They may look old and wrinkled, but they are always young at heart. Perhaps because of that they live a long time."

The military pitched their tents and bedded down for the night. Guards stood by in shifts until the morning. Before dawn they took their tents down. They ate a quick breakfast and were ready to go at first light.

There were tearful goodbyes as they prepared to leave. The grandmothers cried, kissed their cheeks, and went to the well to wave goodbye.

They reached the Silk Road and traveled at a fast pace to reach Guangzhou by night fall. The soldiers surrounded the carriage to keep everyone safe. They kicked up a lot of dust. Everyone in the carriage covered their faces and did not attempt to speak to each other.

As they neared Guangzhou, Fu Ling Yang signaled the captain to slow down.

"The fast pace is exhausting for us. And drive by the docks to see if our sailors returned. We were shipwrecked at the mouth of the Indus River and they chose to get home by sea. Perhaps someone could ride ahead and make inquiries."

"I will send someone immediately. We did not know you were shipwrecked! That is why you came home over the Silk Road. Dangerous choice either way. I am relieved that you are all safe and it is our honor to escort you home."

He and Fu Ling Yang put their hands together and bowed. The captain went to his second in command and a rider started off at full gallop for Guangzhou.

Lishan was nestled next to Shamhar and he held her in his arms.

"Are you well?"

"Yes and it is better now that we have stopped galloping along. I feared we would be too tired to get out of the carriage and need to be carried into the house."

"I will carry you anywhere you want to go."

Chapter 68

MYSTERIES OF GUANGZHOU

———— ❦ ❧ ————

The sky was darkening as they approached the city. They could hear the music and see the light from the lanterns at the marketplace. A very long and dangerous journey was coming to an end.

They drove past the markets and on to the docks. Fu Ling Yang stepped out of the carriage. A ship's captain came to meet him and confirmed that he had brought their sailors home on his freighter that morning.

"They have had harrowing experiences such as pirates, illness, and being abandoned on an island. But the island had a port and they found passage again on a fishing boat. They have survived and their families are overjoyed to receive them home. Welcome home to you, Master and your family. Your journey over land must have been most taxing as well. Again, welcome!"

The captain of the wrecked ship came to greet Fu Ling Yang.

"We prayed to the gods that you would survive your travel on land. Our freighters came in safely and the captains were surprised not to find us here. The news was very slow coming of the wreck and our chosen ways home."

Fu Ling Yang bowed.

"I will take my exhausted family home and return to recount our adventures together. There must be a written report of all incidents."

He returned to the carriage with the good news that the sailors had returned and were with their families. They cheered and applauded.

"I will tell you of their experiences after I meet with our captain again. It has taken far longer to arrive in Guangzhou than a sea voyage should. So there will be much to tell."

Everyone at Fu Ling Yang's home came out to welcome them and usher them into the dining room. Dishes of delicious food were set out on the table and the dancers came out to greet them and dance a celebration for their return.

Ninana was happy to return and still a bit restless. She turned to Fu Ling Yang.

"I understand you are a master in the mysteries of China. I have heard something of the special prayers and incantations for buildings and all other parts of life. I believe it is called the mantic way. Chaoxiang knows something of this and I would like to learn more of this if that is possible."

Fu Ling Yang thought for a few minutes.

"Let us begin with what Lishan can teach you. She is quite knowledgeable. And then we can continue to deeper understanding if you wish to go further. Are you agreeable to this?"

"Yes. I am sure I have asked a great deal of you. The mysteries are not displayed for everyone before they learn. I wish to understand."

Lishan and Ninana spent time in a salon near the pool as teacher and student again, this time about the mysteries.

"Mysteries are about divination and prophecy. These are things that help you understand yourself and your future. They are about protection, the art of living well within yourself, and how to nurture your life. A person of good will and understanding transmits a pattern, sets a position from the grace within them. Your influence on your life is felt from this centered position that you have created.

"You begin by sitting still, attention to your breath, and try to clear your mind of all judgments and emotions. This will take some practice. At first it will seem that nothing is happening. That is a good sign. An inner transformation is taking place that leads you to special knowledge, strength, health, and clarity. It is not about what happens to you, but what happens within you."

"Can it tell me the future?"

"Your future comes from what is within you. The pattern you set in the moment becomes the pattern of your future."

"Will you sit with me as I do this?"

"Yes. At first. We will sit facing each other and I will hold your hands. Every few minutes I will squeeze your hands to draw your attention away from whatever is entering your mind. You will refocus on my hands and still your mind."

They practiced for a while until Ninana was exhausted and frustrated.

"Do not be discouraged my dear friend. You are not accustomed to it. It becomes easier. Let us go into the pool and refresh ourselves. Then we will have food served to us here."

They splashed into the pool and floated around. They giggled and laughed about experiences of the past. Ninana relaxed and let the frustration dissolve in the fragrant water.

Serving girls hurried in with food, towels, fresh tunics, and slippers. They were very quiet and quickly backed out of the door.

"What shall we do now, teacher?"

Lishan laughed.

"Let us go for a walk. We will meet love among the flowers in the gardens. Chaoxiang and Shamhar will be waiting for us. This evening we will spend a short time practicing and then go to dinner. The dancers await us there."

It all seemed like a dream to Ninana. First the shipwreck, then the roughness of the travels on the silk Road, and now the heavenly atmosphere of Fu Ling Yang's home.

They practiced many times that week until Ninana could do it on her own.

"Tell me more about divination, Lishan. How does that come about?"

"It comes to you when you are ready and when you ask it to. I will help you with it soon."

"How will I know when I am ready?"

"When you stop trying to make it happen."

Ninana came out of her meditation one morning and went to find Lishan.

"Something happened. I saw myself in Babylon again as the queen and Chaoxiang was with me. I have not planned to go back to Babylon, ever. The people were told I was dead."

"Has it occurred to you that when Chaoxiang married you, he married royalty? He married the queen who is not actually dead. So he is the king!"

Ninana reached for a cup of rice wine and drank the whole thing in one swallow and coughed.

"I never thought of that! Did he ever think of that?"

"Even I did not think of that until now."

"I guess I am always royalty even if I renounce it. Even if I hide from it. God knows I have tried those things without much success, even now."

"What caused me to think of it is the news from Fu Ling Yang that Cambyses was killed in Egypt. Now there is no regent in Babylonia. Perhaps you are needed there."

Chapter 69

KING OF BABYLONIA

———————— ⟨⟨⟨ ⟩⟩⟩ ————————

Fu Ling Yang and Ninana watched Chaoxiang climb down from the thirteenth level of the pagoda that his architects were building.

"What is this about?"

"News has come from the Silk Road that Cambyses was killed in Egypt. There is now no regent in Babylonia and no longer danger to me from him. You are the king by marriage to the queen, even though she pretended to be dead in her coffin above the Ishtar Gate."

"I am what?"

"Yes, my love. A king! Not only are you the king, but in my meditation a divination came to me that Babylonia needs her queen."

Completely astonished at the turn of events, they sat down in the garden of the architectural school. Serving people brought them rice wine, fruit, and small cakes.

"Ninana, If you decide to go back to Babylon, I will be alone again. If I go with you, I will be the king. Is there not another choice? Any middle ground? Perhaps to stay here?"

"I have not decided what to do, my love. It is all new to me as I study the mysteries. I need more time to discern what the message is and I need you to do that with me."

Fu Ling Yang held up his hand.

"We will all join together in this. I am sure Lishan and Shamhar are involved as well. We will gather at the School of Arts and Mysteries. I will return there today to prepare. My carriage will come for all of you in a few days in the morning when the air is fresh and clear."

Chaoxiang and Ninana stayed at the school of architecture continuing their work there. In the evening they went to the tea house in the back of the gardens where they first made love years ago.

"Are you not happy here, Ninana?"

"I am not unhappy here, my love, but there is a driving force within me that has carried me to all of the places in my travels. None of those places were in my thoughts or plans. I was happy in my city, Babylon. But events took place that changed everything. They demanded that I follow them or die.

"I gave my city to King Cyrus to save it. I lived in Persia. Then I went to Babylon with Cambyses to see my beloved Babylon. I went to Jerusalem to help the people who desired to return there from the settlement I built in Babylon. I went on to Egypt to find Queen Nitocris of two thousand years ago. Again I had to escape Cambyses and Egypt and hid in Jerusalem. Then I hid again in the Arabian desert settlement built by Nabonidus. Then I returned to Babylon and could not stay there, so I went to Uruk, the city of my childhood. Then I returned to Babylon as Queen Nitocris of all Babylonia. When my work was finished there, I came back to China and you."

They sat quietly for a long time.

"And now?"

"And now, this message comes to me, or from within me, with such strong urging and clarity that I wonder if I dare ignore it. If I did would it ever stop?"

They sat quietly a little longer, many thoughts running through their minds. Chaoxiang was the only one who had never been to Babylon and now he was the king, husband of the queen. Presently he began to sort his thoughts aloud.

"Ninana, we have dynasties here in China. They are quite remote from everyday life, but they set forth defenses, create cultural entities, and organize food supplies for the empire. I have not tried to imagine what else. All of my adult life I have been the master of this school. Is that anything like being a king?"

Ninana tried to give him what information she could to support his decision making process.

"My father only knew command and cruelty. He cared nothing for people. They obeyed or died. The Jews were captured and caused to work as his slaves. He did not even remember my name most of the time. My mother was the queen regent and a much gentler soul who did care. But she was Assyrian and was taken from her home in Harran, given to him for political reasons. She went back to Harran when he died. King Cyrus was the only one I knew who had a heart and expressed kindness toward me. This I dared not share with the Amazons since he was not their friend and they killed him when he attacked them."

The sky was darkening and they returned to their quarters in the school. They were still quiet as dinner was served and a musician played quiet but joyful music from another room.

The next day Shamhar and Lishan came to the school. Most of their time in China they had lived there working with Chaoxiang's engineers and designers. They settled into Shamhar's quarters.

Ninana was surprised and happy to see them. Lishan touched Ninana's arm.

"We must speak with you when you have time."

"Have you spoken to Fu Ling Yang?"

"Yes, we have and there is much to discuss with you and Chaoxiang."

Chaoxiang joined them and they sat together in the garden over food and rice wine. They all started talking at once and then broke into laughter. Shamhar began again.

"I had not thought about it, but if you marry a queen you are the king! It does not matter if you are here or there, Chaoxiang. You are now the king of all Babylonia."

Lishan added her thoughts with a giggle.

"Even if you are pretending to be dead, Ninana, you are still royalty and the queen. Dead or alive."

Ninana squeezed Chaoxiang's hand.

"All this being true, we need to discuss what decisions can be made."

"If you decide to go there, Shamhar and I are going with you. We will not be separated again. I promised you many years ago that I would always be your friend and always be with you. Shamhar agrees."

Shamhar nodded and looked at Chaoxiang.

"What are you thinking, my friend?"

"I am still stunned...that I am a king. I have no idea what that means!"

"My love, we are a queen and a king. Neither of us chose that for ourselves. I never wanted to be a queen, or even royalty. It created a barrier between me and the people I loved. I was their friend, but they always saw me as their queen. It was very frustrating. The times I have renounced that and lived as a commoner were a joy and a relief.

"I forced myself to be Queen Nitocris when I went to King Cyrus to save my city. I also went to him to learn what it is to be a queen regent. He kindly and with much patience answered all my many questions. He promised to save my city, but not to save my throne. I was happy with that."

Shamhar reached for his rice wine.

"Chaoxiang, you and I have both married royalty. Ninana is a queen and Lishan is of a royal family. We both must decide with our wives what our roles will be. They must be suitable for who we are and our happiness must not be marred."

"Has a decision already been made?"

"No, my love. We will consult with Fu Ling Yang before we decide anything. He may have information for us that we do not yet know. I am content to wait, but it is hard not to think about it all."

"What do you think about?"

"I think about showing you my city. You have seen my drawings, but you have never seen it. When the sun shines on the blue and gold bricks of the walls, the Ishtar Gate and the palace, it looks like the city is shimmering and floating above the earth. I think about taking you to the building of Yang Light of the Rising Sun where our cultures come together."

"I am starting to like the idea of being your king."

"My king?"

She laughed and hugged him.

Chapter 70

DIVINATION AND DECISION

As he promised Fu Ling Yang came for them in a carriage and with a large guard.

"The rebels are active again and the city police told me to bring a guard."

Ninana flashed a smile at Chaoxiang.

"Oh wonderful, another fight with the rebels. I do not want my Dao to get dull. I shall sharpen it to be sure."

Fu Ling Yang smiled and bowed with hands together.

"I hope we will not have to fight our way into Guangzhou. We will go to the School of Arts and Mystery. They are expecting us and have prepared a room for our meditation and divination. They will give the appropriate prayers to the gods, exhortations, and rites for centering ourselves. Then we will be alone to receive wisdom and speak of our findings."

The ride to the school was uneventful. They stepped down from the carriage and were met by two priests in black robes and hoods. They all bowed and were escorted into the room prepared for them. The priests performed the rites, rituals, and incantations. They bowed and backed out of the room. The room was cool and quiet. There were ornate cushioned chairs and robes for their comfort.

Fu Ling Yang began with a quiet chant and they all followed.

"Clear your minds of all apprehensions, all concerns for the outer world, and trust that which is within you."

It took a while for Ninana and Chaoxiang to let go of their disturbing thoughts. He reached over and took her hand. The energy moved between them and they were able to move into the quiet place of their deepest love.

"I go to where love awaits me. I go to where love awaits me. I will follow my joy. If I forget my joy, then I have forgotten my god. I am safe in God's love."

After a long period of time Fu Ling Yang ended the meditation with a chant and asked each one to speak. Their messages were essentially the same. Love, joy, and safety coming from the cosmic realm into their hearts.

As they concluded the session they were escorted out into a garden for rice wine, sweet cakes and fruit.

Chaoxiang spoke first.

"I will go with whatever Ninana decides. She is more important to me than my life here. I will not be without her. She is my joy and I love her above all else."

Ninana caught her breath.

"I could not go without you. I would stay with you even if the cost were high. But you have spoken first, my love, and it is right that we should go together."

Shamhar spoke next.

"I am eager to return to Babylon. It was my home. Of course I would not be without Lishan and will stay or go, as she desires. After all this is her home and I would stay here with her."

Lishan smiled and squeezed his hand.

"I believe I have already said that I would stay with Ninana, fulfilling a promise of long ago. Shamhar promised to stay with me. I am happy that we will all be together wherever we are. And you Master Fu Ling Yang?"

"China is my home and I will return here to continue my life as Master of the Mysteries and Arts. I feel the decisions made today are right. I will hold you in my prayers as we travel forth. You are my children and I must see you to your destinations one more time. You all have blessed my life. My blessings and love are with you always."

They went back to the School of Architecture with Chaoxiang to set the school up under another director. The one who headed the school while Chaoxiang was gone was chosen by the engineers and students.

The appropriate rituals, incantations, and prayers so familiar to Chaoxiang were new to Ninana. She could feel the energy flowing through everything and it made her shiver a bit. The projects were blessed. Plans for the future were made and blessed as well.

There were sad farewells as they packed their belongings and prepared to return to Fu Ling Yang's house.

Ninana was joyful at the thought that she would finally show Chaoxiang her city, Babylon. She did not let her excitement spill over causing her to forget that he had made the decision that opened the way for all of them. She was watchful lest he should show signs of regret, but he did not.

"I have no regrets, Ninana. It feels right to me. And, as we said before we started on the Silk Road, it will be a great adventure. I am as excited in my own way as you are. I will be seeing a part of you that is new to me. I want to know all about you, wherever it takes us."

Fu Ling Yang stayed very close to them. He knew it was the right decision for everyone, but he was shepherding his beloved family away forever.

Ships were specially prepared to carry the King and Queen of Babylonia and other royalty of China. A fleet of guard ships would travel with them. Everything was carefully chosen including the captain, sailors, and guards. Fu Ling Yang did everything he could think of for them, leaving no detail undone.

There were special celebrations on the river with fireworks and lighted dragons ready to mark the grand farewell of royalty. Queen Nitocris had visited their city and King Chaoxiang from China would accompany her to Babylonia. It was truly a momentous occasion.

Once more they visited the mysterious shop of the man who created the energy for the protection of Ninana's ring. He was old and blind now, but he knew her by her energy. He greeted her as a daughter and blessed her with gifts that carried good omens.

"You will always be blessed by our connection. Your ring and these gifts will keep us connected and I will see you always protected."

"And I pray to my god to protect you, Master, and keep you strong all of your days."

They smiled, put their hands together and bowed in the Chinese way.

Ninana had tears in her eyes as they walked through the darkened front room and out of the door into the bright day.

Chapter 71

A GREAT ADVENTURE

———— ❧ ————

"You must teach me to be a king, Ninana. What are the duties? How should I act as royalty? How should I regard the subjects? What will your people think of me?"

Ninana put her arms around him and kissed his cheek.

"My love, you are royalty just as you are, even before we met. Your duties will become clear as you work beside me for the good of the empire. You regard our subjects as people who depend upon you for safety, sustenance, and kindness."

"And the acceptance by the people?"

"You will certainly be a curiosity since they have not seen any Chinese people except perhaps for Fu Ling Yang and Lishan. Shamhar fell in love with Lishan from the first time he saw her. The people may fall in love with you as well."

"What about Persia? Are they enemies? Captors?"

"We are certainly captives. But the threats are gone for now. All who would rule us are dead. Arakhu is the Governor of the City of Babylon and Karim is his military assistant. They were friends of Daniel and are both faithful to me."

Chaoxiang sat quietly.

"What is on your mind, my love?"

"Tell me more about Daniel. Who was he to you?"

"He was a Jewish captive brought to Babylon when my father destroyed his city of Jerusalem. He was a prophet of his god and taught me what his god had taught him. His teaching was, "If I forget my joy, then I have forgotten my god.""

"I have heard you say that. It sounds profound. I want to know more about his god, too."

"He said the presence of God the Creator of All is within each one of us always. All power is given to those who believe. When we ask for wisdom it is given from the Universe. He translated the writing on the wall that appeared when my son, Belshazzar, was giving one of his decadent feasts. That was the night that Cyrus came into Babylon and Belshazzar was killed in a drunken rage outside of the palace wall. Daniel and I escaped to Susa, Persia, where Cyrus granted us asylum and protection. Years later Daniel died there. He was a dear friend, trusted by kings, and teacher of the mysteries."

"Kindness and being goodhearted, caring for all people? That sounds like Confucius and Mencius."

"And so it does. Wherever truth rises from, they converge into one. Daniel called it God of All. Prophets, seers, and your philosophers travel in higher realms of being. They receive wisdom far higher than what most people will know.

"One more thing, Chaoxiang. You must learn to call me Nitocris and not Ninana. Queen Nitocris or Your Highness. You might hear the Jews there call me their Princess. I was a princess when I built their community in Babylon and they will see me that way until they pass on."

"Aha! And will you call me King Chaoxiang and Your Royal Highness?"

"Yes. And we must not laugh when we say it."

"May I call you Ninana when we are in our bed?"

"Yes. Please do. 'Your Royal Highness' does not belong in our bedroom."

"That is good!

He swept her up in his arms, kissed her, and held her tight. The future was nearly upon them. It held adventure, mystery, danger, and now always joy.

They settled in at Fu Ling Yang's home while ships and everything needed for the journey were in final preparation.

"We will stop in Muziris, India, and I must take you to the pagodas, stupas, and viharas there. That is where I made the sketches for you at the behest of Fu Ling Yang...but I did not know it was for you, just for Chinese architects."

"From what I understand from Fu Ling Yang, he came to trade with your father, saw your drawings and invited you to come to China. He came back for you a few years later and you agreed to go with him. That was very courageous."

"Well, I was still a wide-eyed young girl. Even marriage and a baby did not change that. I did not know where China was or how to get there. He brought Lishan to be my companion and we were instant friends. She knew so much about everything and I was fascinated. I wanted to learn everything. Especially about Chinese architecture.

"My father was happy to see me leave and stop bothering him. He would never recognize my work in Babylon, always dismissing me like a child. You might say he pushed me out into the world, the wonderful world of India and China. Now I should thank him."

"I would thank him as well."

Preparations were complete. They all made a few visits to the ships. Ninana had never seen anything like it. Royalty floating on the high seas. Perfect weather for sailing was approaching and they must not linger and miss it.

She took Fu Ling Yang's arm and reminisced about helping the sailors on her voyages.

"I am sure I will not be allowed to help the sailors now. Royalty does not work with their hands. I may break that barrier, but only by accident or necessity."

Fu Ling Yang laughed, those crinkles appeared in the corners of his eyes.

"I am sure you will continue to be yourself wherever you are, crown on your head or dao in your hands."

"Master, a queen has riches and yet you have given me riches beyond anything royalty can offer. You have given me belonging as I have never known before. You, Lishan, and Chaoxiang have claimed me as your own family and I have claimed you as mine now and for always. I will keep the incense burning in Yang Light of the Rising Sun to acknowledge that our spirits are one."

"I could not ask for more wonderful children. You have completed a lifetime desire of my heart. Now I must send you out into the world one more time. I will accompany you to the Ishtar Gate and then return to China."

One did not touch or hug a master, but she broke protocol again and hugged him. Then they stepped back and bowed, with hands together and some tears.

Chapter 72

THE LAST VOYAGE

Ninana and Chaoxiang stood by the rail waiting for Lishan and Shamhar to come up the gang plank. There were boats all around them with dragons, lanterns, flowers on the water, and music. Bouquets of flowers arrived and behind them Lishan and Shamhar.

"These are the favorite flowers of China and they bring good luck. There are chrysanthemums, Chinese roses, peonies, lotus blossoms, plum blossoms, camellias, azaleas, and hibiscus. Every kind of good luck there is! We could not choose just one or two. They were so beautiful that we brought them all."

The servants onboard rushed to take them to the state rooms. The oars hit the water, began to back the ship away from the dock, and turn it into the main river currents. Ninana felt that familiar lurch of the ship that always carried her away to the next adventure. They sailed down the river to the South China Sea with their fleet of guard ships. Their beloved China slowly disappeared behind them.

With a deep bow Chaoxiang presented a gift to Ninana.

"What are these?"

"They are Chinese royal crowns."

He placed one on her head. She took the second one and placed it on his head.

"The weight of two kingdoms was now on our heads!"

Lishan and Shamhar bowed deeply to the crowned heads of Babylonia and joined them. They sat together in meditation, each giving thanks to their gods for all the good that has blessed them and all that is to come in the new adventure.

They sailed down the coast, through the islands and straits. It was the same hot, humid, and breeze-less place she remembered. Some people on the shorelines stood to watch this amazing royal flotilla as it passed.

Ninana was excited to get to Muziris again with its wonderful harbor, and vast markets.

"Sadly, my love, that is where our child was lost. Even though it was only a small handful of tissue, hardly recognizable as a child, we buried it in a sacred burial place with appropriate prayers. It was Lishan's suggestion."

"Very wise, thank you both. That little soul will find its next body."

A storm was coming up as they entered the Port of Muziris. Chaoxiang went to talk to the captain. Ninana could not resist helping the sailors as they pulled the sails down. She coiled the ropes and stowed tools. The wind was whipping through her hair giving her a wild sense of freedom again.

The rowers steered the ship into a berth. The sailors secured and anchored it. Fu Ling Yang, Chaoxiang, Ninana, Lishan, and Shamhar disembarked quickly and went to the hotel. Rains began to beat down and the markets were shuttered.

"I hope this does not last too long, Lishan. I want to go to the markets again."

"It could last a day or a week. We will have to wait. We cannot set sail until it has cleared."

The wind whipped and the rain beat down for two days and then began to subside. Everything was soggy and tents were blown away or torn up. Some ships were blown across the bay and damaged. The royal fleet was well moored and safe.

Fu Ling Yang met with the captain.

"Can we be of help to any of these with damage?"

"Will you come with me and we can speak to their captains? If the damage is above the waterline, yes. Below the waterline, the ship may sink and take those repairing with it."

"I understand. Let us see if there is anything we can do. Good will on the high seas is a tradition."

"I agree."

Chaoxiang and Shamhar came from the hotel and were eager to help. Ninana and Lishan came behind them. Chaoxiang looked shocked.

"I am also an architect and builder and Lishan is a translator. My father called me 'just a girl' and ignored me, left me behind. I cannot let you do that to me, too."

Fu Ling Yang smiled at Chaoxiang.

"She is your equal, my friend. She deserves to be treated as an equal."

"Good advice for when we become king and queen in Babylonia in Babylon!"

"You are taught that Chinese women are to be protected and kept from harm. Ninana is different. You have seen that she is a great warrior in all areas of her life. It would destroy her to be kept back. She loves you and would do anything for you, even destroy herself. No good would come from that for either of you."

"I should have learned those things when she was training and fighting with the Amazons. Somehow I forgot that when it came to repairing the ships in a harbor."

"Yes, Chaoxiang. When we were attacked the first time we came to the School of Architecture, I was knocked down by a brigand. She leaped over my fallen body, grabbed up a sword, and beat them off herself."

As they walked onto the docks together they were invited to board ships to assess the damages, helping where they could. It was a long two days' work, but rewarding when they saw some of the ships at last get underway.

Ninana reached out and hugged Chaoxiang and smiled up at him.

"Now Lishan and I will do girl things. We are going to the market to shop."

He squeezed her tight.

"I am so sorry that I forgot who you are. I will not forget again."

"You know that I will remind you, my love. Gently of course."

Chapter 73

THE PORT OF UR

All the sails and banners were raised as they sailed into the Sea of Makran, through the Strait of Basora. The mountains rose high on either side of the strait and islands dotted the northern coastline. Ninana and Chaoxiang stood on the prow of the ship letting the hot breeze blow over them.

"We will soon be at the seaport of Ur. They will wonder who is coming with all these banners waving over the ships. They will never guess it is the king and queen of Babylonia. As far as they know, I am dead and in my coffin atop the Ishtar Gate."

"It will be a wonderful surprise!"

"Or they will kill me enroute to Babylon."

"I will fight by your side. We will live or die together."

"They killed my son, Belshazzar, when he tried to enter his palace during the siege of Babylon by King Cyrus. His orders to the guards were that they let no one enter the palace, even if they claimed to be Belshazzar, himself. Then he was drunk and wandered outside of the palace. Of course the guard did not believe that he was Belshazzar and they killed him."

Fu Ling Yang joined the conversation and listened with interest.

"When we dock I will send a message to Governor Arakhu that you are returning. He knows me and he knows you. Hopefully Karim will be there as well. Arakhu can make an announcement and explanation to the local military and they will come to meet you at the Ishtar Gate."

"I understand that Cambyses is dead. Who takes his place?"

"Prince Bardiya, his brother, was to take his place. It is said that after some battles he committed suicide but others suspect Darius killed him in order to get the throne. Darius was the lance bearer for Cambyses. Darius himself claims that he achieved the throne not through fraud, but cunning, even erecting a statue of himself mounted on his neighing horse with the inscription: 'Darius, son of Hystaspes, obtained the sovereignty of Persia by the sagacity of his horse and the ingenious contrivance of Oebares, his groom.'

"Ridiculous! Worse than Cambyses."

"The Persian empire is huge with many conquests added to its territory. It is now called the Achaemenid Empire. My dear, eight kings have met their demise in your lifetime so far."

"I do remember Darius. He was as arrogant and as dangerous as Cambyses. Pray that Chaoxiang and I will not be numbers nine and ten."

"Hold your judgment until we arrive. Remember that in divination you were guided to return. Divination does not send one into death, but life. I know you will be praying to your god and Daniel's god for safe passage."

Ninana and Chaoxiang still sat in the prow of the ship talking about all that had transpired.

"I thought King Cyrus was your friend. Why would your life be in danger?"

"When I was escaping Egypt after Cambyses got himself imprisoned and then escaped, I was headed for the exit from Egypt into Gaza. It is a swamp created by the Mediterranean Sea. When the tide goes out, it leaves a barely passable land bridge between the two countries. I was in a carriage. Cambyses and his guards came out of the hills, tried to take my carriage, which would have left me in Egypt with no way out. I ordered my driver to put the horses into full gallop when he tried to grab their bridles. We sort of ran over him and I got away.

"We hid in a stable in Gaza. Later Cambyses came thundering by on horses and fortunately did not stop to look for us. Then we traded the carriage for a common wagon and drove to Jerusalem. He is so arrogant and paranoid. He thought I was after his throne. Even though I proved to him many times that I was not, he never believed it."

"That is quite a story! Do you think the Persians on the Silk Road were sent by him?"

"Likely. He would not have come himself. They could say I was dead and if they checked in Babylon, it would be verified."

"Do you think Darius has any interest in Babylon?"

"So long as there are no uprisings or battles, his attention will likely be elsewhere."

The Port of Ur was at last coming into view.

"Ninana, is there anything else I need to know?"

Ninana thought for a few minutes.

"Daniel and I built the Jewish community in Babylon so they could live in decent homes with fresh air and water. They could plant their own gardens, have their own marketplace and thrive. I am their beloved princess. When starting for Egypt I took some of them to Jerusalem so they could recover their city. Many of the older ones stayed in Babylon. Most of the younger ones went to Jerusalem with me. They would have gone without me, but Cambyses was leading the way like a charge. He was too far ahead to know what I was doing. He probably hoped I would get lost or killed."

The sails came down and the oars hit the water. They pulled into the dock and were met by some dignitaries from the City of Ur. Fu Ling Yang went forward to meet them. Ninana waited in a state room.

"I told them that we are Chinese traders and our cargo is valuable. So we have guards. Our friend, Shamhar, is from Babylon and will be escorting us there. They seemed satisfied with that, welcomed us, and left."

"Do you think that is all true, that they are city officials?"

"Yes, I checked with the port authority and they verified it."

Ninana put on a Chinese kimono, clung to Chaoxiang's arm, and they all disembarked quietly. Fu Ling Yang rented a carriage, horses, and a few pack animals.

"We will stay at the hotel tonight and leave in the morning. That is what ordinary merchants would do. We will keep a low profile until we get to Babylon. At Uruk we will trade for a larger carriage, put on better clothing, uniforms for our guards, and prepare for a royal entrance into Babylon. Everything we will need is on the pack animals."

Chapter 74

THE WAY HOME

───────── ◌◊ ◊◌ ─────────

They left Uruk and the next stop was Isin for fresh horses. The village of Isin had grown since Ninana was a youngster traveling with Zaidu. The hotel Ninana and Karim had repaired was expanded and busy. The hotel owner came out to meet the visitors.

"Of all the gods, it is you! My hotel repair lady! I remember you. Welcome! Is your friend with you?"

"No, he is in Babylon. These are my friends. Merchants from China. Do you have accommodations for us?"

"Oh, Yes! Please come this way. I am eager to show you the new addition and the rooms we added. You can stay in those."

They settled into the new rooms.

"Ninana, is there another story you have not told me?"

"Yes, there is. I am sure you know that I have many adventures I have not thought to bring up. When I had to escape Babylon for the third time,

I went to Uruk, my childhood home. Karim was with me. It was a time to recover my past, my peace of mind, and my joy. I spent much time in meditation every morning at the top of the ziggurat. When we heard that Cambyses was killed, I knew it was safe to return to Babylon as Queen Nitocris. Babylon needed me.

"We stopped here which is about halfway to Babylon. When Master builder Zaidu and I traveled back and forth to Babylon we stopped here in Isin for fresh horses. Karim and I stopped here as well and found the place nearly falling down. It was not hard to quickly brace it again, barely an afternoon's work.

"It was a happy surprise that Arakhu was governor. I moved into my mother's apartment and Karim became head of the guard. I pulled the Babylonian military back together, set up security for the City of Babylon, and worked with Governor Arakhu until Fu Ling Yang came for me."

"I sometimes feel like a stranger looking through a window to see your life, almost as if I am an appendage, and not a part of you. I envy the men who have been part of your life and adventures. Women in my culture are shielded from all of that. They come into marriages with almost no past."

"My love, I have not been part of your life until now. I know little of all that transpired before we met. You must tell me the stories of your life, list every building you have built, every adventure while erecting them. It was a joy to watch you and your men build a pagoda from my sketches. This is the only way we can share our early lives and feel that we are part of each other in that way."

"A man in my culture does not share those things. We keep them buried deep inside and never speak of them to anyone. It is considered weakness to do that."

"I understand that from the men in the Babylonian culture, but I am a woman that does not fit into any cultural restrictions. You were attracted to me because of my passion for architecture and the energy it engendered. I was and still am different from anyone you know.

"The only one remotely like me is Lishan. Her education is vast and she traveled with Fu Ling Yang, although protected by him. Within her is a universe of learning experience which she expresses as wisdom and love. This is why we love and treasure her. She is like no other."

"I have been a lonely man all my adult life. I worked with engineers and we built wonderful buildings, which kept me busy. I lived at the School of Architecture. Except for Fu Ling Yang and in the last few years, Shamhar and Lishan who look after me from time to time, there is no one else to call a friend."

"How difficult it is to find where we belong and with whom. Master Jarem was my mentor. Zaidu the builder and I worked together all my young life. Daniel was my spiritual guide and teacher. Royalty was ways a barrier. My guards were Persian, but loyally stayed with me. We were a very long way from Persia. Still the royalty was there in the background making it impossible for any closeness. Lishan was my first real friend. Probably her own royalty was helpful in erasing the barrier between us."

Again, you must tell me the stories of your life. Where were you born? How did you grow up? What was your childhood like? How did you become interested in architecture? Who inspired you? List the buildings you have created."

"All that?"

Ninana laughed

"Yes, all that."

"Well, it is not very interesting, not like your life."

"It is interesting to me. Tell me."

"I was born in a province quite far from Guangzhou and my people were tall…"

373

His story was halting at first, but then he lost the self-consciousness that hampered the flow. It became easier and Ninana was fascinated. She began to ask him questions about how his experiences made him feel.

"Are you sure you want to hear all of this?"

"Yes. Please continue."

"Talking about feelings is foreign to me and I have difficulty putting words to them."

But he labored on, Ninana holding his hands.

A messenger came to Fu Ling Yang from Babylon.

"Governor Arakhu has made your arrangements and is very happy that the queen is returning. The military will be notified and all explained to them. He looks forward to a celebration of her return."

Fu Ling Yang carried the message to Ninana.

"Our arrangements are made. Nothing further. Perhaps he did not wish to send anything more with the messenger, which is wise."

"Did you tell Arakhu about Chaoxiang?"

"Only that he is with you. Once again that needs to be worked out privately and not through a messenger who might spread the word to those who could start trouble."

"It is difficult to know what the political climate is exactly. I will speak to Chaoxiang and we will have a conference with Arakhu immediately when we arrive."

Chapter 75

THE ISHTAR GATE

———— ⟐ ⟐ ————

"We are coming to Babylon. Can you see it in the distance? There is the Ishtar Gate. I named it after the Goddess of Babylonia and Assyria."

"It does look like it is floating in the air. How did you make that happen, Ninana?"

"I did not. It is the shiny blue and gold bricks catching the sun. My people were taught to make them when artisans came from Persia. They set up the ovens and bought the materials to be applied that would bake into a hard shiny surface."

"Is there a message from Arakhu?"

"Yes, but nothing was said about you. It would be dangerous to send a sensitive message by envoy. Nothing will be announced until we have decided what the announcement should be and when."

They drove through the gate with no fanfare and went immediately to the palace.

"I will take the carriage and the guards back to my ship at the Port of Ur."

Fu Ling Yang bid them farewell, the carriage was turned, and the guards drove him out of the gate and toward Ur.

Karim and Arakhu met them behind the palace doors. Then they hugged Ninana and welcomed them all back. Ninana introduced Chaoxiang and he was graciously received. They went to an anteroom to have an immediate conference.

Governor Arakhu began the conversation.

"Nitocris, I know that Nabonidus became king because of marriage to you. But he was in the palace as a distance cousin of Evol-Merodach, so royalty was not questioned."

"Except by me! Every day until he died."

"I am sure. I am not sure it is wise to announce that Chaoxiang is the king of Babylonia just yet, or ever. We can call him Royal Consort which would indicate his royalty and relationship to the queen."

"I speak your language, Governor. And I am not insulted. More like I am relieved. In China we do not have kings. We have emperors and dynasties. I understand that your kings are assassinated regularly. Our emperors are not. It might be much safer to call me a Royal Consort, I am sure."

Ninana gasped.

"But you will still be working beside me, king or consort...if you are willing."

"Ninana, I will be beside you wherever you are, and I want to be sure I am alive to do it. Royal Consort is good."

"You are sure?"

"Yes, I am. Thanks to you I know how I feel and this feels comfortable, right."

"My love, you amaze me every day."

The military from the city arrived on the steps of the palace and Queen Nitocris went out to speak with them. Before she could get a word out, they began to applaud and cheer.

"Queen Nitocris! Queen Nitocris!"

"You have been told, I am sure, why it was necessary to fake my death and leave Babylon. Let us continue building the Babylonian army and our defenses. We will not attack anyone, but we will be ready. Cambyses and Bardiya are dead. Darius has taken the throne. So long as we make no trouble they will ignore us and go for bigger quarry. Let us plan a future of peace together. I need every one of you. Thank you for being here and for your support."

They applauded and cheered again.

"I want to introduce you to my Royal Consort and true love, Chaoxiang of Guangzhou, China. He will be of service to Babylonia and work beside me. I hope you will get to know and accept the goodness that he brings."

To her amazement they cheered and shouted "Chaoxiang! Chaoxiang."

He bowed Chinese style.

"Thank you."

The next few days were filled with conferences, plans, and touring the city. Chaoxiang was fascinated by the Babylonian architecture and the fact that Ninana was the designer and architect.

"This is unbelievable. It is beautiful! Cosmic!"

"This is my art. Now I will take you to my heart, the Jewish community. I could not bear to see the Jewish people used as slaves and also to live in squalor. So I chose a corner of Babylon that was not designated for buildings, but had water, air, and open space. The people from Jerusalem sketched their homes for me so I could build something that would resemble home for them. Daniel helped me communicate with them until they began to trust me. Now I am their beloved Princess. Karim, please take us to my home. Is it still there?"

"Yes, Your Highness. It is preserved and cared for by those who remember the gift you gave them. They call it House of the Princess."

Ninana and Chaoxiang stepped down from the carriage and were immediately surrounded.

"Our Princess! Our Princess has returned from the dead."

She explained to them that she was not dead, but away for her protection. She introduced Chaoxiang to them and they hugged and kissed his cheeks as well. The were ushered to a table being laden with food and placed at the head and foot of the table. They were curious about Chaoxiang and he talked to them, patted their hands, and laughed with them.

"Do you remember Fu Ling Yang and Lishan?"

They all nodded and pointed to Chaoxiang.

Chapter 76

MESSAGE TO DARIUS

Word came that Darius, now king of the Achaemenid Empire, was securing his holdings. He was a fierce warrior. He and his army were on the move enlarging the empire. Babylon was the least of his worries. There had been no uprisings or trouble. A Persian was the governor and no problems were expected.

An envoy came to Arakhu with a message asking if the Queen of Babylon was there. Some said she was dead or away. Arakhu send a message back.

"The queen is alive and has not left. She was a great help to King Cyrus in securing the City of Babylon for him with no resistance from the people. She continues to be supportive of the Persians and of King Darius. The empire of Babylonia is at peace and pays regular tribute to King Darius. We are grateful for his protection."

Ninana held her breath as she read the messages.

"Do you think this will keep the peace with King Darius?"

"Yes, it is certain. Darius, like Cyrus, allows his conquered people to live in peace, keep their own religions, and to prosper. He is a builder and creates protections for his empire. He is a great administrator and enhances trade throughout his kingdom."

"We have mentioned my being here and your advice was wise to continue to keep a low profile. My concern is for my people and this looks like I will be able to continue that way in the foreseeable future."

Chaoxiang and Ninana had another conference with Arakhu. They began making plans for their roles in taking care of the city, connecting with other cities in Babylonia, and generally living happily and peacefully.

They made their home in the Jewish community and spent little time in the palace. Their favorite place to spend time was the Yang Light of the Rising Sun building. They kept the incense glowing.

"I am so happy you created this building for Fu Ling Yang. I have heard about it and now I can be in it. It is wonderful. I feel at home in it."

Lishan and Shamhar would meet them there. They were the caretakers and Lishan conducted visitors through it.

"The people of Babylon were a little afraid of the place, but now they enjoy it and come often. I tell them Chinese stories and speak a little Mandarin for them. They think my language sounds very funny."

Shamhar was checking some of the hangings and the strength of the hangars.

"I always do this to be sure the building and everything in it is in good condition and not deteriorating. I bring students here to teach them about the construction and the importance of maintenance. Then we go to the hanging gardens to study them as well. They have been wonderfully refurbished. China has taught us wonderful things about construction. They are endlessly fascinated by the upturned corners of the roofs."

An envoy came from Darius.

"Your reply is received. Tell Queen Nitocris that her throne is honored and her support is appreciated. She is to continue as royalty and keep her people happy and at peace."

"He knows my name! How strange. I have my throne back even though that is not my desire. It is good to know that I am safe for now."

One of the guards came running to Chaoxiang.

"Come quickly! Dam number 15 is in danger of collapsing!

"Go to the palace to get Queen Nitocris."

"Go to the queen?"

"Yes, the queen. She built this city. Now go and tell her. I will meet her there."

Nitocris and Karim jumped into the carriage and dashed toward the dam.

"We must not let than dam break. It protects the Jewish community."

Shamhar was running from the Yang Light of the Rising Sun building. They pulled him into the carriage.

"It is dam number 15."

"I will get the students and some builders and be there immediately."

He jumped out of the carriage near the school.

Ninana and Karim stopped at the top of the dam. Chaoxiang came running to them.

"Is it bad?"

"No, but soon it will be."

"Shamhar is bringing architectural students and builders."

Everyone converged on the dam's weak point and began to work. Ninana brought materials needed to support the area. Chaoxiang was directing the working crews. It was not long before the damage was repaired and the dam secured.

"Now I believe I am really home! Working on Babylon again. It feels so good!"

Chaoxiang came up from the work area and put his arm around her.

"I am home wherever we are so long as you are here with me."

A man from the Jewish community came over the dam smiling and waving at them.

"Come now. We have food for all of you and dancing. Bring everyone!"

"Love awaits us."

"Yes!"

She kissed his cheek and hugged him.

ADDENDUM

―――――――――― ✺ ――――――――――

THE TEACHINGS OF DANIEL

Page 3

"Where is your god? Is there a statue where I can see him?"

"My god is within each one everywhere and also within you. There are no statues because you are the living representation of your creator."

"I am the living...what? How can that be?"

"It is the spirit of the Creator that is within us all and gives us life."

Page 17

"My god is always with and within me wherever life takes me. If I believe that I am forced as you say, then I have forgotten my god and my joy will be gone."

"How does your god lead you?"

"It gives me joy to see my god everywhere and I follow my joy."

Page 71

"Daniel was surely a man of inner peace and followed the ways of peace and love. He stayed so centered and unruffled. He called it the teachings of his invisible god. Did he mean that this god presence was the truth within him?"

Page 72

Something within me comes alive when Daniel speaks of his god, and that same something within me was always crushed by my father.

Page 94

Ninana thought about Daniel and his god, their god. She knew that the blessing of protection came from within.

Page 116

"Princess, I am sure this must be upsetting to you. But you are not forgotten in the great realm of the universe. Each of us is known and precious in the sight of God. He created each of us individually and responds to everyone who asks. Others may forget us, but not God. We are forever in his heart."

"Is that enough for you, Daniel? That your god remembers you, even when my father eventually forgets you, too?"

"Yes. God is forever. Humanity is not. You are remembered forever."

Page 120

"Our path or faith should you choose it, is not to please others but to please God. Others will disappoint you, but God never will."

Page 121

Over time she learned that Daniel was indeed different. He had insight, intelligence, and wisdom. His promotion reflected his keen mind, knowledge, and understanding. He had the ability to interpret dreams, explain riddles, and solve difficult problems.

Daniel was gentle and kind to everyone. Ninana was fascinated with their conversations about his god and the goodness of the teachings. He would speak to her of his god as they worked, and the value of love and compassion for people.

Page 152

It was his fervent prayer.

"They are your people, God. Keep them in the palm of your hand as you have kept me."

Page 156

"That was not fortune but God who always holds me in the palm of His Hand. I never know how He will take care of me. My place is to trust and not fear."

"I do not know if my faith would ever hold up in a lion's den."

"I have spent a lifetime with God. You are new to the faith. Do not worry about it. God loves you as you are and does not hold only favorites in His hand."

Page 157

Daniel stood before the furnaces quietly. He was not afraid.

"Be at peace, dear friends. No harm shall befall us. God is ever present and holds us in His hand."

Page 158

"My God and Daniel's God, I pray that you will show me the path I must take as you always showed Daniel. I will be joyful as he was always filled with joy at your presence in our lives. I will remember the love and wisdom you have showered upon us and be grateful. Shelah."

"Yes, but God never forgets us. That is the blessing. We can always return and God is there."

Page 191

"We will remember and honor Daniel who taught me about a god of love in a city of hate. I have not forgotten his teachings. They live in me and his god is my god."

Page 293

"He said the presence of God the Creator of All is within each one of us always. All power is given to those who believe. When we ask for wisdom it is given from the Universe. He translated the writing on the wall that appeared when my son, Belshazzar, was giving one of his decadent feasts.

"Kindness and being goodhearted, caring for all people? That sounds like Confucius and Mencius."

"And so it does. Wherever truths arise from they converge into one. Daniel called it God of All. Prophets, seers, and your philosophers travel in higher realms of being. They receive wisdom far higher than what most people will know.

REFERENCE

Quote and Image Credit and permission:

1. This work has been selected by scholars as being culturally important and is part of the knowledge base of civilization as we know it.

This work is in the public domain in the United States of America, and possibly other nations. Within the United States, you may freely copy and distribute this work, as no entity (individual or corporate) has a copyright on the body of the work.

Scholars believe, and we concur, that this work is important enough to be preserved, reproduced, and made generally available to the public. To ensure a quality reading experience, this work has been proofread and republished using a format that seamlessly blends the original graphical elements with text in an easy-to-read typeface.

We appreciate your support of the preservation process, and thank you for being an important part of keeping this knowledge alive and relevant.

From Bibliotheca Historica

A description of the tunnel as being built and used by Queen Semiramis is given by Diodorus (fl. 50 BCE) in the *Bibliotheca Historica*:

"After all these in a low ground in Babylon, she sunk a place for a pond, four-square, every square being three hundred furlongs in length, lined with brick, and cemented with brimstone, and the whole five-and-thirty feet in depth: into this having first turned the river, she then made a passage in form of a vault, from one palace to another, whose arches were built of firm and strong brick, and plastered all over on both sides with bitumen, four cubits thick. The walls of this vault were twenty bricks in thickness, and twelve feet high, beside and above the arches; and the breadth was fifteen feet. This piece of work being finished in two hundred and sixty days, the river was turned into its ancient channel again, so that the river flowing over the whole work, Semiramis could go from one palace to the other, without passing over the river. She made likewise two brazen gates at either end of the vault, which continued to the time of the Persian empire."
— Diodorus, *Bibliotheca Historica*, Book II,1 (Translation by G. Booth, 1814)

Philostratus (d. 250 CE) also describes the tunnel's construction in the *Life of Apollonius of Tyana*:

"And [Babylon] it is cut asunder by the river Euphrates, into halves of similar shape; and there passes underneath the river an extraordinary bridge which joins together by an unseen passage the palaces on either bank. For it is said that a woman, Medea, was formerly queen of those parts, who spanned the river underneath in a manner in which no river was ever bridged before; for she got stones, it is said, and copper and pitch and all that men have discovered for use in masonry under water, and she piled these up along the banks of the river. Then she diverted the stream into lakes; and as soon as the river was dry, she dug down two fathoms, and made a hollow tunnel, which she caused to debouch into the palaces on either bank like a subterranean grotto; and she roofed it on a level with the bed of the stream. The

foundations were thus made stable, and also the walls of the tunnel; but as the pitch required water in order to set as hard as stone, the Euphrates was let in again on the roof while still soft, and so the junction stood solid".

—Philostratus of Athens, Life of Apollonius of Tyana, book I,25. (Translation by F.C Conybeare, 1912)

Printed in the United States
by Baker & Taylor Publisher Services